Read Bill

CONR

THE
CHILD
TAKER

GerriCon Books Ltd

First published in Great Britain in 2009
by
GerriCon Books Ltd
Orford Green
Suite 1
Warrington
Cheshire
WA2 8PA
www.gerriconbooks.co.uk

ISBN: 978-0-9561034-5-1

Cover Photos: ©istockphoto.com

Cover designed and typeset in Minion 11pt
by Chandler Book Design
www.chandlerbookdesign.co.uk

Printed in Great Britain by the
MPG Books Group, Bodmin and King's Lynn

1

CONISTON WATER

Hayley watched her twins chasing each other around in a circle. They had been playing outside on the grass all afternoon and their olive skin glowed, kissed by the sunshine. Every now and again the chaser would about turn, and become the chased. They giggled so much as they ran that they could hardly get their breath. Life couldn't get much better than watching her children laughing and playing in such a beautiful place. The evening sun was setting over the lake and the still water looked like a huge mirror set between two mountains. In the distance she could see the peak of Coniston Old Man, where patches of snow still clung to the mountain top despite the glorious sunshine. On the lake two white sailing yachts were anchored close to the shore and the crystal clear water rippled gently around the hulls, but apart from them the Coniston Water was as still as could be.

"Ten more minutes you two, and then it will be sleepy time for little boys and girls," Hayley reached out and ran her fingers through their blond hair as they raced past her. They were nearly six years old and she couldn't believe how fast they were growing up. Hayley treasured every minute that she had to spend with her children. Seven years earlier she had been told that she couldn't have children and the

1

news had devastated her. Her husband had been like a rock at the time but Hayley thought that she could sense a yearning within him, and it tore her apart that she couldn't give him the children that he wanted so badly. Two months later she had conceived. Her husband wept when they received the news that she was pregnant, and they both wept when they were told that they were expecting twins. Things between Hayley and her husband had changed since then, but she soldiered on because of her beautiful twins. They were the most precious things in her world, and she had to try hard not to smother them by wrapping them in cotton wool to protect them from the world.

"I don't want to go to bed yet, Mummy!" Sarah chuckled as her identical twin brother caught up with her.

"I don't want to go to bed neither, Mummy!" Zak agreed with his sister before tearing off in the opposite direction as the chase began again.

"Either, Zak, I don't want to go to bed either; we don't use the word neither," Hayley laughed.

"Either, Mummy, either, either, either," Zak shouted the word as he zigzagged across the grass before heading toward their tent. Her husband had nagged at her for years to try camping in the Lake District. He had been a frequent visitor to the area as a young man, fishing and climbing the challenging peaks that the Lake District had to offer. Hayley had finally caved in to the idea and she was surprised how much she enjoyed the peace and tranquillity. The stresses and strains of everyday life seemed to melt away as they drove through the breathtaking scenery on the way to their camp. The campsite was situated on the lakeshore. It was early in the season and there were only a handful of tents and campervans scattered about the site.

Hayley watched the twins carefully as they careered toward the side of the tent, and the potentially dangerous configuration of guy ropes which held their impressive eight birth tent in situ. Zak ducked beneath the first nylon line and expertly sidestepped the tent peg which protruded from the grass. Sarah was not so flight of foot and she stumbled over the peg before crashing head first into the wall of the tent.

"I've told you not to run around the tent, Zak, you should stay at the front where I can see you. Now your sister has hurt herself because you ignored me," Hayley ran to her daughter and gathered her up into her comforting arms. Sarah had that look on her face that only children can have. She was teetering on the edge of tears but not quite crying. Her bottom lip quivered slightly and her eyes looked watery but she wasn't going to let it go just yet. As soon as she felt her mother's embrace the emotion became too much and the tears flooded down her rosy cheeks. She wrapped her little arms tightly around her mother's neck. Hayley could feel her sticky fingers grasping for some material to hold on to, and then the sobbing began as if it was the end of the world.

"I'm sorry, Mummy," Zak tugged at his mother's blouse with one dirty hand and patted his twin sister's foot, which was just about in reach, with the other hand.

"How many times have I told you not to go behind the tents?"

"Ten times, Mummy," Zak guessed, but he was way off the mark.

"I think it's more like a hundred and ten times, young man!"

Zak looked confused by the use of such a big number. He could barely comprehend sums at the best of times, and a hundred had way too many zeros to begin to work it out.

"I'm sorry, Mummy," he repeated. He was at a bit of a loss for anything else to say, and his little sister was blubbering for England. He patted her foot again but she kicked his hand away grumpily and cried even louder.

"What's all the noise about?"

"We could hear you all the way across the lake!"

Hayley smiled as she turned toward the voices. Her husband, Karl had been fishing on the lake with his younger brother, Steve. They were both wearing vest tops and shorts, and the sun had reddened their skin, especially on their shoulders. Their rods and equipment clattered as they walked. Zak ran to his dad and grabbed his leg with both arms.

"What have you done to your little sister Zachariah?" his father asked in a mock stern tone of voice. He only ever used his son's full name when he was in trouble.

"She tripped over the guy rope, Daddy, and then she crashed into the tent," Zak looked up into his father's eyes and searched them for approval. His sister was a girl after all and she was always crashing into things and crying. Zak didn't think that this was a bad crash by any stretch of the imagination. Sarah had crashed into a glass coffee table at Granddad's house last month, and it had shattered into pieces. Now that was a really bad crash in comparison to this one.

"She tripped over the guy rope, and I wonder who was chasing her?" his father ruffled his blond hair and gently clipped his ear.

"She was chasing me, Daddy, and your hands smell horrible," Zak had gotten a whiff of fish from his father's hand. His father responded by rubbing his hand under his nose. "Poo! Stop it, Daddy."

"How was the fishing?" Hayley asked. Karl put his rod down and embraced his wife and daughter with his strong suntanned arms. Hayley felt herself flinch slightly as he touched her skin; she didn't like the feeling anymore, as it turned her insides out. Karl glanced into her eyes and she looked away, guiltily.

"We caught a couple of tiddlers, but they weren't big enough to eat so we'll all have to eat bread and water tonight. How's my favourite girls?" he said as he kissed his wife and

4

daughter in turn. Sarah stopped crying and flung her arms around her father. She snuggled her sticky face into his neck.

"I don't want bread and water, Daddy," Sarah said forlornly. She forced another little sob to reinforce her concern.

"Okay sweetheart, what would you like to eat then?"

"Alphabet spaghetti and toast," she groaned.

"Okay princess we'll see what we can do," he kissed her forehead and gently moved her fringe from her face.

"Daddy," she whispered.

"What darling?" he whispered back.

"Your hands are smelly," she said. She giggled and pinched her nose to block out the smell. Karl kissed his daughter again and they all laughed.

Fifty yards away behind the tent, in the trees, a figure moved silently with the stealth of a cat. He was tall and thin with a gaunt face. The skin on his face was pockmarked, riddled with blackheads and postulant pustules. His arms were pale and crisscrossed with blue veins. The figure stared through the leaves and branches at the family gathering. He had received a tipoff from a reliable source that the family were heading for the lakes, and so he had waited, and then followed them from a motorway service station two days earlier. The twins had been eating ice cream when he'd first spotted them. They were priceless and too good an opportunity to miss, so he'd tracked them all the way to their campsite.

He had rubbed his hands together with glee when he realised that they were heading to a remote spot for their holiday, it could have been so much more difficult if they'd been heading to a busy hotel in one of the many tourist towns in the Lake District. His internet connections had gone ballistic when he first floated a picture that he'd taken with his mobile phone of the blond haired children. When he had put them up for sale, it created a bidding war between men from four continents. Now he had a buyer in place and everything was set. He looked at the little blond girl giggling in her father's arms and he smiled. The smile became a twisted grin and his pink tongue flicked over crooked blackened teeth. He could feel his heart starting to beat faster, and he ran his skeletal fingers through his greasy black hair. The black dye which he used emphasised how lank and greasy his hair was and the grey re-growth at the roots belied its true colour.

His name had been Ian once, but that was when he was a young boy, years before he'd been sent to prison. When he came out of the penal system they'd given him a new identity, and called him Jack, quite an apt choice he often thought. The gruesome stories of the 'Ripper', or 'Jack', as the police had nicknamed him, fascinated him for all the wrong reasons. Nowadays he used whatever name sprang to mind. Few of the people that he met ever spoke to him anyway especially the children he encountered, they never spoke. He wasn't sure what he should be called anymore but his latest employers used his internet pseudonym. Jack liked the internet very much. It was a world where he could meet deviants with the same interests as himself, some not quite as sick, but some much, much, worse. It was also how he made his living. He had stumbled into his profession, and business was booming. It was very rare that his customers ever knew his real name. They only knew him as Jack Howarth, the Child Taker, and his profession was stealing children to order.

2
MOGADISHU

Thousands of miles away, on the African continent, Grace Farrington felt sweat running down her spine in rivulets. It was nearly one hundred degrees in the full glare of the Somali sun. Her black skin glistened with moisture as the heat of the sun intensified. Midday was approaching and the temperature continued to climb steadily as she walked through the bullet ridden streets of Mogadishu. The buildings around her were built from stone, and then rendered with plaster that was made from crushed seashells. She couldn't help but wonder what the city would have been like before civil war brought it to its knees. Grace had seen many war torn cities during her service, but Mogadishu was in a league of its own.

Grace was the daughter of the first black man to achieve the rank of Sergeant Major in the British army, and as such, she had chosen to follow her illustrious father into the forces. She was a natural soldier, sharpshooter and unarmed combat aficionado. Grace had risen through the junior ranks of the military quickly, impressing her superiors so much that they'd put her name forward for Special Forces' selection programmes. She was successful and spent the next three years flitting from one elite unit to the next, wherever a female black operative was required at the time. Different missions required different personnel, especially in countries abroad where dark skin was indigenous. Soon Grace was chosen to take the selection programme for the combined Terrorist Task Force Unit, which she passed with flying colours, and now she was the unit's number one agent. She had led operations all over the world, but this time Somalia was the theatre in which their unit would perform. The collapse of the Somali government seventeen years earlier had led to a brutal civil war which was still raging, and the outskirts of the city had been reduced to nothing but derelict ruins. The square built buildings were pockmarked with bullet holes of every size and shape that you could imagine. The deserted houses were riddled with shell holes, and black smoke stains crept out of every window and smeared the bricks above them. Grace could hear a petrol engine approaching and the hairs on the back of her neck bristled.

"It's them," her Somali guide whispered nervously as he looked over his shoulder toward the speeding vehicle. He was a nineteen-year-old militiaman, as thin as a rake and dressed in a mishmash uniform, which hung from his skeletal frame. Sweat was pouring from every pore on his skinny body, and the smell that pervaded from him was not a pleasant one. "Give me the money now before they get here."

"You'll get paid when I've met Said Adid," Grace hissed. She stubbed her little toe on a stone and cursed under her breath. Rocks and stones protruded from the compacted sand that formed the narrow streets of the war torn city. Her flimsy sandals offered her very little protection against them, and she stumbled.

"I don't trust you, English bitch!" her guide snarled. He grabbed her elbow and helped her to her feet again. "Pay me my money."

"There are half a dozen marksmen with their sights trained on the back of your head right now. If you don't calm down and stick to your part of the bargain I'll signal them to blow your fucking brains all over this godforsaken road," Grace held him with an icy glare which left him with no doubt in his mind that she wasn't lying. He tried to match her glare, but she was not a woman to mess with.

"Are you okay?" Tara asked concerned. Tara was a twenty three year old white skinned European. She was the newest member of the unit, and she was also beautiful, and today Grace and Tara were being used as the bait in a honey trap operation.

"I'm fine, get on with the job," Grace replied curtly. Although Tara and Grace had worked in the elite counter terrorist unit together for three months now, they didn't get on at all. She turned back to their guide and hissed, "If you make one move out of line, you're a dead man."

The guide nodded his head slowly and swallowed hard. His oversized Adam's apple bobbed up and down. He was sweating profusely and he wiped his eyes with the front of his khaki shirt. A dark wet smear appeared on the material. The vehicle's engine roared as it screeched to a halt ten yards away from them. The driver fishtailed the back of the truck and a wave of grit and sand showered Grace and her guide. The guide rubbed sand from his face as he turned to the vehicle and smiled widely. Grace kept her face lowered as she analysed the situation in a microsecond. The vehicle was a battered red Toyota pickup. There were three men in the crew cab, and three more standing on the flatbed at the rear. They were operating a Chinese made heavy machinegun that was welded to a makeshift tripod. Mogadishu was swamped with improvised military vehicles like this one. They were known to Westerners as 'technicals'.

"Let me see them." The man in the passenger seat spoke. He was sporting a red beret on his head, and was wearing a grimy red vest to match. All the men in the pickup had mirrored sunglasses on.

"She's Jamaican, and she's untouched, very clean," the guide rambled. He put his hand beneath Grace's chin and pushed her head upward so that the men in the vehicle could get a proper look at her. "And this one is Swedish. We took them from a boat." He added, referring to the hundreds of ships that are attacked and held for ransom every year off the Somali coastline. He grabbed a fistful of Tara's blond hair and twisted her head cruelly sideways. Tara grimaced and thought about putting a bullet through him for a moment, but the mission was an important one, and she would have to play along with it for now.

The driver of the pickup studied Tara and Grace and smiled as he punched a number into a mobile phone. He spoke a few words and then nodded his head as he ended the brief call. The driver grinned and then saluted the guide. The engine roared again and the wheels span in the sand before finding purchase, and the pickup lurched forward. Grace stepped backward to avoid the avalanche of grit that it had created.

"What's going on?" she said to her guide. "Which one of them was Said Adid?"

"None of them, he wasn't there," the guide looked wide-eyed and confused. He held his hands palm upward and shrugged his skinny shoulders. He was about to speak again when they heard a second engine approaching.

"They were the reconnaissance crew," Tara said as she looked toward the oncoming vehicle. "If you pull my hair again I'll cut your balls off, do you understand me?"

The guide was about to reply but the look in her eyes made him think again. He was paid more money than he could earn in ten years for guiding the women to this area of the city. The two women were soldiers, which was a concept that he couldn't comprehend. Being told what to do by a female was alien to him, but these women were very different, and they were also very dangerous. Today they were being used in a honey trap to lure a Somali warlord out of his lair. Said Adid was the brains behind the recent spate of pirate activity off the coast of Somalia, which had cost Western governments billions of dollars in ransom payments. Despite the deployment of dozens of allied warships to the area, the pirates were still succeeding in capturing ships at will. Governments the world over were being forced to pay huge amounts of money to ensure the safe return of multi-million pound cargos. Despite several coordinated initiatives, the international community had failed to stop the pirates. A joint government committee had decided to remove Adid from the equation, thus cutting the head from the serpent. The problem was that Adid was just as unpopular in Mogadishu as he was internationally, and there was a huge bounty on his head. He was a ghost like figure, always in hiding, and always moving his hideouts to prevent his rivals assassinating him. Adid was a hunted man and as such, he was forced to be a very cautious man too.

"Shake hands with Adid first, do you understand?" Grace whispered to the guide. A rusty white van appeared from a side street two hundred yards away on the left. The van stopped next to the red pickup truck and words were exchanged between the two drivers. There was a heated discussion going on, and the men who were manning the mounted heavy machinegun on the back of the pickup were gesticulating wildly. Grace thought that their plan may have been scuppered, but suddenly the two sets of men joined in raucous laughter. Whatever the dispute had been about, they seemed to have resolved it.

"I'm not sure about shaking hands with Adid first," the guide was shaking nervously as he spoke.

"What do you mean?"

"I have never actually met him before," the guide confessed.

"You have never met him before?" Grace repeated quietly.

"I've seen him from a distance and I know what he looks like a little bit," the guide swallowed hard again, and his Adam's apple climbed upward towards his chin, before bobbing back to its original position. Rivers of sweat were running down his face, a combination of the burning sun and fear.

"What the bloody hell do we do now?" Tara hissed. The white van pulled away from the pickup and headed toward the strange trio.

"I know that he has a lazy eye, it looks a different way to the other one," the guide said proudly. The van pulled up adjacent to them, and the guide grinned widely at the van driver. The driver didn't reciprocate his greeting, and neither did his colleagues. The driver and the two men in the passenger seat stared expressionless at the two women. They all sported mirrored sunglasses. The atmosphere was electric. This was going to go one way or the other, and Grace knew that it could deteriorate into a melee in a matter of seconds.

"Hey, Boss. Look at the beautiful women that I have brought for you. This one is Jamaican, very clean, no diseases. This one is French," the guide grinned nervously as he tried to sell his wares.

"French?" the man who was sat in the middle of the crew cab repeated.

"Yes, French," the guide swallowed and his huge Adam's apple bobbed up and down again.

"You told my friend that she was Swedish," the man spoke with a deep throaty voice. There was no malice in his tone as pointed out the guide's mistake, but there was caution in his eyes as he removed his sunglasses.

"I was mistaken, Boss, she's French," the guide grabbed Tara's hair again and twisted her face upward, as if he could demonstrate her nationality by doing so. "Tell him where you are from bitch."

"Je suis Francais," Tara lied. The man in the middle nudged

12

the passenger and he opened the door and climbed down to allow him to exit the vehicle. They eyed the women and there was an air of malevolence about them. Every nerve ending in Grace's body was stood on high alert, just waiting for the right moment.

"They are good quality, Boss. No one has used them yet." The guide emphasised the point that neither of his prizes had been raped at any point since their capture. In Somalia that was verging on a miracle and it added to their value because the risk of catching Aids was drastically reduced if another African man hadn't touched them. "I'll give you a good deal boss."

"Shut your mouth," the man said quietly as he approached the two women. The driver and his mate had also exited the vehicle and they approached the trio menacingly. "She is no more a French woman than I am."

Grace edged backward an inch or so at a time. She needed to put some distance between herself and their target. If one of the men was Adid then she had to try to give the snipers a clean shot at him.

"Stay where you are, bitch," the man growled. Grace froze and looked down at her feet in mock fear. She was studying the man's face to try and see his eyes behind the glasses. "Have you somewhere to go, bitch?" The approaching men began to laugh but there was no mirth in it, only menace.

"Look here, Boss, I'll give you the best price I can, because I respect you," the guide stepped backward away from the approaching man, but he didn't move far enough. The man reached behind his back and pulled a fat silver Bulldog revolver from his belt. As quick as a flash he pressed the thick barrel against the guide's chest and pulled the trigger. The .44 bullet smashed through his sternum and shredded his heart muscle before punching a huge hole, the size of an orange, through his back as it exited. The guide was lifted from his feet by the force of the impact and he landed on his back with a thump. A deep red stain began to blossom across his khaki shirt. His eyes were wide open and he stared lifelessly at the blue Somali sky. He was just one of hundreds of young African men that would die that week at the hands of their own kind. The man turned the revolver toward Tara, and he aimed it at her midriff.

"So, bitch, tell me where you are from," he grinned as he spoke to her. His gravelly voice was full of contempt. Tara glanced at Grace to see if she was going to give the signal for the snipers to open fire but Grace was still looking at the man's face. He caught the look that had passed between them, and turned toward Grace. "What?" he snarled. He took his glasses off and put them into his shirt pocket.

Grace immediately saw that his left eye was made from glass. She was about to signal the snipers by raising her hand when the driver of the van stepped between them. He smiled as he approached her and he pushed his glasses up on top of his head. The driver had a turn in his right eye. The young men of Mogadishu were part of a militia as soon as they were strong enough to carry a gun. Violence was a way of life to them, and making it into your twenties with both eyes intact and keeping all your limbs attached to your body was virtually impossible. There was no way of identifying Adid by the turn in his eye alone.

"I asked you where you are from, bitch," the man pressed the Bulldog to Tara's temple. He leaned his face close to hers and licked her cheek with his long pink tongue. Tara recoiled but he pressed the gun harder to her head. "Get on your knees now."

Grace had no way of knowing who the primary target was, but the situation was now beyond redemption. There was no way of taking out Adid alone. She reached for her combat spike, which resembled a sharp screwdriver, and with expert timing she drove it upwards under the driver's chin. The spike sliced up through the driver's flesh, pierced his tongue and the roof of his mouth, before penetrating his brain. He dropped like a stone onto the sandy road. Four sniper rifles, which were well concealed around the area, spat death, and in the space of ten seconds the men from the van and their affiliates in the technical pickup truck were lying dead or dying in the Somali dust.

3
THE CHILD TAKER

The child taker stayed hidden in the trees for hours. He watched the twins and their parents playing and eating their dinner with both a sense of excitement and a tinge of jealousy. His first memories of family life were not happy ones, back in the days when he had been called Ian. Ian was the first child of a young couple who lived in a small town on the outskirts of Manchester called Irlam. The couple had married in their teens. It was a shotgun wedding and his mother was nearly six months pregnant when she walked into the registry office. There were no cheering guests or comedy speeches from the best man, just two sets of scowling parents disgusted that their youngsters had been so irresponsible. All the aspirations held for their offspring had been shattered by premarital unprotected sex. The hopes and dreams of college and university educations, followed by great careers were dashed, and replaced with disappointment and shame.

By the time Ian was born, his young father had followed his own father, and grandfather into employment at the local steel works. The work was incredibly hazardous but well paid for that day and age. His father adored Ian. He was the apple of his eye and even the grandparents eventually relented and doted on the newborn baby. His mother however was a different kettle of fish. She struggled to bond with her son at all. She felt trapped in the two up, two down terraced house that they lived in. Her husband grafted twelve hours a day to earn a living and the long hours of enforced solitude made her resent the child. The grandparents became concerned that Ian was always left unchanged in soiled nappies, and that he was always crying. Ian's father desperately tried to help his young wife to cope with the burden of motherhood, but his shifts were long and the work was physically exhausting. When he came home from work, he needed to eat and then sleep. Life for Ian's mother was lonely and relentless, and she took her frustrations out on the child. Bruises began to appear on the baby and the family were convinced that he was being mistreated, and that he wasn't being fed properly. There were arguments and the threat of bringing in social services was made several times, although it never came to fruition, more is the pity. Just when it seemed that the situation couldn't get any worse, Ian's father went to work one day and never came home. He was crushed to death between two huge ingots of white-hot steel. The ingots were lowered onto a flatbed trailer that travelled on railway lines through the mill to a cooling area. There they were sprayed by hosepipes with water that was pumped from the nearby canal. That particular day Ian's father was in charge of one of the hoses, and he was spraying the white hot steel when a second trailer broke free and crashed into the one that he was working on. The impact tipped the flatbed over and the ingots, which weighed tons, fell on top of the young father. By the time the metal had been cooled down enough for his rescuers to move the massive ingots, Ian's father was welded to the steel. His body had to be peeled from the metal like a burnt sausage from a griddle. For baby Ian things could only get worse.

The grandparents tried to step in and help the young distraught mother but she shunned their efforts and her behaviour spiralled out of control. The death of her husband had brought her a small amount of compensation from the steel mill, and the local community always had a whip-round when a mill employee died. She began to use her newfound wealth to buy the only thing that made her happy, which was vodka. Every time the grandparents turned up at the house, she was drunk and abusive. The house became steadily more and more filthy and disorganised. Soiled nappies were left discarded around the house, and a dirty dish mountain threatened to engulf every flat surface in the kitchen. Eventually Ian's grandparents stopped visiting altogether, especially when a string of men began to frequent the tiny house. She sought company from any man that would stretch to the price of a half bottle of vodka, and she repaid them by giving them her body, and it wasn't long before she fell pregnant again. She didn't have a clue who the father was and she didn't care, all she did know was that the thought of giving birth to another child would only add to her woes. She sought out a private clinic and had the baby aborted, which brought more shame onto her family and she never heard from her father ever again. She was left all alone in the world apart from baby Ian, who she hated.

Ian had no good memories of his childhood. His mother was a violent drunk and he could only remember hoping that she would be so drunk when he got home from school that she'd be asleep. She couldn't hit him when she was asleep. He also remembered being scared and hungry most of the time. School was a blessed relief at first, but it soon became an extension of his living nightmare. The other kids soon spotted that he was always unwashed, and that his clothes were ill fitting and dirty. His school blazer was three inches too short on the arms and there were snail trails of snot on his sleeves formed by his constant runny nose. He was a skinny kid with sticky-out ears and holes in his shoes, and kids are incredibly cruel to other kids. Soon school became so bad that he didn't go anymore. He spent his days wandering around the back streets, or stealing sweets and food from the local shops, until it was time to go home.

Ian, the Child Taker, was eight years old, when after a long list of casual affairs his mother finally met another man. There was a short spell when life became almost normal for the young child. His mother stopped drinking as much, although it was always prevalent throughout his memories. There was a brief period when he enjoyed hot porridge every morning, and he was given dinner money to take to school. Tea was cooked and served for six o'clock in the evening, in time for his stepfather to come home from work. Ian had never been happier at home, and there was a routine for a while, although his memories of that time were always tainted by the fear of receiving a beating if he stepped out of line.

The problems with the new set up began when the school truant officer knocked on the door. Ian hadn't been into school for nearly nine months. His mother was furious when he got home that day, but her wrath paled into insignificance when compared to the reaction of his stepfather. Ian had taken many a good hiding from his mother in the past, and a couple in the schoolyard from older bullies, but nothing came close to the pain he felt that night. His stepfather dragged him by the hair into his bedroom and beat him to within an inch of his miserable life. Ian couldn't understand why he was so angry. His stepfather told him that he was thief and a liar because he had continued to take his school dinner money for all those months without actually going into school. Ian had begged and pleaded with him to stop the assault but the beating was relentless. Even when he'd tried to explain through his swollen bleeding lips that he had bought his dinner every day with the money, the beating continued until he'd lost consciousness. Ian's memories of the next few weeks were hazy and blurred.

His injuries were so severe that his mother reluctantly took him to hospital the next morning. The doctors didn't believe that he had fallen down the stairs and social services were alerted to the fact that he was an abused child whose safety was in jeopardy. A gaggle of disapproving social workers decided that he was to be taken into care when he was well enough to be discharged. His mother and stepfather never visited him in hospital once. At the grand old age of eight and a half Ian was taken to a care home for prepubescent boys, which was run by a catholic priest. It was then that the real abuse began.

4

TERRORIST TASK FORCE

An unmanned MQ-1 Predator drone patrolled the airspace over the ruined city of Mogadishu. It had been tasked with monitoring the operation that was taking place on the ground, and its information was being sent back to the taskforce command centre, which was situated on board an American aircraft carrier, twenty miles off the Somali coastline. The Predator was equipped with synthetic aperture radar, which was capable of relaying detailed digital video, via K-band satellite links, even if the ground was obscured by cloud or smoke. In layman's terms it can see everything, through anything. The plan to draw the Somali warlord Said Adid from his hideaway by using the promise of foreign, disease free, women as bait had been compromised. (Sex in Africa is like playing Russian roulette because of the AIDS virus, and so foreign women were highly valued acquisitions.) The honey trap had worked to a degree, but they were now uncertain of the outcome, as to whether it had been successful or not. All the active members of the unit were unharmed however; they could not confirm that their target had been eliminated. There were several confirmed kills but Adid had been so elusive in the past that there were no up to date photographs of him, so there was no way of knowing if he was amongst the fatalities.

"What's the situation down there Pilgrim one?" Major Stanley Timms used Grace's call sign. The Major was the head of the Terrorist Task Force. The small but elite counter-terrorist unit was called upon only when all other options had been exhausted. Their operations were known as 'black bag operations', which means that the British Government would claim to be completely non-complicit in any of their activities. As far as the general public and conventional law enforcement agencies were concerned, the taskforce did not exist. Their targets never stood trial. They were eliminated.

"We have a number of fatalities but no positive identification of Adid."

"What about your guide?" the Major asked. "Couldn't he identify him?"

"He's dead, and it turns out he'd never actually met Adid."

"What?" the Major was furious. Their intelligence was obviously flawed. The guide had lied to them about his level of familiarity with the warlord, but it was their job to identify quality intelligence and to weed out liars. Somalia was full of militiamen who would trade their mothers for money, and the intelligence units were supposed to be able to qualify their informants. The lives of his unit rested upon it.

"He had never met Adid. He told us that Adid had a turn in his eye, which was not much help in this city."

Young Somali men carried weapons and joined a militia as soon as they were strong enough to carry a gun. Few lived into their teens without sporting scars or war wounds. Glass eyes and facial injuries were commonplace.

"Roger that. Have the bodies been searched?" John Tankersley joined in the communication. He was situated a half a mile away from the scene in the ruins of a derelict building. His colleagues called him Tank, and he was the taskforce's lead agent. On this particular operation, he was consigned to the backup unit, which consisted of him and four other taskforce members. They had to be hidden. The presence of a seventeen stone white male with a shaven head, accompanied by four heavily armed men dressed as Robocop would not have gone unnoticed in the centre of Mogadishu.

"The unit are checking the bodies now, but so far we have zilch," Grace replied.

"It's your call Major," Tank said. The city was a ticking time bomb and their presence there would not go undetected for very long. The sound of gunfire had been kept to a minimum by the use of suppressors but heavily armed militiamen in their technicals constantly patrolled the empty streets. If Adid was amongst the dead then his absence couldn't be kept a secret for very long before his remaining troops realised that he had not returned to his safe house.

"Roger that. Our tech people are analysing the data from the drone. Now that we have the details of the vehicle that he was travelling in, we can trace back through the footage to see where its journey originated," the Major wanted this mission completed and wrapped up as soon as was physically possible. He was on board the Nimitz-class carrier The Ronald Reagan, and although he had served for many years in the Royal Marines, he had never gotten used to sailing. He didn't have sea legs at all. Seasickness was amplified on carriers like the Ronald Reagan because they are powered by two nuclear reactors, which drive a huge water turbine. The turbine propels the vessel through the oceans in virtual silence. The sensation of being below decks without any engine noise added to the sick feeling.

The Major was handed a series of aerial photographs and a Tech pointed to the relevant areas on the operations map. The Major assessed the information from the drone and spoke into the coms unit.

"Pilgrim one, I'm sending in a Heli-vac for your unit. You can't achieve anything more there," he said.

"Roger that, we'll be at the rendezvous point in five minutes." Grace made a circular motion with her right hand and then pointed it toward a narrow street one hundred yards down the road. Her unit moved silently in combat formation toward their extraction point. The dead Somalis were left bleeding in the dirt, and swarms of flies were already feasting on their carcasses.

"Pilgrim two the vehicles started out from a small compound three blocks to the east of your position. There appears to be some activity taking place there," the Major nodded to the Tech and indicated that he wanted the live feed from the drone patched onto the screen in the command centre. The screen flickered to life and the ancient city appeared on it. The aerial view was segmented by gridlines.

"Roger that, what type of activity Major?" Tank asked.

"It's difficult to say, but there are a dozen or so armed men in and around the compound. It looks like an abandoned open air Souk with one main entrance gate on its west wall. The gate is being guarded by two men in a technical," the Major relayed what he could see on the detailed pictures from the drone.

"What is the E.T.A. for the extraction helicopter?" Tank asked. The sight of an American Navy helicopter flying over the city would create mayhem on the streets below. Every militia in the city would call its men to arms. Tank was hoping that its arrival would create enough of a diversion for his unit to take a sneaky look at what, or who was being guarded inside the Souk.

"Six minutes exactly," the Major replied. He already knew what Tank was thinking. They had an understanding that came from years of working together.

"I need ten minutes at least to get to that Souk before the chopper stirs up a storm," Tank made a circular movement with his hand and then pointed his fingers to the east. The four taskforce men moved as a unit to the jagged hole in the building that was once a door. The compacted sandy road had a pinkish tinge to it. The buildings around them had flat roofs and were rendered with yellowed plaster. They scoured the road, and it was clear in both directions before Tank and his men began to slither stealthily between the ruined buildings toward the old market place. At certain points the road narrowed to nothing more than an alleyway, three yards wide, and the path was strewn with shattered bricks and debris.

"Roger that Pilgrim two, you have ten minutes before the extraction. You'd better get in and out of there before the city comes down on you, check out the souk and then lay low until sundown and then we'll extract your unit."

"Roger that, are there any more details from the pictures on the Souk?"

"There are two men with a fifty calibre on a technical at the main gate. The others are either inside, or on top of the walls." The Major noticed a shadow moving at the rear of the building near the market wall. "Wait a minute."

Tank moved with his men through the dusty alleyways and empty streets. There wasn't a single building intact, let alone occupied. This sector of Mogadishu was completely deserted. The families that once lived there, were born there, educated there, married there and ultimately kept the wheel of civilisation turning there, had long since fled the violence.

"There is one x-ray on the north wall of the Souk. I can't see him fully, so I'm presuming that he's in a doorway. He seems to be sheltering from the sun, but it looks like he's a sentry," the Major explained.

"Roger that. That's our way in," Tank clicked the coms unit twice to signal that they were now approaching bandit country, and he could no longer safely speak out loud.

He could hear the familiar drumming of a helicopter engine in the far distance. He could also hear the distinctive rattle of AK-47 machineguns. The militias on the ground were emptying magazines of nine millimetre bullets into the sky, despite the fact that by the time they'd realised what it was that was flying over them, it was too late to fire at it effectively. The taskforce man who was at point suddenly froze and held up an open hand, which was the signal to stop. Tank and his unit crouched low and tried to melt into the crumbling brick walls which surrounded them. The heat was becoming unbearable and dust clung to their sweat covered skin. Tank checked his men visually, all elite agents, and the very best counter terrorist operatives available. They had been trained to fight in extreme conditions and they couldn't be any more extreme than this. Flies buzzed around their heads looking for a quick meal. His men all made an okay sign with their fingers, to let him know that they had no problems at this stage. The uneven ground and intense heat was putting incredible stress on their bodies. He had to check regularly that everyone was 'A' okay. Heat stroke could creep up on a man in this climate, and affect his judgement.

The point man was situated to the left hand side of a ragged doorway. Huge chunks of brick had been blasted away by stray munitions. The point man looked around the opening and then curled his index finger to summon Tank over to his position. The sun was beating down on them through a huge hole where the roof once was. Tank could feel beads of sweat trickling down his back as he slowed his breathing down to a minimum. Sweat tickled his neck and face as it ran from beneath his armoured helmet, and made its way south in tiny rivers across his skin. He reached the point man barely making a sound.

The point man nodded toward the left, and Tank slowly peered around a splintered doorframe. There were two pairs of feet dangling from a wooden platform fifty yards away. The feet wiggled gently and Tank could hear the voices of their owners chattering in Somali. They appeared to be two militiamen sitting on the remnants of a first storey bedroom floor. The front elevation of the building had been destroyed, which had left the upper floor exposed. It offered the militiamen a good view of the surrounding streets, and an excellent position from which to take out rival militias who ventured into their sector of the city.

The militiamen were in between the counter terrorist unit and the market, and the clock was ticking. Tank pointed to the dangling feet on the left, and then he indicated that the agent who was on point should take care of their owner. He repeated the process with the second pair, indicating that he would deal with them personally. Silently the taskforce men advanced through the rubble of what was once someone's kitchen. The air was stifling and Tank's body armour was saturated with sweat as they crept beneath the Somali militia men. The ancient floorboards above them creaked, and then there was a loud bumping sound. Something heavy had landed on the floor above them and dust billowed down onto the taskforce men. Tank froze and held up his hand, a signal to stop.

The Somali men began laughing and there was another loud bumping sound, which was followed by another avalanche of dust and grit. Two pairs of legs wiggled as the Somalis laughed. Tank guessed that they were throwing stones from the rubble at impromptu targets, unseen to the counter terrorist unit below. He motioned his colleague forward again and they were less than three yards away from the dangling legs when the Somalis stopped laughing. There was an excited exchange of words between the militiamen.

The sound of the approaching Heli-vac was now clearly audible, although it was still far away. The drumming of the engines combined with the staccato of distant machinegun fire had startled the two men, and they were obviously debating what their next plan of action was to be. Tank signalled with three fingers held up, and a silent countdown began. Three, two, one, and the taskforce men moved like lightening. Tank grabbed one skinny ankle with his right hand and pulled down hard. The Somali made a squawking noise as he fell through the dusty air, and he hit the rubble-strewn ground with a heavy thump. Tank was surprised how light the man had been, there was barely any resistance. He was on top of him in a flash, his serrated commando knife was hurtling toward the prone Somali's throat, and then his brain registered several things at once. The man was too light, his clothes were too baggy, his eyes were too frightened and his face was that of a boy. Tank pulled the blade to the right at the last second and it plunged into the compacted sandy floor beneath his head. The Somali could not have been any more than twelve years old. The boy stared at Tank with wild frightened eyes, his mouth was open but there was no sound coming from him. Tank looked around to see how the second Somali had fared. He was lying on his back with his head hanging unnaturally to the side, staring with a lifeless gaze. His tongue was lolling from the side of his mouth and his lifeblood was gushing from a deep rent in his throat. Tank reckoned him to be older, not by much, but definitely not a boy. He signalled to the taskforce men behind him. They moved through the doorway as one slick unit and joined them.

"Tie him up next to his friend," Tank whispered. There was a look of uncertainty in the eyes of the agent that he'd spoken to. Tank saw it and asked, "Is there a problem?"

The agent knew better than to question an order from a senior ranking officer, especially if his name was John Tankersley. The problem was that on a mission as dangerous and covert as this one, no witnesses could be left behind, no matter how old they were. The agent grabbed the frightened boy and dragged him to where his dead friend was laid. He took a plasti-cuff from his utility strap and fastened it tightly around the boy's wrists. Tears ran freely down the boy's black skin, making shiny trails across his grimy face. He was shaking like a leaf. The agent reached across to the dead Somali and ripped a strip of material from his shirt. The young boy knew that it was to become a gag and he cooperated without even a whimper. The Somali militias grew up fast, and this young boy realised that his survival depended on being quiet, not being brave. The sight of his friend bleeding out like a pig in a butcher's shop confirmed his logic.

"I don't think that we should be leaving him behind, Tank," the agent whispered into the coms unit.

"You don't need to think, you need to follow orders," Tank hissed back across the coms.

"Pilgrim two, do we have a problem?" the Major's voice broke into the conversation.

"No problem, Sir," Tank replied. "Number three was expressing his opinion," he added sarcastically.

"Number three needs to keep any opinions to himself and get on with this damned mission!" the Major said annoyed that there had been any level of dissent at all. It wasn't tolerated in the military at all, and the Special Forces units were even more unforgiving. "Are you clear, Number three?"

"Roger that, Sir," the agent replied. He looked at Tank as he spoke and wiped a thick sheen of perspiration from his face with his sleeve. The look in Tank's eyes told him nothing. It was like looking into a shark's eyes, as they gave nothing away at all.

"Check that he's secured and then we move," Tank ordered. A second agent checked the bindings, and he added a plasti-cuff tie to the boy's legs as a final measure. The unit moved out of the ruined building and scurried across the narrow road. There was an alleyway between the buildings opposite. Tank checked the compass on his wrist and signalled the unit to move on. A hundred yards down the alleyway, the walls became higher and offered them both shelter from the burning sun, and cover from snipers. They reached a ruin that looked like it had once been a bakery of some type. There were stone ledges fixed to the walls and two large brick ovens. Beyond through an empty window Tank could see the high walls of a compound across the street.

His unit had reached the Souk and they took cover behind the ruins of a stone bread oven. The helicopter would pass over in a minute, and then the fun would begin.

5

THE CHILD TAKER

Hayley sat on a folding camping chair. It was made from tubular metal and rainbow striped canvas, and her husband said that you needed a pilot's licence to erect it. She was reading the story of 'Puff the Magic Dragon' to the twins as they dozed off to sleep snuggled up in a double sleeping bag. They had been asleep for at least five minutes now but she treasured the time that she had with her little angels, and so she read on for her own sake while she watched them. The air inside the tent was hot and stuffy, and it was tainted with the smell of the synthetic chemicals that made the structure waterproof. She didn't like the tent one bit, although the surroundings were fabulous. A squadron of Crane flies were hopelessly trying to barge their way out through the roof of the tent. Occasionally one of the clumsy insects would bounce off the battery-powered lantern that hung from the apex of the tent, and then spiral out of control toward Hayley. She hated insects of any description, but especially flying ones with huge gangly legs. The thought of them becoming entangled in her hair made her feel sick. She lashed out with her children's book as another hopeless insect hurtled towards her. The insect took a direct hit and was launched into an involuntary warp speed freefall, which ended fatally with a collision against a camping stove.

Sarah opened her eyes sleepily, and frowned at her mother. The flapping pages of Puff the Magic Dragon's story book had disturbed her slumber.

"What are you doing, Mummy?" she mumbled.

"Nothing, angel, you go back to sleep," her mother lied.

"Were you killing beasties?" the little girl whispered.

"Yes, but don't worry, they're all gone now," Hayley chuckled at her daughter's perceptiveness. There was no fooling Sarah at all, whereas Zak could be gullible. His sibling had been born first, and so she was technically older than he was, which was something she reminded him of at every point of opportunity. Sarah wrapped her brother around her little finger. She was somehow much smarter, not more intelligent, she was just cannier.

"I don't like beasties, Mummy."

"No, baby, neither do I."

"Do you think Puff the Magic Dragon would eat all the beasties up?" Sarah closed her eyes and licked her lips, and before her mother had contemplated whether the kindly Dragon in her book did actually eat Crane flies or not, she was fast asleep. She turned her head toward her sleeping brother, and he placed his tiny arm over her shoulder, as if he was protecting her.

"Sleep tight little angels, I love you both so much," Hayley whispered and pulled their sleeping bag up an inch. The temperature inside the tent plummeted at night. Hayley grimaced at the thought of reaching through the Crane fly squadron to turn the lantern down a shade, but she was saved by the arrival of her sunburnt husband. The zip on the flysheet rasped noisily as he opened it up to gain entry. "Shush, you clumsy man! They've only just gone off to sleep."

"Good because the barbecue is glowing and the sausages are nearly cooked," her husband clapped his hands together playfully as if he was excited about a plate of charcoaled sausage. Hayley noticed that his hands were black.

"Look at the state of your hands, Karl. I hope you haven't been touching the food with them," she scolded him.

"I had a little trouble starting the barbecue that's all," he opened his hands and made to rub them on her face. She giggled and pulled away from him. "What's the matter? You used to like my dirty hands all over you," he teased.

"Get away from me you tramp!" she laughed. "I never liked your hands on me. I just pretended that I did to keep you quiet."

He pulled her toward him and kissed her cheek. "Oh you were pretending were you?"

"Yes, well not all the time," she said coyly.

He pulled her closer still and felt himself stirring sexually. His flimsy cargo shorts did little to hide his excitement.

"Karl," she leaned away from the kiss, spoiling the moment. Things hadn't been right between them for a long time.

"What's wrong?" he gasped. It had been a long time since they'd made love. His wife didn't seem interested any more. He was hoping that the fresh mountain air would stir emotions in her that had been dormant since she had given birth to the twins. The reality was that it wouldn't, in which case the fishing rod would come in handy.

"Nothing is wrong, Karl," she stepped back out of the embrace completely. "Apart from the fact that our children are asleep two yards away, and your brother and his snooty wife are the other side of that canvas wall."

"She's not snooty, Hayley, and I'm sorry I was just fooling around," he whispered and stepped closer to her again. She tensed as he touched her. He could feel her involuntary physical revulsion to his embrace. Something had been lost between them along the way. He still loved her that was for sure, and he certainly loved his twins, but the fire that they

33

once had for each other seemed to have burned out. At first, he thought it was the arrival of their children that had doused their passion.

Sleepless nights and tiring days took their toll on his wife in the early months, and so he gave her space and time to feel like being a woman again, and not just a mother. Months flew by and when they finally made love, he knew that something had changed in her. She seemed to be mechanical. There was no intensity to the passion like there had been before. It had gone and so far, it showed no signs of returning. He had tried hard to cope with the constant rejection, but he was a red-blooded male with a high sex drive. Karl had turned his attention to other women, and although he tried to be discreet he couldn't help but feel that Hayley knew every time that he'd cheated.

"Your sausages will be burning," she said quietly. She couldn't look him in the eyes. Hayley leaned forward and kissed his lips quickly. He felt like it could have been a kiss from his grandmother, or an old aunt for all the passion that was transmitted through it. "I'll be out in a second," she added.

"Fine you do that," Karl snorted like a sulky schoolboy. He opened up the tent flap and went back outside. Hayley could hear her sister-in-law's voice through the canvas.

"Hey babe, what's the matter, has the ice queen been at you again?" she whispered a little too loudly.

"Shush, Louise," Karl's concerned reply sent a shiver through Hayley. She had an inclination that something wasn't right between her husband and his brother's wife. There was no solid evidence. She just had a feeling about her. There had been several incidents over the past few years where she had seen them exchanging glances, maintaining eye contact a little too long. Now she knew that she called her the 'Ice Queen' behind her back, and that rankled her. The two women had never gelled, never got on or liked each other. Karl on the other hand got on with her like a house on fire, and he defended her far too quickly for comfort. They constantly teased each other to the point of embarrassment.

Hayley had noticed that Karl's brother Steve wasn't all together happy with the attention that his sibling paid to his spouse either. Steve was the quieter brother. He had dark eyes and boyish handsome features, and he was sensitive and thoughtful, but also very dull. Karl was the opposite, selfish and brash, but good company socially. He had a wide jaw and rugged good looks. There was no doubt which brother had the most success with females during their younger years.

Karl had a string of young babes through his university years, and Hayley was flattered when he asked her to go steady with him. She was a stunning blond with piercing blue eyes and Karl was the envy of his friends when they started dating. At first, she revelled in his attentions, and physically she was as keen and eager to explore as he was. Having the twins was like flicking a switch for her, and sex was no longer enjoyable. Hayley was very aware of her short comings in the bedroom, but she didn't think that they justified her husband seeking solace elsewhere, especially with his brother's wife. Her face darkened and she felt her heart beating faster. Anger was rising in her throat. Jealousy is a powerful emotion and she could feel it coursing through her veins. Was it all in her mind? She couldn't be sure they had done anything at all, but she couldn't prevent herself from suspecting them either. She took one last glance at her beautiful twins as they lay sleeping, and then she breathed deeply before she unzipped the flysheet and climbed out of the tent.

"Have the twins gone off to sleep then, Hayley?" Louise asked. She always adopted a baby girl voice when she spoke about the children. It irritated Hayley immensely. Hayley ignored the question and zipped the tent closed. She took another deep breath before turning to face the others.

"Are the twins alright, Hayley? Here, have a glass of wine," Louise picked up a bottle of Australian Chardonnay from a cool box. She tipped the remaining contents into a plastic cup. There was barely enough left to fill it half way.

"Oh my god, we've drunk all the white already," she giggled as she passed the wine to Hayley. Hayley glared at her as she took the cup from her. Louise giggled again and walked away on unsteady legs toward the barbeque. "I don't think your wife is talking to me." She whispered into Karl's ear as she approached him. It was said loud enough for everyone to hear. Karl looked up from the smoking grill and he saw the anger in his wife's eyes. He blushed, and Hayley wondered if it was embarrassment or guilt that made his face flush red.

"The sausages are ready," Karl announced. A forced smile creased his face as he tried to make the best of the situation. The atmosphere was tense to say the least. Karl carefully placed burnt sausages onto four paper plates, but he couldn't maintain eye contact with Hayley.

"I'll nip to the shop and get another bottle of wine if you like," Steve offered. He ripped open a floury bun and handed it to his brother. Karl plonked a frazzled sausage onto the bread and handed it back. "I've only had one beer, so I'll eat this and drive down the hill. Do we need anything else babe?" He bit into his sandwich and burnt his tongue. He laughed and fanned his hand in front of his mouth to cool the food down.

"Get me some cigarettes, I've only got a few left," Louise didn't even look at her husband as she spoke. "You might as well buy some extra beers too. Karl will want another beer or two I'm sure." She put her wine to her lips and smiled provocatively. Karl blushed again. The sound of a baby crying drifted over the camp.

"Why don't you go with him, Louise?" Karl looked at her sternly. He'd had enough of her theatrics in front of his wife.

The wine was starting to affect her better judgement, and she was becoming more embarrassing by the minute. He wanted her out of the way for a while so that Hayley could calm down.

"Yes, why don't you go with your husband?" Hayley stared at her. The look in her eye warned her that she had crossed the line. There was a moment of complete silence as the two women glared at each other. It was a very uncomfortable moment for Karl, although Steve didn't look too happy either.

Steve looked between the two women, bemused by the tension between them. He was a little slow on the uptake, but not completely stupid. The sound of a baby crying pierced the silence and he looked across the campsite toward the sound. There were no tents in that direction, and he wondered where the sound could be coming from.

"I don't know why you two can't get on," he mumbled to himself.

"I don't know why you and Steve don't go to the shops and get some more wine together, Louise," Hayley snarled.

"I think I'd prefer to stay here thank you very much," Louise sneered. She shook her head defiantly and tossed her shiny long black hair. Her hair was jet black, and it had a deep sheen to it. The evening sun's rays gave it a blue tinge. The sun was nearly gone now and the shadows were lengthening. "Steve doesn't mind going on his own, do you darling?" She draped her arms around her husband's neck and kissed him full on the lips. Steve looked more bemused than ever, but he responded in kind and squeezed her shapely buttocks with one hand, while the other clung to his sausage sandwich.

The noise of the baby crying increased a notch, and the cries were becoming more urgent. Karl looked toward a small copse of trees across the campsite. It seemed as if the distressed infant was somewhere in that direction.

"I don't mind going on my own if I get some more of that kind of attention when I get back," Steve cajoled his pretty wife.

She was firm and fit, and attractive to men. She flirted at every opportunity and used her sexuality to wrap her husband, and other men around her well-manicured finger. Louise opened her lips wide and allowed his tongue into her mouth. She kept her eyes open and stared at her husband's brother all the time she kissed him. It was a deliberate act of provocation to wind her brother-in-law up, and she loved every minute of it. Hayley watched her husband's expression for signs of jealousy, but he was otherwise occupied. He was staring into the darkening shadows of a wooded area across the site, and the sound of an infant in distress became louder still.

"Can you hear that?" Karl asked. Hayley nodded and sipped her wine.

"I can't make out where it's coming from, noise travels so far on the breeze," Hayley replied quietly. "Give me the car keys, I'll drive down the hill to the village and get some supplies."

Louise and Steve were still joined at the lips. Alcohol was fuelling their passion. Louise pulled out of the embrace and shook her hair again.

"Steve will go, Hayley," she said tossing her dark mane sexily. "You don't mind do you babe?"

"I want to go thank you, give me the keys please, Karl," Hayley replied curtly without looking at her sister-in-law. Louise pulled a face and stuck her tongue out childishly. Her husband nudged her gently to make her stop teasing.

"I'll come with you," Karl said. He pulled the keys to their BMW estate car from his pocket.

"I'll be fine Karl, just give me the keys please," Hayley needed five minutes away from them all to calm down. Her sister-in-law's antics had annoyed her immensely.

"I really don't mind going, Hayley," Steve chirped. He squeezed Louise's bottom and she giggled like a school girl. She pouted at Karl and thought it had gone unnoticed, but Hayley caught it.

"I'm going to drive to the village, on my own, before I'm sick. Now can I have the fucking car keys please," Hayley held out her hand, and Karl handed her the key fob in silence. "Thank you," she said curtly. Hayley turned and walked toward the estate car.

"I don't think there was any need for that," Karl hissed as he followed her a few steps behind. "That was just plain rude."

"Oh well I wouldn't want to upset Louise now would I, babe?" she replied sarcastically. "The Ice Queen is spoiling the night and having a go at everyone again, am I?" Her tone was acidic.

Karl stopped in his tracks. Hayley turned to face him, and he could see the anger in her eyes, her demeanour warned him that debate was futile until she'd calmed down.

"What's the matter, babe? Did you think that I hadn't heard her?" Hayley imitated Louise's girly voice.

"I don't know what your problem is. Why do you want to cause a scene?" Karl reached out to hold her hands. Hayley pulled away and turned toward the car again.

"Leave me alone, Karl, I do not need that bitch talking about me behind my back, especially not to my husband," she pressed the alarm button on the fob and the lights flashed to indicate that the vehicle was unlocked. Hayley pulled the door open and climbed into the dark blue BMW. Karl grabbed hold of the door to stop her closing it.

"Look, Hayley, she's a drama queen, just ignore her. We're supposed to be on holiday," Karl tried to calm his wife. "She's had a lot of wine."

"I don't care, Karl, leave me alone," she grabbed the handle and slammed the door. Karl stood back from the car as she started the engine. The muffled sound of Dire Straits, playing 'Sultans of Swing', came from the stereo. Hayley glanced at her husband briefly as she drove away. He looked at Louise and shrugged his shoulders, and in that instant Hayley knew that they were sleeping together. She didn't know how, or why, but she knew. Karl watched the estate crossing the campsite. Halfway across the site the headlights flicked on. The sun was fading fast and the shadows were lengthening. The indicator light flashed as the car reached the entrance gate, and then he heard the engine gunning as Hayley pulled the vehicle onto the main road. His heart felt heavy with guilt, but there was something else eating at him too. Hayley seemed to sense that there was something between him and his sister-in-law and that frightened him. He had tried to be as careful as possible to hide it from his wife and his brother, but Louise's antics were not helping one bit.

Karl heard the sound of the infant crying again, but this time it was much more urgent, almost a scream. He looked toward the woods, and the spaces between the trees had become inky darkness. The trees were dark silhouettes against a darkening sky. The first stars were visible in the north above the lake. It was such a beautiful setting that the view calmed him for a moment, and then the child cried out again. This time it was accompanied by a female voice. He couldn't make out the words but it sounded like the woman was calling for help. Karl looked at the handful of tents and caravans that were on the site, but they were all in darkness, their occupants out walking or fishing, or eating an evening meal in one of the country pubs that were spotted around the lake. The site was completely empty apart from him. Steve and Louise had disappeared into their tent. The coals on the barbecue smouldered, and the smoke drifted vertically upward toward the darkening sky. The night was deadly still, not even a breeze moved across the waters of the lake. The child cried out again and the female's cries for help became much clearer. Karl walked toward the copse of trees as darkness descended, and the sound of Louise gasping forced him to glance toward his brother's tent. Her lovemaking was always loud and frantic, and that was one of the reasons why he couldn't leave her alone. Karl knew that their affair was wrong in so many ways that he couldn't believe it some days. Screwing your brother's wife while your partner cares for your twins is about as low as one man can get. He didn't love Louise, and most days he didn't even like her as a person, but he did love screwing her, so much that he couldn't leave her alone. So far his brother and Hayley had no idea what had been going on, but Louise's behaviour was becoming increasingly more obnoxious. Steve seemed blissfully unaware but Hayley was becoming suspicious, and Karl knew that he could be forced to stop the affair before Louise did, or said something stupid, that would lead them to be discovered.

Karl's thoughts were interrupted by a desperate scream. It sounded like an adult woman's voice. The infant's cries joined the female's and Karl broke into a jog as he approached the trees. He slowed down to allow his eyes to become accustomed to the darkness between the trees, but the urgency of the infant's cries was reaching fever pitch. Karl picked a gap between two trees and ducked beneath the lower branches. A sharp pain stabbed him in the soft flesh above the hip. Another stabbing pain emanated from below his left knee.

"Shit!" he said, as he realised that he'd careered into a barbed wire fence. A trickle of blood ran down his shin. The woman's voice screamed for help again, and she didn't sound far away anymore.

"Hello, can you hear me?" Karl cupped his hands together and shouted into the darkness. His question was answered by the infant crying. "Hello, can you hear me?" he shouted again. Reluctantly he climbed between the barbed wire strands then he was engulfed in the darkness of the woods. Karl stared into the darkness and tried to make sense of the shadows before him. Slowly but surely he picked his way through the branches and undergrowth toward the sound of the infant crying.

A tree root protruded up from the soil and he stubbed his toes against it. He fell forward and scratched his face and hands on the low network of branches. Thick tendrils of brambles wrapped around his legs and the thorns pierced his flesh. His shorts offered him no protection whatsoever. He tried to stand but only succeeded in pulling the bramble tighter against his flesh.

"Hello, can you hear me?" he called as he pulled the thorny plants away from his legs and ankles. The thorns scratched his hands and he swore aloud.

"Bloody hell! Can you hear me?" he called again. Blood had run down his shins and was clotting in his socks. "Hello!" he shouted louder, and the infant cried out again. He stumbled on for another twenty yards or so and the female called out for help again. She sounded very close this time.

"Hello, can you hear me?" Karl ducked beneath a thick branch and peered into the blackness. The infant's cries were very close, but the female had fallen silent. He wondered what they were doing in the copse in the first place. "Hello, I'm here to help, can you hear me?"

The infant cried again, but this time it seemed that it was behind him. Karl turned and listened intently. The cries were no more than a few yards away.

"Hello, can you hear me?" The crying was coming from below him, down to the left. There was a tree trunk barely visible in the blackness, and Karl kneeled down and edged closer to the base of the tree. "Hello, where are you?" he spoke gently, so as not to frighten the infant. The cries suddenly became louder and the female shouted for help too. Karl could not make any sense of it. They sounded as if they were right in front of him, but he couldn't see anything. He fumbled in the darkness and his hand touched something hard. His fingers felt blindly around the rectangular object, and he nearly dropped it in fright when the infant's cries screamed louder still from the box. It vibrated slightly as the cries reverberated through the trees. Karl realised what it was and he gazed open mouthed at the wireless speaker. The female's voice cried out again. The sound drifted through the trees and across the still waters of the lake, and it was all the more eerie now that he knew it was a hoax.

"Why would anyone play a stupid, good for nothing trick like that," Karl whispered to himself in the darkness. It was a warm still evening but a cold shiver ran down his spine, and he was suddenly very, very, frightened.

6

THE SOUK

Tank watched the sentry in the doorway of the souk as the helicopter approached their airspace. Curiosity got the better of him and the Somali reluctantly stepped from the shelter of the doorway into the blazing sunshine, and he scoured the cloudless sky for a sight of the enemy aircraft. He was wearing khaki ill-fitting clothes, mirrored sunglasses and a baseball cap, which appeared to be standard issue for the many militias in Mogadishu. Tank figured him to be around sixteen or seventeen, if he was a day. Raised voices could be heard from inside the souk as the helicopter flew nearby, and a burst of machinegun fire came from within the walls somewhere. The sentry peered skyward and turned around through three hundred and sixty degrees. Tank pointed two fingers toward the sentry and one of his men responded by firing two, soft nosed nine millimetre bullets, from a suppressed Glock seventeen. The fat shells punched holes the size of walnuts through the back of the sentry's skull. His face was virtually ripped clean off as the flattened ammunition exited through his forehead. The sentry hit the dust with a dull thud and a pool of blood began to leak into the sand. Tank waved a hand and the unit moved silently toward the doorway.

The walls of the souk were made from handcrafted bricks,

which were the colour and texture of sand. The doorway was low and narrow, and it was fitted with a thick wooden door. The door was grey in colour and the wood was warped and cracked with age. There was a rusted keyhole next to the frame on the left of the door, but no handle was fitted to the outside. It was obviously designed to open from the inside only. A burst of gunfire erupted from the near distance, and half a dozen other weapons soon joined it. The taskforce men couldn't see who was firing skyward but it was obvious that they were in the vicinity of the souk. Tank stepped into the doorway, knelt down, and placed his eye to the keyhole. There was nothing to be seen except a spider's web. He stepped back and nodded to his number four. Number four moved swiftly and within seconds he had fitted a small plastic explosive charge to the keyhole. The unit split, two men each side of the doorway, and they ducked low against the sandy brick wall. Number four counted down with a gloved hand, four, three, two, one, and then the crack of a small controlled explosion joined the cacophony of machinegun fire. It appeared that the small explosion had gone unnoticed by the militiamen inside the old market place, as the gunfire didn't falter.

The wooden door cracked into three triangular pieces. Tank ducked under the low doorframe and broke through the broken door. He moved inside and to the left, into what looked like a dusty storeroom. His colleagues broke right and took up defensive shooting positions. The room was empty except for a small wooden desk in the centre. It was the type of desk a child would have used at primary school in the sixties. The lid was sloped toward the fixed seat, and an inkwell was drilled into the lip of the pencil ledge. Cobwebs hung from the low ceilings like grey curtains. At the far end of the storeroom was a metal door, which had been fitted to prevent thieves from gaining entry to it. The unit approached it and quickly assessed how to breech it. Number four pointed to the hinges, which would be the weakest point of a metal door, and the ideal place to fix an explosive charge. Tank held up his hand, and signalled him to wait a second. He reached for the rusty handle and twisted it downwards. The handle screeched and groaned before it gave way, and the door creaked open slowly. Tank smiled as the door opened and his colleagues chuckled at the irony of the situation, why blow the hinges off a metal door when it isn't locked? The corridor beyond was unlit and empty, and the unit slipped through the door in cover formation. There was a shaft of sunlight shining through a small rectangular window, and dust swirled around in it. At the end of the corridor was a stone staircase. The steps were wide and worn shiny by hundreds of years of use.

Tank and his men reached the bottom of the staircase and he peered through the glassless window into the souk. Inside the old market square was a courtyard made of compacted sand, once packed with stalls and traders selling spices and wares. Now the hustle and bustle of the souk had been replaced with two Technicals and a thick whipping post, which had a poor unfortunate soul shackled to it. The man was limp and hanging by the wrists, and by the look of his injuries he'd been subjected to sustained beatings over a prolonged period of time. Machinegun fire roared skyward again, but this time Tank could see where it was coming from.

Around the market square were high stonewalls, which could be accessed by rotten wooden steps, similar to a medieval castle. Four men were shouting and firing Kalashnikovs into a cloudless blue sky. Two more men were standing in the back of one of the Technicals, firing a fifty millimetre into the air. There were doorways fitted into the inner walls of the souk every ten yards or so, which meant that there were at least two dozen rooms off the central courtyard. It would be like trying to find a needle in a haystack. Tank mulled over the options for a second. They could take out the militiamen and then clear each room one at a time by the numbers, hoping that they would stumble across the pirate warlord. Alternatively, they could bug out of the area and then call in an airstrike on the souk, while they lay low until a Heli-vac could be arranged. He was leaning toward the latter course of action when a door to the left of the window opened, and a man wearing new camouflage combats and a red beret stepped into the square. He shouted a series of instructions to the militiamen and they stopped firing their weapons straight away. One of the men on the Technical barked something back at him, while pointing to the empty sky. Tank could tell by the sound of the helicopter engines that it had picked up its human cargo and was well on its way back to the carrier in the Indian Ocean. He could also tell that this man was a high-ranking officer at least, and possibly their leader, Said Adid. The officer turned his head toward the Technical and Tank caught his full profile. He had a black patch over his left eye, appropriate for a pirate, Tank mused.

"Pilgrim one, we have a possible sighting of the target," Tank whispered into the coms. He watched as the officer picked up a stone and hurled it at the man in the Technical. The stone bounced off his arm and then rattled off the roof of the pickup. The militiamen fell silent, and the officer began to rant and rave again. He was gesticulating wildly with his arms as he hurled a tirade of abuse at the rag tag militiamen.

"Roger that, act accordingly," came the reply from control.

Tank signalled to his number three, by waving straightened fingers across his throat. He moved from the window and allowed the unit sniper to take up his firing position. The Somali officer stormed across the courtyard to the whipping post, and he began to kick the shackled captive in the guts. The man twisted his body to try to avoid the vicious blows but there was no escaping it. The taskforce sniper lined up his target and squeezed the trigger three times, tap, tap, and tap. Two bullets smashed into the officer's chest and the third blew the top of his cranium off. It landed on the floor still inside the red beret. Said Adid tumbled onto the compacted sand at the feet of his shackled captive, and his brains spilled out of his skull. A fourth bullet hit the captive in the centre of his chest and released him from the pain of further torture. By the time the militia men had reached their leader and realised that he had been assassinated, Tank and his unit were already a quarter of a mile away.

7

THE CHILD TAKER

The Child Taker could not have planned it better. He approached the back of the tent where the beautiful twins were sleeping, and he smiled a crooked smile as the sound of Louise reaching her orgasm reached him from the tent next door. She was noisy, that was for sure. It reminded him of his first night in the guardianship of a catholic priest, known to the children as, Father Paul. When he was first taken to the boys home, and the social workers had left, Father Paul had taken him to his office where he'd been forced to strip naked while the priest watched him. Then Father Paul had bent him over the desk and beaten him with a leather-soled slipper.

"You've been sent here so that I can save your wicked soul," the priest had ranted as he spanked him with the slipper. "Say I'm a wicked boy, Father Paul," he instructed him.

"Please don't hit me, Father Paul," he had sobbed between the blows. "I haven't done anything wrong!"

"Shut up you wicked boy, now repeat after me, I'm a wicked boy, Father Paul." Each word brought a fresh blow to his reddening buttocks. Each blow brought stinging tears to his eyes. He was supposed to be safe here, safe from his stepfather's beatings, but now he was being beaten by the man who was meant to protect him.

"Ow! I'm a wicked boy, Father Paul," he'd cried. Unfortunately, the beating had continued, and was merely the prelude to severe sexual abuse that was repeated every night for as long as he could remember. Eventually Father Paul had identified a younger boy to receive his particular brand of salvation, and the abuse became less frequent, although it never stopped. The worse thing was the shame of returning to the dormitory. All the other boys knew what Father Paul did to you in his office, and each of them suffered his abuse at some stage in their miserable lives. The priest made the boys say things while he buggered them, the noisier the better. Louise cried out from the next-door tent and his thoughts returned to the task at hand.

He licked his crooked teeth as he knelt next to the tent wall. The twin's father was climbing into the woods opposite, and the mother had driven off somewhere in the car. The situation was absolutely perfect.

He took a razor sharp blade from his pocket and sliced a cross through the canvas with two deft cuts. In seconds he was inside the tent and next to the beautiful children. His heart quickened and he had to take a deep breath to calm his breathing down. He could hear their gentle snoring in the darkness. They were sleeping face to face which was ideal for what he had in mind. The Child Taker removed a plastic sandwich bag from his pocket. Inside it was a tissue soaked with chloroform, and he took it from the bag and placed it beneath the noses of the twins. Within seconds, their breathing had slowed further still as they slipped into unconsciousness. He grabbed the edges of the sleeping bag and gathered them up into his arms. The groaning in the tent next door was reaching fever pitch as he carried the children out of the tent and into the woods.

8

REALISATION

Hayley indicated and turned the estate car into the campsite. The headlights swept across the open ground between the two clumps of trees that bordered the site. Flying insects of every description hurtled toward the light and splattered across the windscreen. Karl was half way between the trees and the tent, and he carrying a square object in his hand. He was two hundred yards away, but it looked to Hayley as if he was holding a stereo speaker. A chill ran down her spine. What was he doing?

Hayley rounded a small hump and their tents came into full view, illuminated by the headlights. There was no sign of Louise or Steve, and the barbeque was nothing but a dull glow. Karl waved at her as she approached the camp.

"Where have you been?" Hayley opened the door and climbed out of the BMW.

"You will not believe me if I told you," Karl moaned. Hayley noticed blood running from a small cut on his leg, and scratches around his shins and ankles. "Someone is well out of order, their idea of a sick joke." He held up the speaker.

"What are you talking about, Karl?"

"The baby crying before you left, well it got worse, and

there was a woman screaming too." He held the speaker up again. "I went to help and found this in the woods."

Hayley could only think of one reason why anyone would do that, and the blood drained from her face. Her fists clenched tight around the car keys and her knuckles went white. She had read about a serial rapist in America who used recordings of babies crying to lure women out of their homes. Hayley stared past her husband at their tent.

"What's the matter, Hayley?" Karl was alarmed by the look on her face.

"The twins," she murmured. She couldn't speak properly, and her legs were frozen with fear. She literally couldn't move as her body was filled with dread.

"What do you mean?"

"The twins," she repeated, still frozen.

The tent next door wobbled and the flysheet unzipped loudly. Steve and Louise stumbled out half-dressed.

"What's the matter you two?" Steve asked. Louise yawned and looked disinterested.

Hayley managed to gain control of herself as she walked toward the tent nervously. Karl followed suit and realised her concern.

"They're sleeping darling, don't worry," he reassured himself more than anyone else.

Hayley reached down and pulled the zip upward, and she lifted the entrance flap up. The interior was inky black and she couldn't see anything at first. She reached for the battery lantern and pulled her hand away quickly when she felt bugs crawling all over it.

"Shit!" she hissed.

"What?" Karl asked.

"Put the light on. Put the fucking light on!"

Karl reached for the lamp, found the button and flicked it on.

Hayley gasped and drew a deep breath. Karl's voice stuck in his throat as he took in the scene, he stared at the speaker in his hand as realisation hit home. His knees wobbled and he folded onto the floor. Louise and Steve leaned into the tent.

"Oh my god!" Steve whispered under his breath. The back of the tent hung in tattered flaps, and a cold breeze moved the material gently. The tent was empty. Their twins were gone of that, there was no doubt; someone had cut their way into the tent to kidnap them. Karl's life flashed before his eyes as he thought about the type of people that could stage a kidnap such as this, about what they took children for, and his stomach wretched. Thick yellow bile sprayed the floor as he vomited, and the strong acidic taste made him vomit again. Hayley screamed from the pit of her soul, and it was the worst sound a cheating husband could ever hear.

9

MAJOR STANLEY TIMMS

Major Timms and his taskforce watched live pictures, which were being taken by an unmanned Predator drone. It had launched a Hellfire missile strike against the souk when Tank and his unit were a safe distance away. The old market place had been ripped to pieces by the initial explosion, and was then rocked by a series of huge explosions, which indicated that a large cache of weapons and munitions had been stored in the ancient building. The general consensus of opinion was that it was indeed the headquarters of the pirate warlord, Said Adid, and that he'd been terminated.

"Another job well done," the Major turned the pictures off. "We'll be transported by Chinook at 0800 tomorrow to a friendly airbase in Ethiopia, and then back to the UK, from there. You'll be back in your own beds by Tuesday."

"Roger that," Tank said. He slapped a colleague on the back with his huge hand, a little too hard. "Sounds like beer time to me."

"Absolutely, ladies and gentlemen, please make your way to the mess where you'll find that our American hosts have laid on a selection of their finest fare, and a few cases of Budweiser for your enjoyment," the Major opened the debriefing room door and the unit filtered out into the corridor. Everyone was buzzing with the adrenalin of completing a successful operation, everyone except the unit's number three. He was leaning against the carrier's bulkhead with one knee raised behind him, and his arms folded. Tank caught his eye and his number three met his gaze and held it. The Major spotted the silent standoff and stepped into the fray.

"Is there a problem here, Adams?" the Major took his number three by the elbow and guided him away from the others. The debriefing room was emptying fast, and Tank waited until the others had gone before closing the door and turning to face his accuser.

"Yes, Major. I have a problem with leaving eyewitnesses behind when it's a clear breach of our policies," Adams flushed red as he spoke. He knew that his behaviour in the field would be questioned when the unit arrived back at base, and he thought it was best to put his side forward before anyone else did.

"This is the Terrorist Task Force, and we don't have policies," Tank laughed as he spoke, but Adams could see the venom in his eyes was very real. "When were you told that we kill kids?"

"He was an armed militia member, it doesn't matter how old he was."

"Oh it matters alright," Tank stepped closer to him, aggression flared in his eyes. Adams wouldn't last two seconds against a giant like Tank, and he knew it. "You see that's the difference between us and them Adams, we can take out the bad guys without becoming like them."

"I'll deal with this, John, please go and join your unit," the Major said without looking at him. Tank smiled at Adams and turned toward the door. There was no love lost between the two men. Tank didn't rate him, and Adams knew that. It was only a matter of time before he was dumped back into the regular army, which was something that he was desperately trying to avoid.

"He compromised the mission, sir, the boy could have escaped and alerted the militia to our presence in the city," Adams dived in at the deep end.

"I'll be straight with you, Adams, I wanted you to be given your papers months ago. You're a good soldier, but you're not a team player, and the whole unit knows that. John Tankersley was the one who wanted to give you another chance, and he picked you for that operation to see how you would respond to extreme pressure. Unfortunately you have shown your true colours and as such, I'll be arranging for you to be transferred back to your regiment on our return."

"I followed procedure, sir, Tank didn't," Adams snapped.

"John Tankersley is the best soldier, in the best unit, in the best army on the planet Adams, and you're not even the best soldier in this room at the moment. You're dismissed soldier," the Major brushed past him and opened the door. "Join the others for the refreshments, I'll keep my decision secret until we reach base, to keep you from any embarrassment."

Adams frowned and stepped out of the room into the grey metal corridor. It was one of thousands which made up nearly two hundred kilometres that threaded their way through the huge aircraft carrier. The Major followed behind him, and walked with a spring in his step, as a good paratrooper should.

"It's a fabulous vessel this, don't you think?" the Major made chitchat as they walked, as if nothing had happened.

"I haven't really thought about it, Major."

"Did you know that she has two nuclear reactors which power her, and she doesn't need to be refuelled for twenty years, which is amazing," the Major shook his head at the ingenuity of the engineers.

"Fascinating, Major."

"Fascinating indeed, Adams, now let's have that beer," they entered the mess hall which was only one of seventeen others. It was filled with enough long tables to seat five hundred service men at one sitting. The taskforce members sat to the right hand side of the mess hall. Some of them were sitting down and talking excitedly across the long table, while others were gathered beneath a flat screen television, and watching the football results from home.

"Any results?" the Major asked as he helped himself to a cold Budweiser.

"Liverpool beat Chelsea four nil again," Grace replied. The sport finished and a review of the main news was playing. Tank looked at the Major to see if there was anything he wanted to say about Adams, but he remained impassive. There would be time for all that when they got back to base.

"Have you got any fishing trips planned when we get home, Major?" Grace made conversation.

The Major was focused on the news and he didn't reply. Grace followed his gaze and noted the picture of two blond children on the screen. There was a news conference being set up, with a blow up picture of the children behind it. A distraught woman was talking silently to the cameras because the volume was turned down, and her red-eyed partner was seated next to her but an unusual distance away. They didn't appear to be united in their grief.

"Major, have you got any fishing trips planned?"

"Be quiet, turn up the volume on the television," the Major raised his voice and everyone stopped talking.

"What?"

"I said turn up the volume on the television," the muscles in his jaw line were pulsating wildly and he had a panicked look on his face. The volume was turned up and the last few words of a distraught mother's appeal for her children to be returned to her played out across the mess hall.

"Jesus Christ Almighty!" the Major looked like he was going to fall over. His mouth was open, as if he wanted to speak but couldn't find his voice.

"What is it, Major?" Tank moved to his side and poured a glass of iced water.

"Jesus Christ Almighty!" the Major whispered as he looked around at the stirring faces. He felt like he was in a terrible dream, one that he had to escape at all costs, but his limbs were filled with concrete and he couldn't run away.

"What the fuck happened then?" Tank asked Grace, but she just frowned and shook her head.

"He was watching the news then he flipped," she replied quietly.

"Major, what's wrong?"

"The missing twins on the news, I have to get home immediately," he rambled. The colour was returning to his cheeks and he seemed to stiffen up as he composed himself.

"I don't understand, Major," Tank said.

"The missing twins that were on the news; the woman making the appeal was my daughter, Hayley, and the twins are my grandchildren."

10
THE CHILD TAKER

Taking the twins had been one of the easier abductions that he'd executed. Things had fallen into place nicely; with the parents arguing, and then separating, combined with his decoy, of course, which was a stroke of genius he'd stolen from an American serial killer. It had worked like a dream by luring the father away from his children. The other adults were too occupied by their drink-fuelled passion to be of any consequence. Carrying the sleeping bag through the woods with the unconscious twins inside had been physically taxing, but adrenalin and pure greed had driven him onwards to his waiting van. The van was a white Ford, one of millions that congest Britain's roads every day. The journey home was uneventful, and he stopped only to re-medicate the twins, and to change the plates. He had swapped the registration plates three times before he'd finally reached his safe place, in order to prevent the police tracking him via the motorway's closed circuit television cameras. He had a caravan parked up in a quiet lay-by a few hours' drive away. It was inconspicuous enough when he hooked it up to the back of his Ford, and ideal to stay one step ahead of the law enforcement agencies.

He smiled as he watched the portable television. The televised appeal for information by the parents had just finished and the Child Taker knew that his internet inbox would be filling up with messages. The buyer and the unsuccessful bidders would now realise that the merchandise had been acquired, and the bidding war would begin again in earnest. The buyer would be furious of course, after all a price had been agreed and a deal had been brokered, but he wasn't selling microwave ovens, and there was no integrity in this world. It always happened that way in this business. Interested parties were always sceptical as to whether the children would actually materialise, or if it was another internet scam and their scepticism was always reflected in their bidding. There was nothing like a good televised appeal to wet their appetites and stoke up the bidding again. The same thing had happened with the last four children that he'd taken, and the price had more than doubled once the second round of bidding was opened. It was usually the same dozen or so bidders that competed from four different continents, but the buyer this time was also his customer the last time around. In fact, it was them that had mentioned that they would be interested in twins, especially mixed sex twins, and that they would pay handsomely for them.

He checked the pictures that he'd taken with his digital camera. There were twelve in total, three of the twins sleeping in their pyjamas, and nine of them naked. The Child Taker had been tempted to indulge his own sexual desires, but the twins were too valuable to spoil, and as such, he had resisted the temptation. He didn't class himself as a real paedophile, because it wasn't only prepubescent children that he liked to abuse. He wasn't fussy who he abused; men, women or children were all the same to him, as long as they were thoroughly unhappy about what he was doing to them, then he was sexually satisfied. It was ironic that he frowned upon real paedophiles as he saw them as being somehow more perverted than himself. At the end of the day what they did with the children once he'd been paid was their own business. The pictures that he'd taken would fuel their interest further, and he scanned them from the camera into his laptop, and then saved them onto a memory stick. He would need to go to a site with public internet connection facilities to send them, that way no one could trace where the upload had come from if they were discovered on line. It had been forty-eight hours since the twins went missing, and the newspapers and television were full of little else. Police investigations into any associated activity on line would be intense, and so he would have to be careful.

The Child Taker slipped the memory stick into his pocket and slipped the laptop under his arm. He turned off the portable television. A small lamp radiated the only light in the caravan, and it created long shadows in the confined space. He walked from the u-shaped seating area into a small kitchenette. The curtains were closed tightly, which gave the caravan a claustrophobic feel. There was a permanent smell of must and damp which permeated the mobile dwelling, no matter how many windows he opened it always seemed to be there, lingering. He flicked off the lamp and walked toward the bedroom. The caravan vibrated in time with his footsteps. He opened the bedroom door an inch and peeped inside. The twins were sleeping like spoons in their sleeping bag. Zak had his arm across his sister, protecting her while she slept. A pink mobile gyrated above them, and it played a lullaby that he didn't recognise as it turned. The mobile had a subtle nightlight beneath it, which cast the room a pink colour. Under different circumstances, it was a peaceful scene, but the twins were blissfully unaware of the terrible evil that hung over them.

The warm glow of the nightlight and the dulcet tones of the lullaby made him envious. He'd tried to replicate his ideal boudoir for the children he kept, somewhere that he would have liked to sleep, peacefully and safe. His own memories of being a child were nowhere near as comfortable as the scene he was looking at now. The dormitory that he shared with nineteen other boys was cold and dark, and there were no lullabies playing. The only sound he remembered at night was the sobbing of his companions, and the desperate cries of whichever poor soul that Father Paul had chosen to discipline. He remembered the sound of those tormented boys vividly, and it was those cries that had twisted his mind irreparably. Hearing someone else suffering meant that he was safe, Father Paul would not hurt him while he was hurting another. Somewhere along the line of growing up the lessons of his abusive childhood mutated and made him the man he was today. He watched the children sleeping and a tear ran down his face, not for them, he didn't care about them, he cried for himself. The Child Taker closed the door gently, and locked it with a key. He opened the caravan door and stepped outside into the night. There was a fast food restaurant on the outskirts of Warrington, which was the nearest town, and it had free WI-FI connections for its customers. It would be the ideal place to upload the pictures for his potential customers to view. His buyer had offered twenty five thousand Euros for each twin and a ten thousand Euro bonus if they were mixed sex. With the children in his possession and the pictures on line, he could demand double that price, at least.

"Are you going somewhere, Jack?" a gruff voice startled him as he descended the small metal steps, which accessed the caravan.

"What's it got to do with you?" he replied frightened by the sudden interruption to his thoughts. He ran his skeletal fingers through his greasy hair. "Who the fuck are you anyway?"

"That's very rude, Jack, considering my client is your best customer. I'm Alfie, and this is my colleague, Brian," the man stepped from the shadows, and another man appeared from the opposite side.

"I don't know what you're talking about."

"Really?" Alfie smiled. "What about the little Asian boy you sold last month, surely you remember him?"

"Go away, I don't know you. You've got me mixed up with someone else," the Child Taker went pale with fear. He stepped off the last step onto the grass and tried to walk by the two men. They were thickset men and tall too. The Child Taker was no fighter, and he needed to get away from them quickly. He was confused to say the least. He had moved the caravan twice in the last two days, never staying in one place for more than one night. He couldn't understand how they had found him, but he knew that they weren't here to socialise. Jack was careful not to give his location to anyone, especially the people that he did business with. They were dangerous men. He tried to walk past them.

"Where do you think you're going, Jack?" A heavy blow hit him in the solar plexus, and he creased up. The wind was knocked out of his lungs. "Now then, my client thinks that you might renege on the deal again. He wasn't best pleased the last time around, and so we've taken a few precautions to make sure that it doesn't happen again." Jack felt a strong hand on his collar, and it lifted him effortlessly. He couldn't breathe as his jacket garrotted him.

"Let's see what's in the caravan shall we, Jack?"

The two men opened the caravan door and then dragged him up the steps. His knees scuffed painfully on the grated metal, but he didn't cry out. There was no point. He had picked this spot because it was miles away from anywhere. No one would hear him shouting for help, and at the end of the day, he didn't want to attract too much attention to the caravan. He clung to the doorframe for a second, but a sharp kick to his skinny fingers halted his futile resistance.

"Search him," he was dropped heavily onto the floor and he heard the door being closed behind him. He opened his eyes and noticed that the two men were wearing highly polished shoes and trousers. Not the attire of your average mugger. Combined with the facts that they knew his name, and that they knew about the Asian boy he'd sold last month, added up to the fact that he was in deep trouble. He felt rough hands fumbling around in his pockets.

"Keys for the van, a random door key, a wallet with ten pounds in it, and a memory stick," Jack recognised the man's voice as he inventoried the contents of his pockets. He had spoken to him on the telephone during his last deal. The fact that he'd remembered a loose connection to the men didn't offer him any comfort, in fact it had the opposite effect. The people that they worked for were evil sadistic businessmen. They had set up an online live feed where fellow perverts could pay per view and watch the young boy that he'd sold being subjected to things that even the Child Taker himself couldn't stomach to watch. He had watched it, out of a morbid curiosity, to the point when the poor child had died, but when the abuse continued he'd turned it off. Everyone had a line that couldn't be crossed, and while he didn't get any kicks out of necrophilia, it was obvious that some people did, but that didn't mean that he had to watch. These people made him look like an angel in comparison.

"The bedroom door is locked."

"Try this," Alfie handed Brian a key which he'd taken from Jack.

Brian walked back down the small corridor and opened the door with the key. "They're in here."

"So, Jack, or should I call you the, 'Child Taker'?" Alfie said in a gruff voice. He held his face by the cheeks and squeezed tightly. Jack didn't fear torture or abuse, he'd experienced it all his life. His mind switched off and took him to a dark place where it waited until the pain had stopped and then it could return to his body safely. He'd developed the technique when Father Paul was offering him the love of Christ by buggering him. "My client thinks that you may have been about to restart the auction."

"I wasn't. I was about to contact you."

"You were supposed to contact me yesterday, Jack."

"I had a few problems."

"You had a few problems?"

"Yes."

"What type of problems?"

Jack's mind went blank. He didn't know where the line of questioning was going, but he was sure that it was going to involve him being hurt badly, or probably killed. Hurt wasn't too much of a problem, but dead he didn't want at all. He saw death as a place where he would have eternity to dwell on the things that had been done to him, and the things that he'd done to others, and that frightened him.

"I asked you a question."

"I'm sorry, what did you say?" his thoughts cleared and he focused on the situation.

"I asked you what type of problems?" Brian stepped in and slapped him hard with the back of his hand. Jack's head snapped sideways but he barely felt it. He looked at his aggressor and thought about the answer.

"I had a puncture."

"When?"

"What?"

"I said when did you have a puncture, Jack?"

"Why does it matter?" Jack asked with a sigh.

"It matters because my client needs to know that you're not reneging on the deal again, Jack, he doesn't trust you."

"The twins are there, give me my money and go," Jack tried to stand up, but he got a vicious kick in the ribs for his efforts.

"When did you have a puncture, Jack?"

"Yesterday," Jack gasped, his breath had been kicked from his lungs, and he struggled to talk.

"When, Jack." He was slapped hard again.

"About two o'clock," Jack snapped and shouted.

The man looked at his colleague. His colleague shook his head in disagreement. "He's lying."

"You're lying, Jack, and that's not good." A highly polished shoe smashed into his face. Jack felt his blackened teeth crack and he could taste the coppery flavour of his own blood.

"What makes you think that I'm lying?" Jack shouted in desperation. He spat blood onto the linoleum kitchen floor. "I had a puncture, what's so unusual about that?"

"We took the liberty of fitting a tracker to your van, Jack, during the last deal, because our client said that you're a dishonest man, Jack." Alfie sat down and crossed his legs, while Brian continued to rain blows down on Jack. "So, because of the tracker, we know where you went and where you didn't go yesterday, and you didn't stop anywhere at two o'clock, Jack."

"That's how you knew that I was here?" Jack asked feeling very offended that he'd been fitted with a tracker during a deal which involved the sale of a nine year old boy to an online paedophile ring. How dare they?

"Terrible infringement of your human rights, Jack?"

"Take the twins and go," Jack wiped blood from his lips with the sleeve of his shirt.

"I'm afraid that it's not that simple, Jack." The man pulled out a revolver. Jack thought that it looked ancient, like he'd seen in cowboy films when he was a boy. Father Paul had let him watch a few cowboy films in his room, which was the only room with a television in it. Of course he'd have to earn it, but sometimes the abuse was over quickly and then he could watch the films in peace. He loved cowboy films, especially Clint Eastwood movies. If ever there was a cowboy, it was Clint.

"Are you going to kill me?" Jack asked.

"No, Jack, because you're good at your job, unfortunately you're not honest. What you need is discipline, and then you can go back about your business a better man." The man stepped over him and pointed the gun at his groin. The Child Taker closed his eyes and went to his dark place to wait.

11
FAMILY LIAISON

Hayley walked through the front door of her semi-detached townhouse. She had to run the gauntlet of the growing crowd of newspaper reporters who had set up camp outside their home. It was a four storey red brick building with white framed windows. They were becoming the building of choice for property developers across Britain because they were tall and narrow, more homes could be built on any given piece of real estate. Karl thought it was trendy to live in a townhouse, but Hayley hated the small windows and shoebox sized bedrooms. She could barely fit a vacuum cleaner around the beds, and although it was new, it felt cramped. She kicked off her shoes and hung up her coat. Her face looked pale and gaunt, and there were dark circles beneath her eyes. She felt completely numb one minute and the next she would cry so hard that she thought she would choke to death. Karl had tried to comfort her in her grief but she couldn't stand him anywhere near her. He was grieving himself, but that was irrelevant, she didn't want him to touch her, and that was that.

Karl stepped in the front door and kicked off a pair of black ankle high boots. Behind him was a pretty woman, with strawberry blond hair tied up tightly in a bun on the back of her head. Her name was Sylvia Lees, and she was a police officer. Her role was Family Liaison Officer, and she had to stay with the family as the point of communication between them and the investigation. She also had to monitor the family's behaviour and report anything suspicious to her Senior Investigating Officer. Most child abductions are family related, and as such, the police liked to have eyes on the inside of the investigation. Sylvia had worked on several cases like this one, and she was picking up some unusual vibes from Karl and Hayley. She hung up her leather jacket and straightened her jumper. It was open at the neck and stretched provocatively over her firm breasts. She had noticed Karl looking at her inappropriately on more than one occasion already. The undue attention was ringing alarm bells in her mind.

"Is everything alright between you and Hayley?" Sylvia asked.

"Things are a bit strained at the moment, but under the circumstances I'm not surprised." Karl wouldn't meet her gaze as he answered her, and he continued to look down at his socks awkwardly.

Sylvia nodded and left him in the hallway. She walked into the kitchen and saw Hayley staring at her own reflection in the window. She was holding the kettle under the tap, and was completely unaware that it was filled to overflowing, and that the tap was still running. The pretty police officer turned the tap off and touched her shoulder. Hayley flinched a little and her eyes filled with tears again. Sylvia placed the kettle on the draining board and hugged her gently, while she sobbed. Outside it was growing dark and she saw Karl's reflection in the window. He was standing in the doorway watching the two women, and Sylvia thought that it was very odd for a husband to standby while his wife grieved openly for her children. It was odd that he made no attempt to comfort her.

"Go and sit down. I'll make us all some tea. I need to talk to you both," Sylvia looked at Karl for a reaction but he turned and walked away without saying a word. Hayley ignored the request and opened a cupboard. She took three matching red mugs out and they clinked as she placed them near to the kettle.

"I'm okay if I keep busy, I'll make the tea, or would you prefer coffee?" Hayley said. Her voice was thick with grief.

"Coffee would be good. Is everything alright with you and Karl?"

"What?"

"You seem very distant from one another."

"Is it that obvious?" Hayley bit her lip to stop the tears from coming again.

"You should be carrying each other, but there seems to be a barrier between you," the officer explained things as she saw them.

"He's been having an affair with his brother's wife, and he left my babies alone, and now they're gone. Apart from that everything is fine," Hayley took a jar of coffee from the cupboard and twisted the top of it aggressively. She dug a teaspoon deep into the granules and chucked a spoonful into each cup in turn.

"You mean Louise?" Sylvia was shocked, but she had to follow the line of questioning now that she'd started it. "Louise is Steve's wife right, the woman that was with you at the campsite?"

"Yes. Do you want sugar?"

"One please. Are you sure about the affair?"

"Yes."

"How long has it been going on?"

"What?"

"How long has the affair been going on?"

"I'm not sure, why?"

"Because it could have a bearing on the case, Hayley. It's

very important that you're both honest," Sylvia reached out and touched her hand. "Most child abductions are carried out by a member of the family. Removal by a stranger is the most unusual form of kidnap Hayley."

Hayley looked the police officer in the eyes and spilled the sugar off the spoon. She tutted and reached for a damp dishcloth to clean up the mess with. There was a dull thud in the hallway and the sound of the front door closing.

"You have to be sure, Hayley. How long has the affair been going on?"

"I'm not sure. You can't possibly believe that Karl has kidnapped his own children for god's sake," Hayley wiped the sugar up with the cloth and then tossed it back into the sink.

"Stranger things have happened, Hayley and if you want us to get your children back then we have to keep an open mind and explore every avenue that we can."

Hayley poured boiling water into the cups and then went to the fridge for milk.

"Milk?"

"Hayley, are you sure he's been having an affair?"

"No I'm not sure. Do you want milk or not?"

"So you think that he's been having an affair?"

"Yes."

"What makes you think that? Have you confronted him?"

"No, I just know."

"How do you know, Hayley?"

"I just do, women can sense these thing, can't we?"

"Woman's intuition, I'm not sure a divorce lawyer would put any faith in it," Sylvia said pointedly.

"What are you talking about divorce for?" Hayley stared at her with her mouth wide open. She was shocked, but she wasn't sure why. Karl was having an affair after all, and surely, divorce would be the next step. The thought hadn't entered her mind until now.

"If Karl was thinking about divorcing you then he would have motive to take the twins, Hayley," Sylvia had to spell it out.

"Why are you saying this?" Hayley started to cry again. Her mind was befuddled with Sylvia's theory.

"When did you first suspect that he was having an affair?"

"I think she's answered enough questions for now, Officer," Major Stanley Timms was stood in the kitchen doorway, and from the look on his face he'd been standing there a while.

"Dad," Hayley put the milk down and ran to her father. She threw her arms around his neck and cried like a baby. He held her tightly and stroked the back of his daughter's head, like he used to when she was a child.

"It's very important that we get to the bottom of this Mister..?"

"Major," he said. "Major Timms."

"I see, Major. It must be a terrible shock for you but we must rule out every possible option that we can."

"Not tonight you're not, Officer. Go home and get some sleep."

"I'm under orders, Major, to remain with the family until the Senior Investigating Officer decides otherwise," Sylvia stood her ground.

"You're here at the family's request?"

"Technically, Major."

"Then technically leave. You're welcome back here in the morning, but I need to be with my daughter alone tonight," the Major spoke with a clear crisp authority in his voice.

Sylvia was about to speak when a monster of a man walked into the kitchen. He looked like he'd been carved from an oak tree. There was a look in his icy blue eyes as they held her gaze.

"Problem, Major?" Tank said.

"Hi, John," Hayley reached out a hand and touched his. He leaned over and kissed her cheek gently.

"Hello trouble," Tank replied, as he squeezed her hand.

"This is, Officer..?" the Major said.

"Lees, Sylvia Lees, and I'm the Family Liaison Officer."

"Sylvia was just leaving," the Major said coldly.

"I'll get your coat," Tank smiled, but there was no warmth in his smile.

Sylvia realised that she was flogging a dead horse and walked toward the doorway. She paused and looked at Hayley before stepping into the hallway. Hayley tried to smile at her through her tears but she couldn't manage it, she buried her head into her father's chest again. He smelled of Old Spice and pipe tobacco, he smelled safe.

"I'll walk you to your car, Officer Lees," Tank smiled again and Sylvia almost went weak at the knees. He was tall and handsome, and built like a battleship. "Is this your coat?"

"Yes, thank you," she felt like a schoolgirl and giggled nervously. She struggled into her jacket and Tank straightened it at the collar for her. "Thank you," she blushed.

Tank moved toward the front door and opened it for her. She stepped out into the evening air and Tank followed her. There was a torrent of questions fired from the melee of reporters who were being held at the end of the driveway by uniformed officers.

"It looks like the circus has arrived," Tank said, looking toward the clicking cameras.

"It's par for the course on a case like this, missing children are big news I'm afraid," Sylvia sighed.

"What can you tell me about the investigation, Sylvia?"

"Nothing," she stopped and turned toward him. "It's obvious that you're a friend of the family, but I can't share any information with you."

"My name is John Tankersley, I'm lead agent for a counter-terrorist unit," He flashed her an identity badge unlike any that that she'd ever seen before.

"I'm sorry, which constabulary are you with?" she asked confused.

"I'm not in the police force, Sylvia."

"But you said you're with a counter-terrorist unit?"

"Yes, I'm military."

"Oh, like Special Forces?" she walked toward her car.

"Yes, like Special Forces."

"Well, Mr Special Forces, I still can't tell you anything about the investigation. She opened the car door and climbed in. She sat holding the steering wheel for a moment as if she were thinking about something. Tank brought himself level with her and crouched down.

"Look off the record, have you got any suspects?" he asked.

"Suspects are about all we have at the moment," she said looking into his blue eyes. She could get lost in them, she thought.

"Forensics?"

"I really can't talk to you about the investigation, John," she shook her head.

"I'm not asking you to tell me anything that a hundred people at your police station, and their families, don't already know," he laughed. His eyes sparkled when he smiled, and lines creased the corners of his eyes.

"It's too early for any forensics yet. We should have the first reports in tomorrow," she replied without committing herself.

"What have you got to go on?"

"Two missing children, taken from a campsite in the Lake District, and evidence of a sophisticated decoy," she reached into the glove box and took out a packet of menthol cigarettes.

"What type of decoy?"

"Someone placed a wireless speaker in the woods and used it to play the sound of a baby in distress," she flipped open her Zippo and lit it, Tank moved back from the smoke. She inhaled it deeply and then blew it out before speaking again. "According to the father's statement he went to help the distressed baby, found the speaker and when he returned, the children were gone."

"It was well planned and well executed," Tank said.

"That's how it appears," she nodded her head and drew deeply on the smoke again.

"You must have a list of suspects who are capable of pulling this off?"

"We do, but it's a very long list," she replied.

"Have you ruled out kidnap?"

"No one has asked for a ransom as yet," she shrugged.

"What other avenues are you going down?"

"We haven't ruled anything out yet, including family members," she blew smoke toward him.

"It seems unlikely, considering the decoy," Tank mused, fishing for more information.

"It wouldn't be the first elaborate hoax manufactured by a family member, and none of the family adults were there at the time of the abduction, so we have to keep that door open," she rolled her eyes toward the press. "This lot don't help one bit. People see missing children convert into pound signs very quickly."

"Do you think they were stolen to order?"

She looked at him hard, and swallowed. The cigarette had burned to the filter and she tossed it onto the lawn before answering. Tank frowned and picked it up. He rolled it between his finger and thumb.

"It doesn't matter what I think happened, we have to keep an open mind," she started the engine and smiled sadly. "There is a Major Investigation Team working flat out on this case, which is thirty senior detectives headed up by our most experienced Detective Inspector. I'm a very small cog in a very big wheel."

"Granted, but I'd appreciate your opinion," he stepped away from the car. She closed the door and opened the window so that they could still converse.

"Okay, yes. I think that they were stolen to order," she said slowly.

"And you must have details of the usual suspects when this type of crime occurs?" he pushed.

"Do you have any idea how many paedophiles are on the sex offenders' register in Cheshire alone?"

"Surprise me."

"Over five hundred, and another four hundred inside doing time," she took a deep breath. "That is just one county."

"That's a lot of scumbags to look at," Tank sighed at the enormity of the task before the police investigation. "What are your thoughts, about the chances of recovering them?"

"Alive?"

"Well that would be the most favourable outcome surely?" Tank raised an eyebrow at her frankness.

"We have a guideline when we're dealing with child abduction, and it's called 'The Golden Hour'. The odds of recovering an abducted child outside of that first hour get progressively lower and lower. The length of time that the twins have been missing means that their chances are slim."

"How slim?"

"Anorexic, in child abduction murder cases, over ninety five percent of the victims were dead within three hours of being kidnapped," she explained. The statistics were frightening, but he needed to know what they were up against.

"If they were stolen specifically to order then the percentages become more favourable?"

"Yes, but if they were taken to order, then it's either paedophiles, or someone wants a readymade family, either way they need to get those children out of the country pronto," she shook her head as she realised just how negative all this must have sounded.

"I'm assuming there's an all ports warning in force?"

"It's one of the first things the Major Investigating Team would have done, as soon as they were allocated to this abduction. They deal with cases like this every day you know," she sounded sarcastic.

Tank stood up to his full height, and leaned on the roof of the car. He looked toward the house and saw Karl watching them from the living room window. He looked tired and alone.

"I'm sorry if I sounded patronising, I didn't mean to. You know that if you come up with anything, that we may be able to help you," Tank said.

"How do you mean?"

"I can get access to things that the police cannot."

"Well I'll bear it in mind, but I'm just a lowly constable, on secondment with family liaison, I'm no detective," she replied cautiously.

"Okay but if anything comes up which hampers the investigation then let me know, I can make it go away."

Sylvia looked into his eyes again and saw steel in there, which frightened her a little. She wasn't sure what he had meant by his last comment, but she was sure that every word was true. Tank waved and walked back toward the front door. He paused to look back a second before stepping into the house and his huge shoulders filled the doorframe. Sylvia picked up her cell phone. She needed to tell her boss that Karl was possibly having an affair with his brother's wife, and about the arrival of the grandfather and his friend, who were both members of a Special Forces unit.

Tank watched her leave through the throng of paparazzi, and the camera flashes gave a strobe effect as she drove by them. He closed the door and reached into his pocket for his cell, and made a telephone call of his own.

"Grace, are you nearly there?" he asked.

"We're pulling into the campsite now," she replied.

"Good, are the police still there?"

"No, it's deserted. There's some crime scene tape to the left near the woods, but the forested area on the opposite side is clear. Have you spoken to the police?"

"Briefly," he said. Karl walked into the room and then realised that Tank was making a call.

"Sorry, I didn't realise," he said embarrassed in his own home. Tank waved and said. "No problem, it's work, I'll be a minute." Karl left the room and closed the door behind him.

"Sorry about that, but I need to be careful about what I say," he said quietly.

"Okay, what leads have they got?"

"Nothing," he sighed again. "The family liaison officer indicated that the investigation team are looking at the family for the abduction, none of them were actually there when the kids were taken, and so they're all suspects."

"Oh my god, that's ridiculous," Grace was shocked.

"Not so ridiculous, I overheard the liaison officer asking Hayley if Karl was having an affair with his brother's wife," Tank whispered into the phone.

"Oh dear, that puts a different perspective on it," she said slowly.

"Exactly, you can see why the investigation is focusing in on the family," Tank said. "I don't buy it one bit, all they are doing is wasting time and allowing the trail to go cold."

"We'll have a good look at the scene, and I'll call you if we find anything."

"Grace," Tank said.

"What?"

"We need to get one step ahead of the kidnappers, and at the moment the police are miles behind them, and looking in the wrong direction."

"I understand, if we find anything, then you'll know about it first."

12

CONISTON WATER

Grace Farrington crouched down and touched a clump of flattened grass. It was about a yard away from a barbed wire fence, which separated the campsite from the woods. To the left the grassy slopes ran gently down toward the lake. To the right was the road which led to the nearest village, and directly behind her was the woods through which the twins were carried off, or at least that's what the police thought so far. It was a cloudy day and across the lake in the distance, the peak of Coniston Old Man was shrouded in mist.

"There's a footprint here," Grace said. Tara was a few yards away studying the area.

"Could be where the father entered the woods?"

Grace moved closer to the fence and looked at the sharp metal barbs. There were two barbs with a dark brown substance on the tips of them.

"Someone entered here. I think this is blood," she said as she took a small plastic tube from her belt and swabbed the barbed wire. She placed the swab into the tube and then sealed it. Beyond the wire, the undergrowth was thick, and there was a green carpet of brambles. "I spoke to the campsite owner earlier, and he said that the only time animals graze on this land is through the winter months, so anything we find, tracks or blood is human."

"What about pets?"

"No pets allowed."

"Well the brambles look pretty dense here, and he was badly scratched around the ankles, it would fit," Tara pointed into the trees.

"Let's see if we can follow his trail."

Grace pulled the top wire up, and Tara climbed through the fence. When she got through, she reciprocated the action to allow Grace to follow suit.

"The branches are broken there," Grace pointed to the base of a sycamore tree. The lower branches were snapped off, but the exposed wood was still pale in colour and slightly damp to the touch. "It's a recent break."

"It looks like he's gone in at an angle," Tara noted. In daylight, the most obvious route was straight on, but the evidence said that Karl had progressed through the trees at a tangent to the fence.

"Well it was dark, and he was moving blindly toward the noise," Grace mused.

"The brambles are ripped over there, and his statement said that he'd stumbled over and then got up again." There was a thick swathe of undergrowth and thorny brambles ripped from the forest floor and clumped together. Tara moved to the right and they walked on for twenty yards or so. There was a gap between two oak trees and the vegetation on the floor looked damaged and torn. The woods opened up a little beneath the majestic oaks, competition for floor space was fierce in the natural world, and there was little vegetation that could survive beneath them. The brambles didn't extend this far into the woods, and the forest floor was a dark mat of rotting twigs and leaves, in various stages of decomposition. There were clear scuffmarks leading away from the clearing toward a dry streambed.

"Over there," Grace said. At the edge of the dry stream was a large chestnut tree. Its roots were exposed by the power of the flowing water that had once run by it.

"What can you see Grace?"

"The perfect hiding place." She approached the tree roots and bent down to touch a dark line on the bark. "Look here, something was resting against this for some time."

"I see, and it was rectangular in shape judging by that line in the moss."

"Exactly, just like a speaker."

"Why didn't the police look in here?"

"Because they had the speaker, and their priority was the wood through which the twins were taken and finding a getaway vehicle. They've planned to come back here at a later date."

"Okay, so we think we know where the decoy was hidden, now what."

"Well my theory is that the speaker was put here well before the abduction was attempted, and then they waited for the right time to turn it on," Grace stood up and looked around the clearing. "We followed the father's tracks easy enough, so let's try and find the kidnapper's trail. They had to come here to leave the speaker," Grace walked along the dry streambed in the opposite direction to the one that they'd come in. Tara walked the other way at ninety degrees to Grace's path.

"How far away would the source of the signal have to be?"

"Wireless speakers generally fall into two categories," Grace answered as she walked. "Infrared and radio frequency operated by remote control, which then beams a signal to the speakers. If they used infrared, then there couldn't be any obstacles between the source and the receiver."

"So we have to assume they used radio frequency."

"We'll assume that for now, but unless we locate the source

we'll have to wait until the police have done their forensic tests." Grace noticed a boulder in the streambed had been dislodged. The exposed soil beneath was dark and damp. Someone had walked here recently.

"Over here," Grace shouted. She crouched next to the boulder and followed the streambed with her eyes. "Since infrared requires a direct line of site, and any objects in the way can prevent the wireless speakers from receiving. I'm guessing that wireless speakers using radio frequency waves to transmit the signal would have to be no more than a hundred metres from the source. You take that side of the stream, and I'll take this side."

Tara nodded and stepped carefully down into the dry stream. They paced slowly heads down, studying the ground before them.

"There," Tara pointed to the top of a rock where the moss had been scraped off. Grace followed her lead. "Do you think that the source will still be here?"

"Well, think about it. If you had snatched two five year old children from their tent, would you hang around to retrieve it?"

Tara shook her head. She spotted a piece of paper in the long grass, which lined the dry stream. It was a chocolate bar wrapper. She moved the grass away from it and looked again.

"Have you found anything?" Grace asked.

"No, all the ink has been washed away from it. It's been here for months." She left the wrapper where it lay and moved on. "I haven't been evidence gathering since I left the Met." Tara had joined London's Metropolitan police force as a degree entrant, and was a promising young officer until she was seconded into the Armed Response Unit. She quickly became one of the top ranking sharpshooters, and she had reacted well in live fire situations, gaining a commendation for taking down a bank robber during a shootout. Although she loved the unit, when she was approached to trial for the Terrorist Task Force she had jumped at the chance. She had no regrets despite the move costing her marriage. The relationship had always been shaky as her husband was intensely jealous of her working with men, and of her success. One day Tara had enough and she packed a small case and left without so much as a goodbye, and she hadn't spoken to him since. Their divorce had been brokered via solicitors, and she had never looked back. Her work mates were her family now, Grace could be prickly to say the least, but the rest of the counter-terrorist unit were friendly and supportive.

"Look here," Grace's voice interrupted her thoughts. On the floor was a cone shaped red plastic top, which was less than an inch in length. "What do you make of that?"

"It looks like the top from a tube of glue, super glue?"

"My thoughts exactly."

"We shouldn't be looking for something on the floor, he's stuck it to a tree," Tara looked around the immediate area and checked the trunks of the trees that were close by. "I'll check back to the clearing, you take the streambed." Tara could tell by the look on Grace's face that she didn't appreciate being told what to do, and she smiled to placate her. Grace turned and walked in the other direction without saying a word. Tara reached the clearing and then tracked backwards checking the trunks, boughs and branches of the trees that she past.

"Over here," Grace's voice called. "We've got something."

Tara walked back up the streambed to where they had separated, and she saw Grace twenty yards on. She was crouching next to a thick oak tree. As Tara approached, she could see the silver glint of a metallic object.

"What is it?"

"Some kind of voice recorder."

"Glued to the tree?"

"Yes, just like you said Sherlock," Grace joked, her animosity to her colleague forgotten for the moment. "And look what else we have here."

Tara bent low and brought her head level with Grace's. The glue had hardened into a clear plastic resin, and behind the recorder was a tiny fibre shimmering in the light. "Is it hair?"

"I think so," Grace took a small evidence blade from her belt pack and prised the recorder from the wood.

"Shouldn't we inform the police?" Tara smiled.

"We test it first, and then we'll inform them, agreed?"

"Agreed, let's get this stuff back to the lab."

13

THE CHILD TAKER

The first kick slammed into his groin with a sickening thwack. Blinding white lights went off in his brain as the delicate tissues that made up his testicles were crushed and torn. Jack went deeper into the darkness of his mind to escape the pain, but a second heavy blow sent sparks searing through his nervous system. He tried not to cry but this time tears ran freely from his eyes. When he was a boy Father Paul seemed to get more turned on if the boys cried, and so he learned not to. If he remained impassive like an automaton then the abuse was over much quicker. Like anything else challenging in life, the human psyche adapted to sexual abuse, and found ways to survive it. Jack survived by building mental doors in his mind. The doors led to rooms, dark rooms deep in his mind where the abusers couldn't reach him. It didn't matter what they did to his body while his mind shut down to protect him.

A third kick ruptured his right testicle and he screamed louder than he'd ever screamed before. He couldn't catch his breath and thought he was going to choke to death. His mouth was open and he was gagging, but nothing came up. He could feel his ruined testicle swelling badly and the pain seared through his abdomen to every nerve ending in his body. The blood was pounding through his brain and his heart felt as if it was about to explode. Unconsciousness gripped him and dragged him down as the pain became too much for his body to bear.

Through the darkness, he could hear gruff voices. They were laughing and unsympathetic, and one of them joked about what Jack had been sent to prison for when he was a boy. They were laughing about what he had done to the priest when he was a boy. He wondered how they knew so much about him and his life. Their employers must have done their research well. His arrest and incarceration seemed like such a long time ago now, a different life when he was Ian, and when he was the abused and not the abuser. The things that he'd done to Father Paul would be well documented, and the details would be easy enough to find in the public records. Jack wasn't daft enough to think that his exploits were untraceable, despite the fact that he'd been given a new identification on his release.

Father Paul's body had been found in his study by the school's early morning cleaners. The post-mortem recorded that he'd been stabbed with a set of mathematical compass over a hundred times, mostly in the eyes and face, and an umbrella had been inserted so far into his anus that his internal organs had been severely damaged. The police said that it was one of the worst crimes that they'd investigated, and that the injuries were consistent with violent rage attack, carried out by someone well known to the victim, with a personal gripe against the priest. As the police investigated the murder, it became obvious that there was no shortage of suspects, as one by one the tales of sustained abuse began to be told. They also discovered that two of the home's residents were missing from their dormitory.

When Jack was called Ian, his life in the care of Father Paul was a living nightmare. The boys under his protection were beaten for the slightest reason, and subjected to sexual abuse at every opportunity. There was no escape from it. On one occasion, a visiting Bishop took prayers in the morning, and then joined the boys for breakfast at first break. He was friendly and appeared to be caring and interested in their welfare. Later that day at lunch, Ian and his best friend Clive, took the opportunity to tell the kindly Bishop what Father Paul had been doing to them at night. His caring facade led them to trust in him, and as such, they appealed to him for help. The Bishop was furious, and told them to keep it a secret until he'd had chance to speak to the other boys, and to Father Paul. The boys placed their trust in him and were repaid later that evening when Father Paul and the Bishop took them to his study where they were beaten and buggered by both men until the early hours of the morning. Jack wasn't surprised that yet another adult gifted with his care had let him down, and hurt him physically; it had become par for the course to him. Clive was never the same again after that night. It was as if his hope and trust in humanity had been shattered completely, and a week later he was found hanged by his dressing gown cord from a tree in the grounds, aged just eleven. Clive was Ian's only real friend and his death turned something in his mind.

Ian couldn't stand anymore, and when Father Paul had finished giving him his special kind of bible class that night, he'd waited until the priest bent down to pull up his underpants from around his ankles, and he stabbed him in the back of the skull with his own compass. Once he'd stabbed him the first time, he couldn't stop, and he continued to plunge the compass point into the priest until he finally stopped moving. The priest had moaned and shouted for help but the boys were used to hearing wailing coming from his office, and his cries for help went unheeded. One boy had heard the priest's cries and investigated by looking through the keyhole, only to see Ian ramming the metal geometry device into Father Paul's eyes. The boy opened the door and closed it behind him, Ian had been oblivious to him, even when he joined the attack and began to kick the priest and stamp on him. The boys became wrapped up in type of hysteria, inserting over fifteen pens and pencils into the priest's skull. Finally, they inserted the umbrella into the priest as an afterthought, ripping his internal organs to shreds. Covered in blood the pair ran from the home with a few pounds that they'd found in Father Paul's desk. It was two days later they were caught sleeping rough in a park nearby, where Ian confessed immediately to killing the priest. He had talked for hours on tape about the abuse he'd received at the hands of the priest, but it bought him only a little compassion from the trial judge. It was twenty years later when he was released back into society as Jack, who went on to be called The Child Taker.

His release into the busy world of normal law-abiding citizens had been traumatic, to say the least. The years of violence and abuse at the hands of Father Paul were replaced by a similar regime in prison. Eventually he began to grow taller and stronger, and he developed long-term relationships with people similar to him in jail. There was strength in numbers and soon the dynamic changed and the abused became the abuser. Despite the years of abuse that he'd suffered he felt no sympathy for his own victims, only excitement and a feeling of power and control. The first man that his twisted posse held down and raped in prison was a turning point for Jack. It released him from the years of being a victim.

Twenty years passed in jail, and a panel of experts decided he was ready for release into society, under the close scrutiny of the probation service. There were many restrictions placed upon his liberty, but none that denied him access to children. He had been convicted and sentenced as a murderer, not a sex offender. It was the system itself that had created his bizarre sexual desires, and because the probation service was so pressured by its workload, nobody noticed him spiralling out of control. His development from a victim to the most dangerous kind of sexual predator was a slow one. He evolved.

The first abduction that he'd carried out was purely an opportunist one, motivated by his own lust. When his desires had been satiated, he was left with a very tearful young girl covered in his DNA, semen, hair follicles and saliva. He knew that they would find him, lock him up, and throw away the key this time around. His instinct to survive took over and he killed her and disposed of the evidence where she would never be found. Months later when the press furore had died down, and the little girl had never been recovered, it dawned on him how simple it had been. It also dawned on him how many paedophiles were talking about the abduction in the chat rooms on the internet. It was a simple progression from the first one, to the second, and then the rest of them. It had made him a man of means financially, and as long as he remained transient, always moving on, then they would never catch him. A hard slap around the face brought him back to the real world, a world of pain.

"Wakey Wakey, Jack," a gruff voice broke through to his consciousness.

"He doesn't look well," Alfie's voice said concerned.

"Shut up and get the kids into the car."

"The Moroccan said teach him a lesson not kick him to death." Jack opened his eyes. One of the men was stood over him, and the other was coming out of the small bedroom with one twin in each arm. They looked cosy and unconcerned as they slept, and the man carried them out of the caravan and down the steps. Jack was doubled up in pain and he knew that he'd been seriously hurt, but he remained still. He heard the boot of a car being closed, and almost felt sorry for the twins. Almost.

"Jack," Alfie shouted at him. "Talk to me, Jack."

Jack looked up at the man but the world was becoming blurred and his voice sounded like an echo, talk to me Jack, talk to me Jack, talk to me Jack. His head began to spin as if he was drunk.

"He looks grey." Brian said.

"Shut up will you," Alfie sounded worried now.

"Jack!" he shouted in his ear.

Jack opened his eyes again, but closed them just as quickly as the world spun violently. He felt vomit rising from his guts, and he groaned as it filled his mouth and then splattered all over the floor. The taste of blood made him wretch again.

"Shit he's throwing up blood."

"What the fucking hell does that mean?"

"It means that you're dead you fool. If the boss finds out that you've ruined his supply line by killing this scumbag, you'll be wearing concrete boots, and looking at the fishes."

"What should we do?"

"What do you mean, we?"

"Let's get out of here."

Jack could hear the men leave, and they turned out the lights and locked the door, 'thoughtful of them', he thought. He heard their engine fire up, and then the car roared as it sped away down the country lanes. Darkness descended on him as the pain in his abdomen intensified.

14

THE TASKFORCE

Tank and Major Timms sat at a wide teak desk in Hayley's study. She used it as her base to run a re-seller business on the internet, so that she could combine work with being a mother to five-year-old twins. The desk had a thin layer of household dust across it, a sign that the study hadn't been used since the twins were snatched. Tank fired up the computer and the screen flickered through a series of different backgrounds as the broadband connected. Hayley's home page appeared and an automated voice informed them that the e-mail box was full. Tank scanned the headers in the inbox to see if there was anything suspicious in there. It all appeared to be innocent. There were no ransom demands, 'mores' the pity', he thought. A kidnap case would increase the chances of recovering the twins unharmed. He checked his watch and nodded to the Major before typing in a secure web address that was only accessed by members of the Terrorist Task Force.

"We're in, Major," Tank said. They were using a webcam to conference call with Grace and Graham Libby, the taskforce's forensic maestro. The taskforce was based in an underground bunker beneath the headquarters of the Merseyside police force, on the banks of the River Mersey. In the seventies a network of subterranean traffic tunnels were built to facilitate the movement of commuters beneath the river. The bunker had been built in secret, at the same time as the Mersey tunnels were constructed, and it spread for miles beneath the city centre. It had been built to house the government in the event of war, and contained intelligence gathering departments, and forensic facilities second to none. The Mersey Estuary opened out into the Irish Sea, and the depths of the Atlantic Ocean were only a few hours away in a nuclear submarine. The idea was that in the event of a Third World War, the bunker could be used by the government in safety, and could withstand a nuclear attack. It was also only yards to the river, where in the event of an imminent enemy invasion key personnel could escape by nuclear submarine.

"What have you got for us, Professor?" Tank asked.

"The blood samples that Grace found on the barbed wire fence match the father's DNA profile," Graham Libby said. He scratched his baldhead and removed his glasses. There were thick tufts of wild grey hair growing unkempt above his ears, which gave him the look of a mad scientist. In reality he was one of the country's best scientific investigators. "That doesn't tell us much on its own. The results of the tests which we carried out on the hair follicle that was removed from the adhesive are far more interesting."

"The blood on the barbed wire could confirm to the police that Karl was in the woods when the children were taken," the Major commented. "It could take the focus off Karl."

Tank nodded his head in agreement. The general consensus of opinion was that the police were spending too much time looking at Karl for the abduction. The hint of an affair with his sister-in-law had added fuel to the flames. The Major was convinced all four adults that were present at the time of the abduction would be hauled in for detailed questioning, especially now that Hayley had mentioned the affair to Sylvia Lees.

"It would indicate that he was away from the tents at some stage, but it's not definitive proof that he ventured any further into the trees," the scientist corrected him. He placed his spectacles back on, and continued.

"Hayley witnessed him walking across the field with the speaker in his hands," Tank argued.

"The police would argue that he could have placed it close to the fence prior to the abduction, and arranged for another party to take the twins. The sister-in-law coerced her husband into their tent with the offer of sex, to allow the abduction to be carried out unhindered," the scientist replied abruptly. It was difficult to argue with the fact that family involvement couldn't be ruled out by the police.

"Let's leave the finer detail to one side for now," the Major interrupted. "Tell me about the results from the hair please."

"The hair follicle was from the hand, or fingers of a Caucasian male, probably in his sixties."

"I thought you had more than that," Tank interrupted impatiently. The how and why of a scientific investigation didn't interest him. He wanted to know the results.

Graham Libby looked over the top of his spectacles and took on the appearance of an angry headmaster. "I have much more than that, Agent Tankersley, if you'd demonstrate some patience then I'll explain." He shook his head angrily and his cheeks and jowls wobbled.

"We haven't got time to play with, Professor," Tank retorted.

"We ran the DNA through our database, and discovered a match. The hair belonged to a man called Ian Thomas. Grace has the details," the scientist said deflated that he'd been forced to rush his information. "I hope you catch him, Major, and I hope that your grandchildren are returned safely."

"Thanks, Graham," the Major replied. "What have you got Grace?"

The study door opened and Hayley tentatively walked

a few paces into the room. She looked a stone lighter than she had before the twins had been taken. Her pretty features looked sunken and gaunt, and her eyes were lifeless and dull. She was wearing a baggy grey jogging suit, which hung loosely from her hips and shoulders, and her beautiful blond hair looked unwashed and lank.

"What have you found out, Dad?" she asked. Her voice was cracked and hoarse. Tank raised his eyebrows in surprise. He thought that she must have been listening to their conversation at the door.

"Give us twenty minutes, Hayley, and we'll talk," the Major turned away from the computer screen and walked toward his daughter.

"I want to hear what they've found out, Dad."

"We've done some background checks into the investigation, that's all. I'll come and tell you in a short while," he reached out and placed his hands on her shoulders. He could feel the bones beneath her clothes. She was wasting away.

"They are my babies, Dad. I need to know what you know."

Tank shifted uncomfortably in his chair. The Major looked back at the screen. Grace had heard Hayley's voice in the room and she didn't look happy. The Major tried to read the expression on her face. Judging by that, he gauged that the news that she had was not good.

"We don't know anything yet, Hayley."

"Bullshit! Don't treat me like a fool," her top lip quivered like it used to when she was a child. The Major felt like his heart was breaking as he watched his only child being torn apart. "I heard Graham say a name, Ian Thomas. Who is he, and has he got my babies?"

The Major closed the study door and then held his daughter's hand. They stepped back to the desk together. Tank coughed and tried to smile at her but she wasn't looking at him. She was looking at the screen.

"Tell me, Grace, who has got my babies." She leaned her head into her father's chest and a tear leaked from the corner of her eye. She held a piece of well-used tissue paper tightly in her right fist.

"Perhaps we should do this later, Major," Grace looked decidedly uncomfortable about revealing the details of their investigation in front of Hayley.

"She needs to know," the Major prompted her to continue, against his better judgement.

Grace looked down for a moment and then took a deep breath before beginning.

"Ian Thomas was born in Irlam, Manchester. His father died when he was seven years old and shortly afterwards he was identified as a child at risk, and placed into the care of the authorities. He was placed into a catholic boys' orphanage where he remained until he was arrested and jailed, aged fourteen."

"Slow down a second, Grace. Jailed for what?" Tank asked.

"He was sent to a young offenders' institution, until he was sixteen and then transferred to Parkhurst for the remainder of his sentence."

"Jailed for what?" Tank repeated himself. The mention of Parkhurst indicated that the offender had serious mental issues.

"At the end of his sentence, he was released under licence and given a new identity, Jack Howarth. As far as we know that's the name he uses now. "

Tank frowned at the Major. Grace was obviously skating over the facts for Hayley's sake.

"I need to know, Grace. Who is this man that has taken my babies, who is this man, somebody please tell me who has taken my babies..!" Hayley's knees buckled and the Major grabbed her to support her. "Please tell me who has taken my babies, Dad, I want my babies, please!" Tears streamed from her eyes and she folded at the waist. "Why has he taken my babies....?" She sobbed uncontrollably. "Please don't let him hurt my children......" her voice trailed off to a choked sob.

"Later, Grace," Tank stood and helped the Major guide Hayley to the study door. Karl had heard the commotion and he was standing in the doorway when they opened it. He looked as tired and shattered as his wife did.

"What's going on?" He asked nervously.

"Take her to lie down, Karl," Tank put Karl's arm under Hayley's elbow and allowed him to take her weight.

"They know who has the twins, and they won't tell me who has taken my babies!" Hayley whined hysterically.

"What?" Karl was incredulous. He looked from the Major to Tank and then back again. Their expressions said everything that he needed to know. "I'm going to call the police, right away," he said exasperated.

"Hayley, calm down," Tank glared at Karl as he tried to calm her.

"How can you know who has taken the twins?" Karl took Hayley's weight and led her away from the study door. She was crying so hard that she was struggling to breath. Saliva dribbled from the corner of her mouth onto the grey hooded top. Karl couldn't take in what had happened. His mouth was wide open in shock, and he was shaking his head in disbelief.

"Karl, take Hayley to lie down, we're trying to help," the Major attempted to calm the situation down. "The doctor gave her some tranquilisers, give her two, and we'll talk to you when she's calmed down."

"How dare you interfere in this, how dare you?" Karl had flushed purple with anger. "They're our children!"

Tank stepped forward and took a hold of Hayley. "Put her to bed, Major, I'll talk to Karl." The Major picked his hysterical daughter up in his arms and carried her toward the bedrooms at the rear of the townhouse. She kicked her legs frantically as if she were being abducted.

Tank towered over Karl, and he could see him flinch visibly as he neared him.

"Karl, we are trying to help find your children," Tank tried to calm him.

"What can you do that the police can't?"

"We can speed things up Karl, we're not trying to hamper their investigation," Tank held his hands palms down to placate him.

"Well then you can tell them what you know when they get here, because I'm calling them now."

"We're going to pass on everything that we know, as soon as we know that it's relevant, Karl."

"Who are you to decide if what you know is relevant?"

"We think that the police have been looking in the wrong direction, and we're looking at the bigger picture, and trying to help."

"This the Major's doing. He has to take control of everything! Well he's not taking control of this, they're my children, and I will not stand by and watch you endanger them," Karl poked Tank in the chest. It was a huge mistake.

"No one is trying to take control, Karl, he's trying to find his grandchildren," Tank took a deep breath and tried to remain calm, but Karl poked him in the chest again as he spoke.

"He has to stick his nose into everything we do, well not this time, I'm calling the police."

Tank tensed his pectoral muscles as Karl made contact, and he grabbed the offending digit with his huge fist and squeezed it painfully. Karl gritted his teeth against the pain in his offensive digit.

"Don't poke me, Karl, it's very annoying. Now calm down and listen to me," he released Karl and he stepped back away from him.

"I'm calling the police!" Karl shouted angrily.

"Okay call them, and we'll deny everything. The police cannot arrest us, in fact, Karl, they can't even talk to us unless we agree to. If we do agree they'll ask us what we know about your affair, and then we'll confirm that we know that you're fucking your brother's wife," Tank shrugged. "Do you know who their number one suspect is at the moment?"

"No, of course I don't."

"You are, Karl."

"What are you talking about?"

"Ninety percent of child abductions are perpetrated by the family, or a close friend of the family. The Major anticipates that all four of you will be taken to the station tomorrow to be interviewed about your affair."

"I've heard enough of your bullshit," Karl stepped forward and thought about poking the big man again, but common sense prevailed and he kept his finger to himself.

"The police are wasting time looking at you, Karl," Tank spoke calmly, trying to get his message across.

"Oh for god's sake man! Why would I abduct my own kids?"

"Because you're having an affair with your brother's wife, and you were worried that Hayley would find out, divorce you, and stop you seeing them."

"Why would the police think that? Where have they got that from?"

"Hayley told Sylvia Lees."

"What?"

"You heard me the first time. Your wife told them."

"I don't understand why she would say that, it's not true," Karl lied.

"You don't have to convince me, Karl," Tank shrugged. "But while there is even a suspicion that it's true then you'll be a suspect."

Karl's jaw opened as if he was about to retaliate, but no words came out. He walked into the sitting room and flopped into a brown leather armchair.

"You can see why they think that, can't you?"

Karl looked winded. He shook his head and his eyes filled with tears.

"We checked the woods where you found the speaker, Karl, and we think we know who put it there," Tank said. "I'm asking you to give us until tomorrow morning to investigate this lead, and then we'll give the police everything that we have."

"What is it exactly that you and Hayley's father do?" Karl was still reeling from the shock of being told that his dirty secret was out, but Tank's revelation that they had impunity from the police had him intrigued. Hayley had said very little about her father's military career throughout their marriage, but he had already come to his own conclusion that he wasn't a Major in the regular army.

"All you need to know is that we're very good at finding people that don't want to be found."

"I believe you," he said shakily. "If you get nowhere then you promise to hand over your information to the police?"

"I promise that we'll let them have anything relevant."

"Find them, Tank. Find my kids." Karl held out a shaking hand toward the big man, and Tank shook it.

"Go and see your wife," Tank said.

The Major walked into the room. He looked through his son-in-law as if he wasn't there. The betrayal of his daughter couldn't be forgiven. Karl looked hunched and deflated, and Tank could only guess what turmoil there must be behind his reddened eyes.

"Are we all square?" the Major said to Tank, ignoring Karl.

"Yes, sir," Tank replied.

"Hayley is sleeping, I think she would appreciate you being there when she wakes up," the Major said to Karl. He nodded and walked toward the stairs. At the bottom of the stairs, he paused and turned to say something, but then he thought again and climbed the stairs in silence.

"What have you told him?"

"That the police are wasting time looking at the family," Tank headed back into the study.

"Is he calling the police?"

"I said that we'd hand over anything that we find to the police tomorrow."

"Tomorrow? That doesn't give us much time."

"I said anything, relevant."

"It gives us some time, let's get back to Grace and see what information she has."

Tank closed the study door behind them and they sat down in front of the webcam. Graham Libby had gone from the screen and Grace was talking on her mobile.

"I'm sorry about that interruption, Grace," the Major said.

Grace ended her call quickly. "No problem, sir. It's perfectly understandable."

"Can we start at the beginning?"

Grace scanned the papers that were in front of her to recount the information that she'd skimmed over earlier.

"Okay, he was given a life sentence with a minimum twenty year tariff attached to it for the murder of the catholic priest that ran the home he was in," Grace began to fill in the gaps.

"A twenty year tariff for a schoolboy sound unusual," the Major frowned.

"It was a particularly brutal murder, and according to the probation reports he never showed any remorse. There were accusations made against the priest of serious long term sexual abuse made by the boys in the home," she continued.

"How many?"

"According to the police reports, all of them."

"Was it investigated?"

"No, the local Chief Superintendant was a good friend of the Bishop of the Diocese, and from the records I have pulled it appears to have been brushed under the carpet to protect the integrity of the church."

"That's all very sad, but what do we know about him now?" Tank butted in. He couldn't stomach all the psychobabble, which excused sex offenders from their behaviour, because they had been abused themselves. Tank was of the opinion that we all have choices, but not everyone makes the right ones. He was intelligent enough to appreciate that human sexuality is complicated. Gay men are attracted to men, simple. Gay women are attracted to other women, equally simple, but there many people of both sexes that swung from one sex to the other, never settling into one specific group permanently. Society seemed to be embracing both gays, and bi-sexual as equals, but those born with internal mental wiring, which made them sexually attracted to children could never be tolerated. The problem was that they could no more control their sexual orientation than anyone else could. He admired the policy for dealing with paedophiles, adopted by the Chinese. They give the sex offender a nine-millimetre bullet through the base of the skull, job done.

"We need to know his recent history, and where to find him."

"He was released under an extended supervision order which was in force for a period of five years. After that, his whereabouts are sketchy to say the least. He was free to travel wherever he liked."

"Why is he not on a register?"

"Because he was convicted of murder, not a sexually related offense," Grace answered. "There have been plenty of incidents over the years where his name has cropped up in police investigations, but nothing ever sticks."

"How many investigations are we talking about?"

"Dozens of missing person reports, and a handful of sexual assault cases," Grace read from a computer report.

"Where is he based?"

"That's why it's so sketchy. They're all over the country, two in Scotland, one outside of Dublin, two in Cork, Bristol, London, York, Warrington, Carlisle, the list goes on and on," Grace turned the pages as she spoke.

"Any patterns at all?" Tank asked.

"Only one thread runs through it all from what I've seen so far," she looked at a separate sheet.

"What is it?"

"The majority of these complaints have been made by gypsies, and travellers."

"That would explain why he keeps disappearing and evading the police," the Major said.

"It's very rare that travellers would trust the police, let alone make a formal complaint. It would make sense if he's moving in the travellers community, that he could prey on them without detection," Tank added.

"Exactly, that's what stood out to me," Grace explained. "Jack Howarth's name has been put forward as a suspect by the travelling community dozens of times over the last ten years."

"Is he part of the travelling community?" the Major asked.

"No, I think not. He seems to find an unsuspecting group of travellers and then follows them to their sites. He's befriended numerous groups of people over the years gained their trust and then he disappears just as quickly when there's a problem."

"That would suggest that he's using a caravan to live in," Tank said. "The gypsies would have an instant affinity with a fellow traveller."

"He could be using travelling fairgrounds as a disguise, or moving from campsite to campsite in a motor home," the Major suggested.

"Are there any details about what type of vehicle he used to travel around, or live in?" Tank leaned forward to the screen.

"Our people are trawling through witness statements as we speak. I'm sure we'll find something useful in them," Grace answered.

"How much information do we have on the missing persons' complaints?" Tank asked.

"We're still collating and cross referencing information from every force in the country, as well as similar abduction incidents from holiday camps, and gypsy communities over the last twenty years," Grace shook her head as she spoke. Her facial expression looked grim.

"I appreciate that, Grace, but what do we know for definite?"

"It's not looking good, Major," she replied tight lipped.

"We're wasting time, Grace," Tank pushed.

"Okay, out of the cases of abduction that we've looked at so far, when Jack Howarth's name is put forward none of the children were recovered," Grace frowned and carried on. "There are several incidents where witnesses reported hearing children crying, and went to investigate, only to find that their own children were missing upon their return."

"The same modus operandi," The Major's face darkened. The wrinkles on his forehead furrowed as he mulled over the shocking news. "Why hasn't this pattern been picked up for god's sake?"

"Travelling communities don't hang around long enough to see out a full blown investigation, and witnesses are both reluctant to testify, and impossible to trace once they move on," Tank said. The counter-terrorist units across Europe and Asia had struggled for years trying to find terrorist suspects who melted into gypsy communities. They met a wall of silence every time they'd approached the travellers.

"It's hard to believe he's got away with this for so long," the Major commented sadly.

"There were a few cases where he was arrested and interviewed, but a lack of evidence led to his release each time. All bar one," Grace paused.

"From the information you have what's the difference that time around?"

"I've only skimmed through the case, but it looks like a young boy, aged nine was sexually assaulted by Howarth. The police arrested him and were set to press charges, but suddenly the family wanted the incident dropped and they moved on. The local Sexual Abuse Investigation Squad traced them and asked them why they had asked for the case to be shelved. The father became abusive and violent, and so the team closed the file, however they did note that the family were living in a new caravan, which was being towed by a new Mercedes van. They also noted that the nine year old victim was riding around the site on a mini-motorbike."

Tank looked at the Major and raised his eyebrows in surprise.

"Someone paid them off?"

"It certainly sounds like they did."

"I wonder how many others have taken a bung to drop charges against him?" Tank asked quietly.

"It would imply that Howarth has money to burn," the Major added.

"And where would he get money like that to flash around?" Tank shrugged.

"Stealing children to order," Grace interrupted their conversation. "I've looked into several witness statements and one of them started alarm bells ringing, Major."

"Go on."

"In two thousand and five a young gypsy girl was abducted from a caravan site in Rhyl, North Wales. She was one of a group of children who were playing in an inflatable paddling pool, which doesn't sound unusual until you realise that none of the gypsy families on the site actually owned a paddling pool," Grace explained.

"He used the paddling pool to attract the local children?" Tank asked aghast.

"Someone placed it near the perimeter of the community, and everyone assumed it belonged to one of the other families."

"This guy is planning every move," the Major mumbled. He clenched his fists beneath the desk, and his stomach clenched into a tight ball. It was becoming obvious that the baby-crying decoy was not the first child trap that he had used. The more he learned about this 'child taker' the more frightened he became about the safety of his grandchildren.

"Carry on, Grace," Tank prompted her.

"According to the police files no one can actually pinpoint when she went missing. It was a sunny day, and her mother assumed that she was playing with the other children in the pool."

"No witnesses then?"

"Not for the abduction. The key piece of information was received over a week after the event, and it was received from an interesting source," Grace explained. "A convicted paedophile was being questioned at a police station in Leeds, Yorkshire, about a breach of his bail conditions. He had seen the media blitz about the missing girl, and offered up some information about her whereabouts in return for leniency."

"Sounds like he was desperate to me?" Tank said.

"That's what I thought at first, but when I looked further into the file there's corroborative evidence," Grace explained. "He said that a fellow paedophile had seen the girl being abused on a pay per view website."

"Did they investigate?" the Major asked. He was shaking with anger now.

"They did but they couldn't find the website. It had been removed and all its footprints erased as soon as the show had finished. They had nothing to follow, no electronic trail, no money trail, but they did get the name of the paedophile who said that he had watched the abuse," Grace turned another page for the details.

"Did they find him?" Tank asked.

"Better than that, they interviewed him and he admitted watching it, which was a breach of his bail, and he was returned to custody to finish his sentence, including another two years for the breach," Grace looked worn out by the research. "They offered to lower the sentence if he could give them something that would prove that the missing gypsy girl in question and the abused child were one in the same person."

"So, he's yet another paedophile clutching at straws by offering up information in return for leniency?" Tank was sceptical.

"That's exactly what the investigating detective thought until he interviewed him in prison," Grace held up her hand. "The convict described an unusual birthmark on the victim's hip, and it matched the distinguishing marks which were given to the police by her parents."

"And it hadn't been released into the public domain?" the Major asked.

"No, it had been withheld to filter the real culprits from the phoneys," Grace closed the file. "It all points to the fact that the little girl had been stolen to order, and sold to a sophisticated internet paedophile ring for profit."

"Why is Howarth linked to this particular abduction?"

"He was staying on a lay-by nearby on the edge of the campsite, and one of the community leaders remembered seeing the packaging for a paddling pool in the refuse that he'd left behind when he left the area," Grace shrugged, it was tenuous at best. "It was innocent enough before the abduction, but after the event it was obviously incriminating evidence."

"The police didn't agree?"

"   It could have been dumped by any of the travellers," Grace shrugged again. "By the time it had been brought to their attention Howarth was long gone."

The three Taskforce members remained silent while they thought over the different scenarios that were unfolding in front of their eyes.

"What do you think?" the Major sighed.

"I agree with Grace," Tank said. "Howarth is the key to this abduction, and if we find him, then we find whoever has the twins."

"I want every resource at our disposal used to find this bastard John. Do whatever you have to do to find my grandchildren," the Major stood up and left the room without saying another word.

15
THE MOROCCANS

Hajj heard the Mercedes engine approaching, and he could see the headlights sweeping across the night sky as the vehicle neared. He was a Moroccan national, his skin was dark, his eyes were olive green and his hair was jet black and greased backward to his head. Hajj had smouldering Arabian good looks, and a smile that men found sickening, and women found irresistible. He looked ten years younger than his forty years, and he was dressed in a tailor made, grey mohair suit, from Carnaby Street, over an open necked black shirt, which revealed a heavy gold chain that he wore around his neck.

"They're here boss," a man named Rahid, informed him. He was wearing a white polo shirt, beige jodhpurs and black riding boots. Like his boss he was of Moroccan origin, although his features were more African than Arab. His nose was flat and wide, and his skin was deep brown.

"Good, move the horses," Hajj ordered. Rahid walked toward a large blue horse transporter and he barked orders to three men that were loading the vehicle with hay and tack. The rear of the horsebox had a wooden ramp that had already been lowered, and the smell of horses and manure wafted on the evening breeze. Hajj could hear the horses' clip-clop, as they were lead from the horsebox onto the farm road by several of his employees. One of them was a woman called Ramah, and she calmed the powerful animals as she led them from the transporter, and Hajj eyed her shapely body as she worked. Moroccan gangsters had been the biggest exporters of hashish for as long as records go back, and they often used animals to mask their contraband. Horses and camels were often force fed condoms full of opium before being transported across the world's borders. Once they arrived at their destination, they were given veterinary laxatives to flush out the contraband. The Moroccans had made an art form of smuggling drugs from Africa, and their biggest customers were Europeans, Spain, France, Germany and the United Kingdom all consuming thousands of tonnes of dope every year. Their smuggling routes were well established, from the Moroccan port of Agadir, Columbian cocaine and hashish were shipped by the boatload to the Spanish ports of Barcelona and Malaga. Small open motorboats known as Zodiacs sailed return trips nonstop from North Africa to Spain, carrying drugs, arms and people. Hajj worked in Britain for one of the biggest Moroccan exporters, and he'd been handpicked for the job because he was a ruthless gangster with a good head for business. The Moroccans used a system called 'road buying', a term used to describe the bribing of border guards and customs officers, to allow their cargo safe passage, no matter what was contained inside. The most lucrative cargos that they smuggled were women and children, stolen to order for the sex trade in Marrakesh. Hajj wasn't a paedophile, this was business; the children were just valuable commodities that he was charged to smuggle.

The Mercedes turned off the main road and began the bumpy journey up the farm track toward the stable block. The driver turned off the headlights and Hajj followed their progress along the track by listening to the engine noise. The stable yard was a concrete square lined on three sides by wooden stables. The concrete was sloped toward a central drain in the middle of the square, so that the yard could be hosed down and kept reasonably odour free. Rahid had the horse transporter parked in the yard, with the cab pointed toward the farm track. As the Mercedes entered the stable square, he switched on the headlights and illuminated the area. The two men in the Mercedes held their hands up to protect their eyes from the blinding light. They brought the vehicle to a halt and turned off the engine.

"Get out of the car and put your hands on the roof," Hajj shouted. He took a Cuban cigar from his inside pocket and rolled the tube that held it between his fingers. He twisted the cap and sniffed the cigar inside. It smelled smooth and moist, as a fresh cigar should.

"Do we have to go through this bull shit every time Hajj?" Alfie shouted from the Mercedes. Alfie was a small time hashish dealer from Liverpool. He sold the substance in kilo blocks to doormen and dealers all over the city. The Moroccans supplied him with drugs, and threw extra work his way every now and again. He wasn't in the slightest bit happy about picking up kids from that scumbag Howarth, but the money that they paid was ridiculously good. When he'd asked Howarth where the children were being taken to, Howarth had told him that they were being sold to rich families that couldn't have children of their own, and that they'd be better off with their new adopted parents. Alfie believed him because he didn't want to think about the alternative. He loved the fact that he was a gangster, smart suits and polished shoes, bling and all the young women that he could handle, but he hated the Moroccans with a passion.

"You know the routine, Alfie, get out of the car," Rahid approached the Mercedes from the rear. Two Moroccan affiliates jumped down from the back of the horsebox and moved to opposite sides of the car.

"Do I have to listen to this arsehole?" Alfie shouted to Hajj. He respected Hajj because he was a decision maker, high up the chain of command within the Moroccan syndicate. Rahid, on the other hand was a foot soldier, and Alfie didn't like taking instructions from a man in his lowly position.

"You are so uncouth, Alfie," Hajj scolded him. "Rahid is one of my top men, worth ten of your idiot lowlife dealers."

"Put your hands on the roof of the car, 'arsehole'," Rahid mimicked him, and pulled a nine-millimetre Tokagypt automatic from his waistband. It was a standard issue weapon in the Egyptian military, and was part of a stolen cache that had found its way to Morocco. He pointed it at Alfie.

"Now he is really out of order, Hajj, he has absolutely no respect," Alfie whined. His Liverpool accent grated at the back of his throat, as if it were full of phlegm.

Rahid ran a scanner beneath the car, under the sills and over the seats inside. He wasn't going to pat down the British gangsters; there was little point as they were undoubtedly armed. He was looking for tracking devices or recording equipment. Alfie tutted and began whistling an inane tune to demonstrate how bored he was with the routine.

"The vehicle is clean," Rahid announced. He glared at Alfie provocatively. Alfie grinned at him like a fool, and then raised his middle finger aggressively.

"Fuck you, Rahid," he laughed nervously.

"When you two have finished behaving like kids, we have business to attend to," Hajj lit his cigar with a match. The tip glowed red in the darkness. He pulled deep on the smoke and puffed it out in a grey cloud.

"The kids are in the boot. They're chloroformed," Alfie walked to the boot of the vehicle and opened it. "Take them so that we can get away from here. I can't stand the stench here." He sneered at Rahid, and the Moroccan moved forward angered by the insinuation that he stank. Alfie pulled his own pistol from his shoulder holster and the two men faced each other in a Mexican stand-off.

"I swear to god I'll drop this prick, Hajj," Alfie growled. His sidekick, Brian, pulled a Mach 10 machine pistol nervously and pointed it toward Rahid. Alfie was in the direct line of fire and he stepped clear of Rahid. The Mach 10 was a small compact weapon, but it sprayed nine hundred bullets an minute and was renowned for its inaccuracy. He didn't fancy being caught by a couple of stray nine millimetre slugs.

"Gentlemen, please, do we have to go through this testosterone filled charade every time we do business?" Hajj puffed his cigar again.

"Tell this prick to put the gun away before I take it off him and stick it up his arse," Alfie was losing his composure. His hatred of the Moroccans was clouding his judgement.

"Charming, Alfie," Hajj blew smoke rings. "Get the children and give them to Ramah to look after. She will stay with them."

Alfie stepped back from the trunk of the car, and two Moroccans carried the twins into the horsebox. Ramah followed the men into the vehicle cooing at the children as she climbed up the ramp. Above the driver's cab was a sleeper unit big enough to fit a single bed and a cot bed. False panels, fitted with rows of hooks and brackets, which were then covered by leather bridles and saddles, had hid the compartment. Ramah took the children one at a time and placed them into a cot. She handled them as if she was their mother, gently and lovingly. She spoke softly to the slumbering children as she laid them down, but they barely stirred. The men slid the panels over the cabin and replaced the bridles onto the hooks. With their cargo hidden, they led the horses back into the transporter one at a time. By the time they'd finished there were four, fifteen hands high geldings, between any would be inspector and the secret compartment. The wooden ramp at the rear of the transporter was pushed closed and bolted into place. Without another word, the Moroccans started the engine and the blue horse transporter trundled out of the yard toward the main road, leaving Rahid and Hajj alone with the deliverymen.

"Very good, gentlemen, another consignment has been successfully despatched," Hajj clapped his hands together, gripping the cigar between clenched teeth. "There is one more issue that we need to discuss, Alfie."

Alfie slammed the boot of the Mercedes and looked annoyed. He winked at his partner, Brian.

"I thought there'd be something else, there always is with you fucking camel jockeys," Alfie sneered. He was pushing his luck but he didn't really care. Delivering the twins would net him twenty grand, which would be loaded onto a pre-paid Master Card and given to him any minute now. He wanted the card and then he wanted to get away. The whole exercise had made him feel nauseous. Brian had nearly kicked Jack Howarth to death, and he'd be very surprised if he wasn't already dead. It wasn't the first time he'd gone too far. The man was a liability. He was a veteran Paratrooper, invalided out of the Army on mental health grounds, and Alfie could understand why. Brian was a psycho.

"Watch your mouth, Alfie," Hajj dragged deep on the Cuban. He straightened his jacket collar and approached the Mercedes. "I need to know that Jack has been taught a lesson, because the boss is very insistent the next deal doesn't have the same issues as the last one."

Alfie glanced sideways at Brian, and Brian blushed red. It didn't go unnoticed by the Moroccan gangster.

"Is there a problem?" Hajj asked.

"No, there's no problem, Hajj," Alfie replied, but his facial expression belied the truth.

"So, he was reprimanded?"

"Yes."

"Why am I detecting a problem with this, Alfie?" Hajj chewed the cigar in the corner of his mouth.

"Like I said, there's no problem," Alfie looked uncomfortable. Brian had beads of sweat running from his temples onto his cheeks.

"Brian, you look hot my friend," Hajj switched his attention to the big ex-Para.

"Alfie has told you twice now," his voice cracked nervously. "Are you deaf or something?"

"I see that your monkey has the same good manners as you, Alfie," Hajj eyed him coolly. He could sense that something was amiss. "I'm concerned that our asset has not been debilitated completely, Alfie?"

Alfie sighed and shook his head. He looked at Brian and shrugged his shoulders. He was backed into a corner, and he knew that the truth would come out eventually.

"Look, Brian was a little, over enthusiastic I'm afraid," Alfie shifted the blame straight away.

"Alfie, you fucking grass!" Brian hissed.

"Shut up, Brian, it's best that we get it out in the open," Alfie smiled at Hajj. "These things happen."

"I hope you're not telling me that he's dead?"

"Not quite," Alfie smiled again, unsuccessfully trying to use his scouse charm.

"Alfie, I'm not playing games here."

"I realise that."

"Then you will understand that I need to be certain that I can inform my employers that their very valuable asset has been reprimanded but is still operational," Hajj blew smoke rings. The muscles in his jaw line twitched with tension.

"Come on, Howarth is a low life nonce, nothing more," Alfie tried to devalue the child taker.

"What he 'is' can be of no consequence to me, Alfie," Hajj walked toward them. "However, he possesses a set of skills which are extremely valuable to my employers."

"How badly beaten is he?" Rahid piped up.

"Shut up arsehole, no one is talking to you," Brian pointed the machine pistol at Rahid. Rahid responded by lowering his own gun, and raising his hands slightly to calm the ex-Para. Brian nodded and lowered the Mach 10.

"My employers have built up a substantial international following for their particular kind of entertainment. Jack Howarth ensures that there is a broadcast every month, without fail," Hajj sucked deep on the cigar. The smoke was smooth and had a calming effect. He had to find out what had happened to their main supplier.

"I'm not sure that I follow you," Alfie said. The hairs on the back of his neck were standing on end, and a shiver ran down his spine.

"Oh come now, Alfie. I'm sure that you get the gist of it," Hajj was becoming increasingly concerned, and increasingly annoyed.

"No, I'm not sure that I do, to be honest," Alfie felt sick. The use of the word 'broadcast' indicated that the children weren't going to rich childless families at all.

"The child taker guarantees our supply."

"I'm not sure where we are going here, Hajj," Alfie could feel the tension rising.

"It's simple, Alfie. Is Jack Howarth alive?"

"He was when I last saw him."

"Is he likely to be able to deliver the next consignment in three weeks time?"

"That's debatable," Alfie wiped his forehead with his sleeve. It was one thing getting lippy with Hajj, but another all-together crossing the Moroccan Mafioso. His life would be shortened considerably, and his death would be a slow and painful one.

"Stop fucking me around, Alfie," Hajj snarled. His temper

was being tested to the limit.

"He'd had a good kicking which is what you wanted, but Brian might have gone too far," Alfie mumbled.

"Explain."

"He was unconscious and coughing blood," Alfie said.

Hajj walked around the Mercedes puffing on the cigar. He stopped in front of Alfie and he blew smoke in his face. Alfie stepped back but did not react. The Moroccan walked past Rahid and tutted. He was shaking his head in fake dismay as he approached Brian. The big Para couldn't make eye contact with Hajj. Despite being a much bigger man than Hajj, he was scared. Hajj had an air of menace about him, which made him uneasy.

"You have seen action many times, yes?" Hajj spoke to Brian.

"Yes, so what if I have?" Brian tried to maintain his composure. Showing fear would not be good now.

"You will have seen many men injured, yes?"

"Yes."

"I have never been to war, but I've seen many men die. Can you tell when a man is about to die?"

"What are you asking me?" Brian said nervously.

"I'm asking you a simple question," Hajj blew smoke into Brian's face. "Will Jack Howarth live to fulfil his commitments to my employers?" Hajj smiled and puffed smoke through a false smile.

"He'll need medical attention," Brian confessed.

"And what if he doesn't stumble across a doctor?"

Brian remained silent and shook his head slowly, indicating the worst. Hajj tugged deeply on the cigar and looked at the glowing tip. He moved like lightening and stabbed the glowing cigar into Brian's left eye. Brian screamed and grabbed at the burning object. He dropped the Mach 10 in the process. Hajj chopped him in the windpipe with a knife hand karate strike, and the big man buckled at the knees.

"Whooah!" Alfie shouted as the attack began. He moved quickly, but Rahid was quicker. He swooped behind him and clubbed his gun from his hand. A swift kick to the back of knees had Alfie neutralised on the floor in seconds.

"Where was Jack when you left him?" Hajj picked up Brian's machine pistol, and he switched it to single shot mode. Brian didn't respond he was writhing on the floor clutching his ruined eye, and gasping for breath.

"Alfie, where was Jack?"

"He was in a caravan on the outskirts of Warrington," Alfie was on his back with his hands raised in surrender, staring down the barrel of Rahid's pistol.

"How long would it take you to get back there?"

"You can't be serious?" Alfie spat the words.

Hajj squeezed the trigger of the Mach 10, and a fat nine millimetre bullet smashed into Brian's left foot. He screamed like a banshee. The gunshot and the screaming had disturbed the stabled horses and they whinnied and stamped their hooves on the concrete. Brian cursed Hajj in a stream of expletives that Alfie couldn't even understand.

"How long, Alfie?"

"For fuck's sake, Hajj! About an hour," Alfie was more frightened than he'd ever been in his life.

"Do you have any idea what is at stake?" Hajj asked calmly.

"I don't give a fuck, Hajj, just leave him alone!"

"Over two million Euros, every month," Hajj explained. He pulled the trigger again and another bullet ripped through Brian's left kneecap, shattering the bone, ripping ligaments and liquidising cartilage as it bounced around inside him.

"Jesus Christ!" Brian screamed and it was a sickening wail. Alfie wanted to get up and run as fast as he could but he couldn't move for fear of his own life. "Stooooop!" He cried again.

"Hajj, I'll go back and get Jack, just stop this now," Alfie pleaded. He glanced across at his injured colleague and grimaced as he saw a dark pool of blood spreading beneath him.

"Two million Euros, every month, guaranteed. Easy money for everyone, ruined by this gorilla," Hajj fired a third bullet. It penetrated his left elbow and shattered the joint into a dozen fragments. The arm bent backwards on itself in the wrong direction. Brian cried out in agony and writhed like an eel across the stable yard.

"Hajj, you'll kill him, please stop, I'll do anything you ask," Alfie thought that it was already too late for Brian. He was more concerned for his own safety.

"Can you tell when a man is about to die, Alfie?"

"Yes, Hajj. Yes I can, please stop, we made a mistake," Alfie closed his eyes as Hajj raised the machine pistol again.

"Do you think Jack is dying, Alfie?" Hajj walked around Brian's writhing body.

"No, Hajj. I'll go back now and get him to a doctor," Alfie stared at the night sky. The clouds drifted lazily east to west, bright stars twinkled between them He wished that he could be up there with them. He had stepped into a world that was far too scary for him. He didn't mind selling a bit of blow for the Moroccans, but this was getting way out of hand.

"I suggest that you go now, Alfie, immediately," Hajj spoke calmly. He didn't take his eyes from Brian.

Rahid waved the pistol in his face, indicating that Alfie should stand up. He stood up on shaking legs, his knees felt like they were going to buckle at any second.

"What about Brian?"

"I think he's about to die. What do you think?" Hajj pointed the Mach 10 at the critically injured Para. Brian was fading into unconsciousness, and his life force was spreading across the stable yard toward the drain in its centre. There was so much blood that Alfie didn't think that Brian would last much longer.

"Let me take him to a hospital, Hajj," Alfie brushed straw and muck from his suit as he spoke.

"I don't think that's a good idea," Hajj pulled the trigger again and Brian's skull exploded like a ripe melon. Grey brain matter mixed with viscous blood splattered across the concrete in a crimson plume. "Brian won't be going anywhere, he's dead, Alfie."

Alfie buckled at the knees and he wretched. He wretched again but nothing came up. The sight of his sidekick still twitching in his death throes was too much to stomach. He felt like he might pass out. Rahid grabbed his elbow and pulled him to his feet roughly. He grabbed the scruff of his neck and turned his head toward his friend's ruined body and forced him to look at the sickening scene.

"Tell me, Alfie," Hajj walked toward him. "How is your father?"

"What?"

"You heard me, Alfie," Hajj was a foot away from his face now. Alfie could smell Armani aftershave, mixed with the pungent odour of cigars on his breath.

"What about my father?"

"How is he?"

"He's fine, Hajj," Alfie tried to break away from Rahid but he'd been badly weakened by the shock, and the Moroccan's grip was tight.

"Do you still take him to the British Legion on Sundays?"

Alfie tried to pull free again but he was held tightly. Hajj rammed the barrel of the Mach 10 painfully under his chin. His face was just inches away now.

"He asked you a question, arsehole," Rahid pulled tightly on his collar, choking him.

"Yes, I still take my father for a drink on a Sunday

afternoon, Hajj," Alfie stopped struggling. Talking about his elderly disabled father had frozen him to the core. He wasn't sure where this was going, but he knew that things were about to get considerably worse than they were already.

"He lives in Woolton Village with your mother, yes?"

"What?" Alfie dare not answer.

"You heard him," Rahid twisted his collar tighter. "They live in Woolton Village, in a bungalow next to the park."

"Yes."

"He walks with a stick, yes?"

"How the bloody hell do you know all this?" Alfie was flabbergasted.

"Because we are professionals, Alfie, unlike your dead friend here," Hajj snarled in his face.

"Okay, okay. He walks with a stick," Alfie felt his eyes filling up with tears.

"Well unless you want to be pushing him for his Sunday pint in a wheelchair, then you'd better get Jack to a doctor, quickly," Hajj spat the words very slowly. "If Jack dies I'll send Rahid to Woolton Village and he'll cut your father's legs off in front of your mother, understand Alfie?"

Alfie nodded his head in the affirmative and the tears in his eyes spilled over and ran down his face. He wretched again and this time thick yellow bile sprayed down the front of his suit. Hajj was not a man to be messed with by any stretch of the imagination, and Alfie knew that he was serious about hurting his father. He had opened a Pandora's Box which was threatening everything that was precious to him, and all for greed, money that he didn't really need. His head span with the events of the night so far.

'Had he really taken two sleeping children in the boot of his car, and delivered them to the most ruthless men that he'd ever met, so that they could be sexually abused for an international audience of paedophiles?' his thoughts whirled across his mind in turmoil. Rough hands pushed and dragged him toward the driver's door of the Mercedes. He sensed the door being opened and his head banged painfully on the roof as he was forced into the vehicle.

"Alfie," Hajj growled at him. He felt like he was in a giant washing machine set to spin.

"Alfie," a hard slap across the face brought him back to the real world momentarily.

"Go and make sure that Jack is alive and well enough to deliver the next consignments," Hajj looked straight into his eyes, and Alfie could see madness in them. He looked like he was enjoying every minute of his pain, and feeding off his panic. "Alfie, make sure that the police aren't involved, and that they don't know who he is."

"I will, Hajj," Alfie croaked. He nodded and tears dripped off his chin onto his dirty suit. Alfie took one last look at Brian before he closed the driver's door and engaged first gear. One sightless eye stared at him accusingly. The other had rolled toward the grid when his head exploded. Hajj smiled brightly as Alfie pulled away down the farm track. It was going to be a long drive back to make sure that the 'Child Taker' didn't die in his caravan. Alfie knew that his life and the lives of those precious to him, depended on him getting there quickly.

16
THE CHILD TAKER

Jack Howarth drifted in and out of consciousness as the waves of pain washed over him. He opened his eyes and tried to gather his composure. Congealed blood caked his face and mouth and there was a sickening ache in his abdomen. Memories of the evening's events came flooding back to him. The twins had been taken and he'd been beaten badly, but he was alive and that was the main thing. He needed medical attention of that he had no doubt. His ruptured testicle had swollen to the size of an orange and even the slightest movement sent unbearable stabbing pains through his body. His mobile phone was still in his pocket. He pulled it free, sending a new wave of sharp pain through his groin. He moaned and held his breath until the pain subsided. Jack looked at the telephone screen and realised that two and a half hours had elapsed, he had six missed calls, all from the same number, Alfie Lesner.

Jack closed his eyes again as a wave of nausea hit him. The caravan seemed to close in around him, threatening to suffocate him. The faces of children that he'd suffocated over the years floated in and out of his mind. They stared at him with empty eyes, accusingly. He could not remember how many there had been as he'd developed his sexual perversions into a lucrative business. Jack was an intelligent man, always thinking of new and ingenious ways to attract children, and to detract their guardians. Some had worked better than others had. Puppies and sweets attracted younger children, but older kids were so much more suspicious of strangers these days. Jack was a chameleon, and he adapted his methods to suit his current surroundings. His use of props, such as paddling pools, rope swings, even bicycles left anonymously had always paid dividends. Finding the Moroccans had changed everything. He had been a sexual predator for many years, but now he had turned his hunting into a science. The money was useful, but it was the thrill of the chase that drove him now. Sexual urges were satiated by his success in capturing children to order. His cell phone vibrated, waking him from his disturbing thoughts. He pressed the green button.

"Jack?" Alfie's scouse accent sounded concerned.

"What do you want?" Jack's voice was thick and slurred. He was confused by the fact that his attackers were making contact.

"Are you alright, Jack?"

"Never felt better," Jack croaked sarcastically. "What do you want?"

"I'm coming back to take you to hospital," Alfie was flapping. The events at the stable yard had rattled him badly.

"That's nice of you," Jack grinned in the darkness through blood smeared teeth. "Hajj wasn't happy with you then I assume?"

"I'm half an hour away, just hang on," Alfie snarled. He was sickened to the core by the brutal murder of Brian, but more disturbed by the fact that he had been duped into helping an international paedophile ring trafficking children.

"You've been lying to me, Jack," Alfie felt foolish saying it, but he couldn't believe how gullible he'd been.

"Did you really think all those children were going to be adopted, Alfie?"

"Yes, I did you sick bastard. I knew you were a fucking pervert, but I didn't think that you could sink that low." Alfie wanted to kill him, not get him medical attention. The problem was Hajj's threat to hurt his parents was still echoing around his mind, alongside the mental image of Brian's death mask.

"Alfie, did you really believe what I told you, come on, are you telling me that doubts never crossed your mind?" Jack's voice was breaking, and his breathing was laboured.

"You're sick, Jack," Alfie was shaking as the reality of what he'd done began to sink in. He had a large extended family, and visions of his beloved nephews and nieces being kidnapped and abused taunted him.

"You're as guilty as I am, Alfie, I bet you fancied some of them yourself, eh?"

"Fuck you, Jack," he thought that he could hear Jack choking, but he realised that he was chuckling to himself. Alfie looked at the cell phone in disgust, and hung up the call.

"Bye, Alfie," Jack chuckled in the darkness. He coughed and a thick blob of congealed blood and phlegm filled his mouth. He spat the offending liquid onto the floor, and the effort gained him a bolt of pain through his abdomen that brought tears to his eyes. Hajj must have forced Alfie to come back and get him medical attention. At least the Moroccans valued his skills. There was one big problem that he had to ponder, and that was the Moroccans had ordered that he be beaten. He couldn't accept that from anyone, he'd suffered at the hands of others long enough as a boy, and he would not tolerate it now, for sure. They had also ordered the electronic tagging of his vehicle. Jack was not happy with that. He wouldn't be anyone's puppet ever again. The Moroccans had disrespected him, and treated him like a common drug dealer who peddled their drugs for them. He was better than that, cleverer than that, and he would demand their respect again. In the beginning, he had dealt directly with them, but now that the consignments were to become regular, they had insisted that he dealt with their minions. Jack was not prepared to do that anymore. His days of being beaten and abused without recompense were long over. He decided to take control of the situation himself. Jack punched three numbers into his cell phone and pressed send, nine, nine, nine. He chuckled throatily in the darkness.

"Hello, emergency, which service do you require?" an operator answered sounding robotic and disinterested.

"I need an ambulance. I've been attacked, I'm badly injured," Jack croaked.

"Can you tell me where you are?"

"I'm in my caravan, parked in a lay-by near Walton Gardens, on the outskirts of Warrington."

"Do you know the name of the road you're on?"

"Chester Road."

"There's an ambulance being despatched now. I'll connect you to the police, please hold." The line became static for a second.

"Cheshire police emergency, can I take your name please."

"Jack Howarth."

"You've been attacked?"

"Yes, he's kicked me, and I'm injured quiet badly."

"Do you know who your attacker was, Jack?"

"Yes, his name is Alfie Lesner, and he's coming back to finish me off."

"Okay, Jack, keep calm. How do you know he's coming back?"

"He called me."

"We'll be there in a few minutes, Jack."

"Be careful, because he's armed."

"What is he armed with, Jack?"

"He has a gun."

"Are you sure?"

"Yes."

"Are you shot?"

"No, I'm badly hurt to my stomach and groin."

"How far away did he say he was?"

"He said he'd be half an hour."

"Okay, Jack, relax. We'll send an armed response unit to protect you. Do you know what vehicle he's driving?"

"It was a dark Mercedes."

"Okay, Jack, that's very useful."

"There's one other thing," Jack croaked.

"What is it?"

"He took those children."

There was a shocked silence on the line.

"What children, Jack?"

"He took the twins from the Lake District. The twins that have been on the news all week," Jack coughed blood and phlegm again. "He took them."

"How do you know that, Jack?"

"He was staying in my caravan, and he brought them here, I didn't know anything about them until he turned up with them."

"When did you see them, Jack?"

"Two hours ago, that's why he attacked me, because I saw them."

"Are the children still there, Jack?"

"No, he took them in the car I think, I was kicked unconscious, so I can't be certain," Jack spluttered and pain racked his body. The injured testicle throbbed white-hot pain, and sweat ran down his face into his eyes.

"Do you have any idea where he's taken them, Jack?" the police operator was trying to grasp as much information as he could from the injured man. He had no idea how badly hurt he was, and there was no way of knowing if he'd still be alive when the ambulance arrived.

"I don't know," Jack grinned in the blackness, and he had to cover the receiver to stop the operator from hearing him chuckle. The movement triggered a bolt of pain, which sliced upward from his groin to his brain. He moaned in agony.

"Are you okay, Jack?"

"No, please hurry," Jack pressed the red button and ended the call. He curled up into a foetal position and tried to block out the pain while he waited for the emergency services to arrive. The accusations that he had made on the phone would bring an army of armed police officers down on the small caravan. The transit van had been expertly cleaned of any evidence and DNA. All traces of the children had been bleached away from his van, which would leave only the evidence in the bedroom to prove that they'd ever been there at all. Alfie would walk right into their clutches, and he wouldn't know what had hit him until it was too late. Jack knew from experience how the police treated paedophiles, and he chuckled again through the pain, as he imagined the look on Alfie's face.

17
TANK

Tank sat in the front passenger seat of the taskforce chopper. He had issued a code red search order, which stipulated that every police division across the nearest six counties, within three hours drive had to send up their helicopters. They were tasked with searching for a white transit van, which was being used to tow a white four birth Lunar caravan. Grace and the evidence team had searched through police records for hours, and the same description of Jack Howarth's living quarters kept coming up. They had to assume that he was still driving the same vehicle and still living in the same model caravan. They had predicted that he would be parked somewhere remote, and so the remit across four police forces was to use heat-imaging scanners to search for the twins and their abductor by scanning any mobile homes that they found. Tank commandeered the taskforce chopper in the slim hope that they might stumble across something. The odds on finding them were slim and becoming slimmer with every hour that past. So far, everyone had drawn a blank, until the radio began to buzz with emergency services' communications from the Cheshire division.

"Cheshire police have had a call concerning the twins," the pilot turned to Tank as the information came through.

"Tune into their band, I want to hear what's going on," Tank ordered.

"Roger that, an ambulance and an armed response unit have been despatched to a caravan parked up on Chester Road, on the outskirts of Warrington," the pilot relayed the communications as they unfolded.

"How far away are we?" Tank checked his watch.

"We are twenty five minutes away at least."

"Did the caller say that the twins are there?"

"Negative, he said they were there, but that they'd been taken somewhere else. The caller is Jack Howarth."

Tank patched the coms unit through to his helmet, so that he could listen to real time coms. The ambulance and the armed response unit were arriving on the scene. The ambulance crew were told to wait at a safe distance from the caravan until the police had cleared the area. The armed police were outside the caravan. Tank followed their progress.

"Unit one, check the van," the team leader ordered.

"Roger that," there was silence for a moment. "The vehicle is locked, driver's cab is clear."

"Unit two, enter the caravan."

"The door is locked, sir."

"Roger that, force it."

The coms went silent as the armed police unit carried out their business quickly and efficiently.

"How long?" Tank asked the pilot.

"Five minutes, not far now," the pilot replied. Tank could see the lights of Warrington twinkling yellow to the right. They seemed to go on forever as they blended into the mass of lights that was Greater Manchester in the distance. There were golf courses and acres of farmland on the left hand side. To the left the ground below them was inky black, broken only by the odd cluster of electric lights here and there. The coms crackled into life again.

"We're inside the caravan, sir, and the area's clear. There's one casualty, he's tachycardic. Better get the ambulance guys in here sharp," the response team leader reported to his superior officer.

"Roger that," the reply came. "Give the ambulance team a green light."

Tank could see flashing blue lights in the near distance as they approached the scene.

"Get me as close as you can," Tank ordered.

The pilot took the chopper over the site and then banked sharply onto the fairway of Walton golf club. Leaves and bunker sand were blasted skyward by the downdraft. Tank opened the passenger door and jumped out. He ducked and jogged toward the flashing lights.

"Who the fuck is in the helicopter?" a police voice came over the coms.

"It's not ours, sir," a confused reply came back.

Tank jogged across the manicured fairway until he reached a copse of trees. A narrow path ran through them to the perimeter fence. He leapt a wooden gate, which accessed the main road, and headed toward the control vehicle. It was parked two hundred yards from the caravan. A senior uniformed officer stood open mouthed as he approached. He was wearing a pristine police uniform and a flat officers peaked cap. Tank recognised him as an officer that he'd had some dealings with previously. Their previous encounters had never been polite or pleasant, and from the expression on his face, Tank had no reason to believe that this encounter would be any different.

"What the bloody hell brings you here?" the officer asked.

"I need to know everything that you know about Jack Howarth's condition," Tank replied guiding the officer away from his colleagues.

"The taskforce has no jurisdiction here, and you know it," the officer protested.

"You and I both know that I can take over this scene with one phone call," Tank kept his voice low, so as not to attract too much attention. The counter terrorist units were always given priority access over traditional law enforcement departments, much to the annoyance of the uniformed divisions.

"Why would you be interested in this?"

"Let's just say that we need to speak to Howarth urgently," as Tank finished his sentence the ambulance sped off toward the town's general hospital, sirens blaring and blue lights flashing.

"He's in the back of that," the officer pointed after the speeding ambulance. He grinned sarcastically.

"What can you tell me about the call that he made?"

"Why, Agent Tankersley?" the officer walked back toward his men, tiring of the interference from the counter terrorist agent.

"Forget it," Tank took out his cell phone and dialled. "I'll have control of this scene in thirty seconds."

"Okay," the police officer waved his hands. He didn't want his crime scene taken from him. This was a high profile case and he wanted to keep hold of it as long as he could. Careers were made and broken on cases like this one. He turned and walked toward the caravan, waving to his men as he went. The uniformed men began to move away from the scene in a well-rehearsed series of actions. The police vehicles that were at the scene were driven away, and hidden from view.

"What's going on?" Tank asked.

"Jack Howarth called us and reported a serious assault," the officer began. He guided Tank toward the rear of the scene behind the transit van. There were six armed police officers in full black body armour ready and waiting for something. Tank wasn't sure what though.

"What's with all the hardware?"

"Howarth gave us the name of his attacker, and he told

us that he was on his way back to finish him off," the officer continued.

"You think that he's coming back?"Tank asked.

"Well that all depends on whether or not he's been scared away by your fucking helicopter or not," the policeman growled at him.

"Why would he return to an assault?" Tank ignored the obvious dig at him.

"Howarth accused his attacker of taking the Kelly twins, that's why he attacked him. He must have been panicked into moving them, and now he's coming back to finish off the only witness," the officer explained his theory.

"I don't buy it," Tank said, more to himself than to anyone else. He knew that Howarth's DNA had been found at the campsite, but he couldn't tell the police that he knew that. Not yet anyway.

"Look, Agent Tankersley," the police officer hissed. "I don't give a toss what you buy and what you don't. I still haven't got a clue what you're doing here, but while you are here you will not interfere with my crime scene."

"Who has Howarth fingered?" Tank knew that there were some shenanigans going on.

"The name he gave us was, Alfie Lesner," the officer didn't give away anymore than he had to.

"Have you run him through your records?" Tank pushed.

"You know that never crossed my mind, perhaps we should do that when we get back to the station," the officer shook his head in disbelief. "Of course we have, what do you take us for, fucking amateurs?"

"Look, I'm not trying to rain on your parade. I need to know what you know and then you can have your precious crime scene to yourself," Tank tried to appease the offence that he'd caused.

"He's a small time drug dealer from Liverpool, previous for

assault, fraud, and possession with intent to supply. We don't know who he works for, but we do know it's not one of the Liverpool based gangs," the officer kept his voice low.

"Doesn't sound like your typical child kidnapper to me," Tank commented cynically. The uniformed officer was about to bite back when the coms unit hissed.

"Vehicle approaching," a voice whispered.

"Do you have visual?"

"Affirmative, it's a navy blue Mercedes. You'll have an eyeball in twenty seconds or so," the coms hissed again.

A vehicle turned a long bend and its headlights swept across the stationary vehicles. It was travelling at speed as it approached the scene. The driver brought the Mercedes to a screeching halt outside the caravan, dirt and grit sprayed the area. The driver's door opened and Tank heard footsteps running toward the caravan. The door opened and he heard a Liverpool accent.

"Jack," the driver stepped into the caravan.

"Armed police!" a shout came from the officers who were positioned inside the caravan. Several officers shouted it as they swooped on the confused driver.

Tank and the police officer moved out of the shadows and walked around the caravan to the scene of the arrest.

"What's your name," the senior officer asked the man as he was bundled down the caravan steps, and handcuffed.

"Alfie Lesner," he replied. He looked shocked and weary, and didn't put up much resistance at all.

"Where are the Kelly twins?"

"I don't know what you're talking about."

"The five year old twins that you kidnapped from the Lake District?" the officer snarled into his face.

"I didn't kidnap anyone, fuck you!" Alfie spat and a globule of saliva hit the police officer on the lapel. It dribbled toward his chest. The officer raised his hand to strike him and then thought better of behaving in such a manner in front of his junior officers. The case was too big to jeopardise.

"He's carrying a weapon," a uniformed armed response officer searched him and discovered the concealed pistol.

"Read him his rights," the officer ordered, and Alfie was dragged off toward a waiting police car. Tank watched as he was led away. He'd seen many men captured under these circumstances, and he'd learned to read the way that they reacted. Alfie had been surprised, that was obvious. He hadn't expected the police to be waiting for him. Why would he? Who could have called them except Jack Howarth or him? Alfie had reacted violently when he was accused of taking the twins from the Lake District, and Tank could tell that it was genuine anger, not staged. When he'd said that he didn't know anything about the twins he was lying, of that Tank was certain. He had to speak to Alfie before he was processed and lost in the legal system, and then he had to speak to Jack Howarth. First, he had to work out how he was going to get to them, and if the twins were being moved he had to do it quickly.

"I want to take a look inside the caravan," Tank walked away from the uniformed officer.

"Do not touch anything," the officer muttered under his breath. Tank shook his head at the childish remark. Three ambulance men and at least three members of the armed response unit had entered the caravan. A defence lawyer could now challenge any evidence found in there as the integrity of the scene had been compromised. Tank had a feeling that Jack Howarth knew all about that, and that was part of the reason why he'd called the police.

He reached the metal steps which led up to the caravan and looked at the shoeprints in the soil using a small pen sized Maglight. There were several sets of boot prints. Tank recognised deep ridges left by the moulded soles of combat boots worn by the armed response unit. There were other tracks too, including flat prints left by dress shoes. Alfie Lesner had been wearing a sharp suit and highly polished shoes. They could belong to him. The rest of the ground had been mashed by the emergency services, and there was nothing there that could help him.

Tanked stepped up into the narrow doorway and had to turn sideways to navigate his way in. He located the light switch and flicked it on using the end of the Maglight, so as not to smudge any latent prints that may have been left behind. The caravan was clean and tidy, apart from thick dark stains on the carpet; there wasn't a thing out of place. There were splatter marks across the pale carpet and up the lower edges of the upholstery. Tank could tell that it was blood, and that it wasn't from an open wound. It was too dark and too thick, which indicated that it had been vomited by the secretor, and not dripped from a cut. The bleeding was consistent with a sustained attack on a prone victim, broken ribs or a stomach rupture could have caused it. There were several blood stained swabs discarded in the sink, probably left by the ambulance men after they'd treated the victim in situ. Apart from that, the interior looked remarkably bland. There were no personal items, photographs, ornaments, books or magazines. Tank knew that was the classic sign of an intelligent predator, sexual or otherwise. Many of his terrorist adversaries had lived the same way, never leaving anything behind them that could be used to identify them later. He opened the kitchen cupboards, and then the fridge, empty.

Tank stepped down the corridor toward the sleeping areas. The smell of a chemical toilet grew stronger as he neared the bedrooms. He opened the first door. It was a toilet closet the size of a small wardrobe. Tank could not have used the convenience without keeping the door open. The smell of deep blue camping disinfectant cloyed at the back of his throat. He closed the door and moved on.

The next door was already ajar. Tank moved it with the end of the torch. He reached inside and flicked on the light. The room was empty apart from a narrow cot bed. There was a thin mattress and a grey woollen blanket covering it, the type that makes your skin itch. It looked like a prison cell from an old spaghetti western. If Jack Howarth had slept in there recently then his DNA would be all over it. Tank stepped into the tiny room and studied the bed. There was a dark blue inflatable travel pillow under the blanket. Tank noted a human hair on it. One end was black, probably dyed, and the other was greyed by old age. It belonged to a man of Jack Howarth's age, no doubt. He left the hair in place, as it couldn't tell him anything that he didn't already know. Tank backed out of the room, flicked off the light and left the door ajar as he'd found it.

The main bedroom was next door, and its entrance was the end of the corridor. He opened it and repeated the process of illuminating it by flicking on the light using the end of the torch. The room was decorated in stark contrast to the rest of the caravan. The walls were pastel colours, pinks and blues, and a child's mobile hung from the light fitting. On the bed was an empty sleeping bag. Tank remembered the mother's evidence, and she stated that the twins had been taken in their sleeping bag. He leaned over the bed and studied the material. Sure enough, there was fine blond hair there. From the presence of the hair, he could guess that the twins had been kept in this room. He couldn't make any sense of it. Maybe Alfie Lesner had been an accomplice in the abduction, and then the Child Takers had fallen out, resulting in Jack Howarth receiving a severe beating. There was only one way to find out, and that was to ask them. He needed to speak to both of them, tonight, and that would not be easy, especially now that they were both in police custody. Tank reached for his cell phone, it was time to apply some Terrorist Task Force priority.

18

THE CHILD TAKER

Jack Howarth awoke to the strong odour of antiseptic. Through the haze of anaesthetic, his senses started to function. His sense of smell told him that he was probably in hospital. He could feel clean crisp cotton against his skin. There was no pain anymore and he was numb from the belly button down. Jack moved his left hand and he heard a metallic rattle against the bed frame. There was a metal bracelet around his wrist, handcuffs. He opened his eyes and the glare of the strip lighting hurt him. His mouth was bone dry and he could still taste the coppery flavour of his own blood.

"He's coming round," a voice said. He didn't recognise it.

"Shame, it's a pity the scumbag isn't dead," another voice answered the first.

"I'll let the inspector know, and inform the nurse," the first voice spoke again.

"Inform the blond nurse will you, she's fit. She could give me a bed bath any day."

"Do you ever stop? Give it a rest will you."

"Could I have some water please?" Jack hardly recognised his own voice. His mouth and throat were so dry he could hardly speak.

"Shut up you nonce," a voice replied. Jack's vision began to clear and he focused on a fat police constable who was next to his bed. The police officer was wearing black combat pants, boots and an armoured stab vest over his tee shirt. On his hip was a holstered Glock 14.

"I'm thirsty," Jack croaked.

"I couldn't care less if you choke to death," the police constable crossed his legs and picked up his newspaper. Jack tried to sit up but his muscles were still immobilised. A pretty blond nurse entered the room. She walked quickly as if she didn't have much time to waste. The fat constable put his newspaper down and breathed in to lessen the bulge of his beer belly. He smiled at her as he eyed the curves of her body through her starched navy blue uniform.

"So he's woken up has he?" the nurse chirped without actually looking at the policeman.

"Yes, mores' the pity," the constable scoffed. The nurse ignored him and reached for Jack's pulse. She checked it against her watch.

"How are you feeling?" she asked him abruptly.

"Tired, unappreciated, underpaid, and my wife doesn't understand me," the constable answered her question, trying to make a joke. The nurse looked at him as if he was stupid. "I was talking to the patient."

"I'm very thirsty, nurse," Jack croaked.

"That's to be expected after anaesthetic," she poured water from a jug on the bedside cabinet into a paper cup, and put it to his lips. Jack gulped greedily at the cool liquid, savouring it as it rehydrated his mouth. "The doctor will be with you any minute."

The nurse put the paper cup into a waste bin, and then she picked up a chart at the end of the bed and scribbled Jack's stats in the relevant boxes.

"You couldn't put your number on there could you?" the police officer tried a more direct approach.

"Do you know I'm not sure who is the worst pervert, you or him," she looked at him frostily as she hung up the chart again, and then she walked out of the room without saying another word.

"Silly bitch," the police officer muttered.

No sooner had she left the door opened again and a tired looking doctor walked in. He looked way too young to be a doctor, and his wavy brown hair was clipped back from his face by a black elastic hair band. His white coat was opened, showing faded blue jeans and a dark tee shirt underneath.

"How are you feeling?" the doctor picked up the charts and analysed it as he spoke.

"Numb," Jack croaked.

"You're a lucky man, Mr Howarth, any longer and you'd have lost both testicles," he sounded disproportionately happy about it.

"What do you mean?"

"I'm afraid we had to remove your right testicle, but we managed to save the left, and one is better than none," he chirped.

"That's why I feel numb from the waist down?"

"Believe you me, it's better to be numb at the moment. I'll pop in and see you in the morning."

"I can still taste blood in my throat, doctor," Jack coughed. "I'm really thirsty too."

"You had a pretty bad beating, Mr Howarth. A rib punctured your left lung, but we've fixed you up, and with some rest and recuperation you'll be up and about in no time," he placed the chart on its hook and left the room without acknowledging the police officer was there.

"Pity they didn't cut both your bollocks off," the constable goaded him, and turned back to his newspaper.

"The nurse had you sussed out all along," Jack croaked. The police officer flushed red with anger. He stood up slowly and folded his newspaper, before placing it on his chair. Jack tensed his body as the fat constable approached the bed. He expected the officer to strike him for daring to ridicule him. A huge shadow filled the obscured glass in the door, and the police officer stepped back away from the bed.

"There'll be plenty of time for you, nonce," he hissed as the door opened. The Chief Inspector walked into the room flanked by a huge man with a shaven head. Jack looked from one to the other trying to make out who they were, and what they wanted.

"Is there a problem, Constable?" the Inspector asked. He removed his peaked cap as he entered.

"No, Sir."

"Go and get yourself a coffee," the Chief ordered. The fat constable looked Tank up and down. Tank eyed him coldly and he left without a word.

"I'm not one bit happy about this, Agent Tankersley," the Inspector snapped as the door closed. Jack could sense the animosity between them.

"Where are the Kelly twins?" Tank ignored the police officer and walked to the bed.

"I don't know," Jack shook his head.

"Where were they the last time you saw them?" Tank leaned against the bed and Jack realised that this giant of a man was no police officer. He did not know how he knew, but he did, and that worried him.

"They were being carried out of my caravan by Alfie Lesner and his thug of a friend."

"Who was his friend?"

"I don't know him."

"Where did they take them?"

"I really don't know, officer, what's your name?" Jack fished for the big man's rank.

"You took the twins from the Lakes, Howarth," Tank told

him. It was not a question.

"No I didn't, Alfie must have taken them. The first time that I saw was when he brought them to my caravan."

"You're a liar, we know that you were in the woods," Tank's eyes were still and piercing like a shark's. Jack's expression flickered, and Tank knew that he was about to lie again.

"I've never been to the Lakes," Jack coughed again. "Am I under caution?" He looked at the uniformed officer. The Inspector blushed and shook his head.

"Not at the moment," he said.

"Then I don't want to say anything else until I've spoken to a solicitor."

"Leave us," Tank looked at the Inspector.

"I'm afraid I can't do that. He's my prisoner," the officer blustered.

"Then I'll have him removed from the hospital immediately," Tank stepped toward the door.

"Five minutes, Agent Tankersley, and I mean it," he put his hat back on and stormed out of the room. Tank waited until he'd gone before turning back to the Child Taker.

Jack had never seen any senior ranking police officer surrender a prisoner as easily as the Inspector had, and he knew that this big man was incredibly dangerous.

"I want a solicitor," he croaked, trying to gain the initiative.

Tank approached the end of the bad and grabbed his right foot. He raised it high into the air and then slammed it back down on the bed. Jack felt flashes of pain in every nerve in his body, and he opened his mouth to scream. Tank moved like lightening and pressed his huge hand over Jack's mouth.

"I've got your DNA in the woods, and your caravan has a nursery in it. Now if you know what's good for you then you'll tell me where Lesner took the children," Tank spoke quietly and looked into the Child Taker's eyes for sign of a reaction. He could see fear. "Now I'm going to remove my hand, shout

141

anything and I'll have you taken from this hospital in less than half an hour. I'll send you to our Albanian interrogation centre, which is situated in the dungeons of an eighteenth century jail."

Jack's eyes registered confusion, pain and fear. He could not understand who this man was. A Chief Inspector did as he was told, under duress, and now he was threatening to make him disappear. Who had that kind of authority?

"You'd like Albania, Jack, because the people there are descended from the Romany Gypsies," Tank's voice was cold and monotone.

Recognition flickered in Jack's eyes, recognition and more confusion.

"You know gypsies don't you, Jack."

Jack's eyes widened and he shook his head.

"Oh, yes you do, because you've been preying on their children for years, you pervert," Tank squeezed his face hard as he kept him silent. Jack was starting to panic, short of breath and racked with pain. He was also very confused as to how this brute of a man knew as much as he did.

"The Albanian interrogators, and the inmates would love to spend some time alone with a child molester like you, Jack, especially one who preyed on their kin," Tank let his words sink in, and then let go of his face. "I've known men who have been interrogated in there for years on end, Jack. You'd be begging them to kill you."

"Who are you?" Jack gasped.

"I'm your worst nightmare, Jack. Now where did Lesner take the children?"

"I really don't know," Jack closed his eyes and waited for pain, but none was forthcoming.

"Have it your way, Howarth."

Tank walked away from the bed and took out his cell phone. He punched in a speed dial number and placed the set next to his ear. He had his back to the Child Taker.

"This is Agent Tankersley. I need that extraction from Warrington General Hospital. Do it now. Interrogation, Albania, labelled rendition." Jack could not make head nor tale of what he was saying but he'd heard enough to be certain that this man wasn't messing around.

"Wait, I want a lawyer," Jack cried.

"There's no lawyer where you're going, only pain," Tank ignored him and ended his call. He stepped toward the door.

"I don't know where he took them, honestly," Jack's voice was cracking up. He couldn't go to a foreign prison where he would be identified to the general population as an abuser of gypsy children. The memories of his terrible childhood, and the pain and degradation that he'd suffered at the hands of the catholic priest came flooding back to him, and he couldn't survive it again. He didn't know how this man was able to threaten him with rendition, but he knew that it went on, and he didn't want to be a victim of it.

"I don't care what you have to say anymore, Jack. I'll ask Lesner himself. Enjoy Albania, Jack," Tank opened the door. The Chief Inspector was at the end of the corridor talking to colleagues. He was also talking to Sylvia Lees, the family liaison officer. They stopped talking as he looked at them, and she pointed toward him.

"Okay, I'll tell you," Jack croaked.

"You've got sixty seconds starting from now," Tank closed the door and turned around to face him. There was a crimson stain spreading from between his legs. Tank thought that he'd burst his stitches, shame.

"The children were bought by a Moroccan gangster, who calls himself Hajj," he began.

"So you did take them?"

"No, Alfie must have taken them."

"Your DNA was in the woods, Jack."

"Did you find it on recording equipment?" Jack asked.

Tank remained silent, and waited for him to continue.

"Alfie stole it from my van," Jack was trying to cover the story that he would tell the police, if he got the chance to.

"Where did he take the children, Jack, last chance?"

"Alfie took them, and he sold them to Hajj," Jack lied.

"What's the Moroccan's real name?"

"Hajj Achmed," Jack replied. Tank typed the name into his phone and sent it to Grace as he spoke to the Child Taker. She would take it and run it through their files while he continued his interrogation.

"Where are they taking them?"

"Morocco."

"How do they transport them?"

"I really don't know that."

"How do you get in touch with Hajj?"

"I don't, I've told you that Alfie sells them, not me."

"So how do you know that they take them to Morocco?"

"Alfie told me," Jack's eyes flicked up to the left as he spoke, indicating that he was creating his answers, lying.

Tank looked at him and shook his head slowly. The blood stain was spreading quickly between the Child Taker's legs, but he seemed to be oblivious to it.

"I'm going to speak to Lesner now, and if you've lied to me I'll come back and kill you," Tank stepped to the side of his bed.

"You can't kill me," Jack croaked.

"I can, and I will," Tank tipped the heavy metal bed as if it were made from cardboard. Jack flapped frantically trying to maintain his balance but gravity got the better of him and he was left dangling from the wrist off the side of the bed.

"Nurse! Help me!" Jack shouted as loud as his parched throat would allow him to. "Nurse!"

The door opened and the blond nurse came running

in. The Chief Inspector followed close behind her. The fat constable and Sylvia Lees stood in the doorway open mouthed at the scene. Jack was still scrabbling to gain his balance, and his feet were slipping in his blood on the tiled floor.

"What the hell is going on?" the nurse said as she tried to lift Jack back onto the bed.

"He slipped trying to reach his water," Tank stepped past her and walked toward the door. The fat constable stood in his way.

"If you don't want to be drinking your Mars Bars through a straw for the next six weeks then you need to get out of my way fat boy," Tank glared down at him. He swallowed hard and stepped aside.

"I need to have a word with you, Agent Tankersley," the Chief Inspector growled.

"Where are you holding Alfie Lesner?" Tank turned to face him.

"Why didn't you say that the Kelly twins were the Major's grandchildren?" he blustered.

Tank looked at Sylvia Lees and didn't need to ask where that gem of information had come from.

"They recovered evidence from the woods," Sylvia added fuel to the fire.

"A word right now!" the Chief said pointing to the corridor. They all stepped out of the room, leaving the nurse to tend to the struggling patient. She pressed the alarm button to summon help and doctors came running down the corridor toward them.

"You have no jurisdiction here if you are acting purely as a vigilante, Agent Tankersley," the Chief removed his hat and pointed his finger at Tank. "I have every sympathy with the Major, but this is not helping us to find his grandchildren."

"Where are you holding Alfie Lesner?" Tank repeated his question.

"Are you listening to me?" the Chief said angrily. "I could have you arrested right now for what you've done so far."

Tank decided to cut his losses and walk away, but the Chief had other ideas. He grabbed Tank by the arm and pulled him backwards.

"I want you to hand over every speck of evidence that you have taken from that crime scene, and then you and the Major need to stay well out of my investigation, do you hear me?"

Tank shook his arm free and turned away without speaking. There was no time to lose arguing the toss with the inspector. He needed to get to Alfie Lesner.

19
HAJJ

Hajj watched Rahid and his men hosing down the stable yard with caustic soda. Brian's body had been stuffed into a large oil drum and set alight with five gallons of unleaded, and a quarter drum of diesel engine oil. It would burn for hours leaving nothing but grey ashes and a black sludge. That would be disposed of in a river that ran through the farmland. It's a simple but effective way to dispose of enemies, and they'd tried and tested it many times before. The smell sickened Hajj; it was sweet like pork burning.

"Rahid," Hajj shouted him.

The wiry little man shouted a series of instructions to his men and then jogged over to Hajj.

"Yes, Boss."

"Alfie has been arrested."

"How do you know?"

"Our contact in the custody suite has just telephoned me."

"What about Howarth?"

"He's not sure, but he thinks that he may have been taken to hospital," Hajj lit a cigarette and breathed the smoke in deeply.

"Do you think they'll talk?"

"Do you?"

"They could ruin everything if they do," Rahid did not want to go back to Morocco, but he didn't want to go to prison either.

Hajj watched the flames flickering from the oil drum, and burning embers climbed high into the night sky.

"It would be easy enough to get Howarth out of a hospital, but how would we get Alfie out of a police station?" Hajj pondered.

"It would take an army of men to do that, Hajj."

"You're right, that wouldn't be an option, but we need to stop him from talking."

"He would be easy to hit in prison."

"That would be too late, Rahid."

"What else can we do?"

"If they had to move him then we could spring him from a prison van, right?" Hajj mused as he watched the flames jumping. Flesh crackled and bones splintered in the intense heat.

"Easy, but why would they move him?" Rahid followed his employer's gaze and smiled. They both laughed and nodded in agreement. "I see, they're going to have a fire, right?"

"Right, Rahid my friend, they're going to have a fire," Hajj laughed again. "We need to move quickly."

20

ALFIE LESNER

Alfie Lesner sat in a prison cell eight foot long by six foot wide. He sat on a thin mattress that was covered in red vinyl to prolong its life. The cell stank of urine and it was cold. The walls were covered in dark green tiles, probably put there by the Victorian tradesmen that had built Warrington police station in the eighteen hundreds. In the corner was a stainless steel lavatory without a seat or toilet paper. The smell from it permeated the tiny holding cell. Alfie had been charged with grievous bodily harm, possession of a firearm and kidnap upon his arrival in the custody suite. The custody officers stripped his belt and shoelaces from him, so that he couldn't hang himself, and they bagged and tagged his belongings. That was only an hour ago, although it felt like weeks since he'd been processed. He still couldn't fathom out who had called the police. Hajj, maybe, but he could see no reason, plus he wouldn't know where Jack's caravan was exactly. Brian was dead, so that ruled him out of the equation. Jack must have called them, but why would he turn himself in? The longer he thought about it the more frightened he became that Jack was going to wriggle out of this by blaming him. His head was reeling with the night's events, and he couldn't see any way of walking away from this untarnished. The custody officers had been rough and aggressive to him. They believed that he was involved in child abduction, and treated him accordingly. Alfie had a feeling that prison would be worse still.

Alfie wasn't an angel by any stretch of the imagination, but he was no paedophile. He'd been a promising footballer at school but a bad knee injury ruled sport out as a profession. Academically he wasn't dim, but he was no rocket scientist either. He was close to his elderly parents, one younger brother and his two older sisters, and he loved their children dearly. The family had an inkling that he was involved with some unsavoury characters. He had no full time job, and yet he drove a Mercedes, dressed in designer suits and always had wads of cash on him. He kept his business close to his chest, and no one pried too deep because he was a lovable rogue. If his family thought for one minute that he'd been involved in child trafficking then he would lose everything that was dear to him, and he couldn't see any way out.

The viewing hatch clanged open and he heard keys being inserted into the lock. The heavy metal door swung open. It was odd but he always marvelled at how thick prison doors were. King Kong could not break through one of them.

"Get up," a burly police officer grunted. He had a keychain dangling to his knees. "Your solicitor is here, I hope he's a good one."

Alfie stepped out of the cell into a wide corridor with a high vaulted ceiling. The walls were covered with the same green tiles as his cell, and there were at least a dozen cell doors on either side of the corridor. The smell of urine didn't fade at all. It still cloyed in his throat.

"Move it," the officer pushed him hard in the back, and Alfie walked down the corridor. There were two men dressed in plain clothes leaning against the wall.

"In here," one of them instructed him. He was wearing a dogtooth patterned sports jacket and black trousers that had become shiny with age. Alfie reckoned he was dressed head to toe in Matalan budget clothing. The second detective shopped at the same store, and he was sporting a bottle green ill-fitting suit, and brown shoes.

Alfie stepped into the interview room and immediately felt claustrophobic. There was barely room to swing a cat in there. A duty solicitor was already sat at the table, and Alfie realised immediately that he was a state appointed brief, and therefore useless. The table and the four chairs around it were fastened to the floor with metal brackets to prevent a prisoner using them as a makeshift weapon. Alfie's solicitor remained seated and he shifted a pile of loose papers that were on the table in front of him.

"I need a moment alone with my client," he said to the detectives. The officer in the dogtooth jacket rolled his eyes to the ceiling and tutted.

"Five minutes," the detective replied looking at his watch.

"I'll need longer than that, Detective," the brief replied.

The detective marched up to the table and placed both hands on it, leaning aggressively toward the solicitor. He looked at Alfie as if he were something that he'd stood in.

"This man is involved in the kidnap of five year old twins. Every minute you're fucking about means they're a minute further away, five minutes is all you've got," he snarled.

The solicitor was a young man, not long out of university. He was learning his trade by taking defence jobs for pro-bono clients on legal aid. He couldn't look the detective in the eye, and he certainly didn't have the stomach to defend this Child Taker.

"Of course you're assuming that my client is in fact guilty," the brief tried to be assertive.

"You got five minutes," the detective turned and headed toward the door.

"I am guilty, and I'll help you to find them if I can," Alfie called after the detective.

"I must advise you to say nothing until we have spoken in private," the solicitor stood up.

"Shut up, Williams," the detective span in the doorway. He pointed to Alfie and said, "you'd better not be messing me around sunshine."

"I'm not," Alfie shook his head.

"Get the tape on," he ordered his colleague. "Sit down." He told Alfie as the other detective opened fresh cassettes and inserted them into a tape recorder that looked like it had sailed on the ark.

"I must repeat that this is against my advice, Mr Lesner, and that I would like it noted that my client has volunteered to assist you with your enquiries," the brief sat down again and ruffled his papers nervously.

"This interview is being conducted, on July the second, two thousand and nine, at three o'clock in the morning, by Detective's Crab, and Wilson. Also present is duty solicitor," he waited for the brief to introduce himself.

"Alan Williams," he said.

"The suspect is Alfie Lesner, and he is being interviewed under caution. What can you tell me about the whereabouts of the Kelly twins?" detective Crab interlinked his fingers and looked Alfie in the eyes.

"I didn't kidnap them, let's get that straight," Alfie began nervously. He didn't know what to say for best but he had to get his side over to them before Jack started shifting the blame.

"Who did?" Crab asked bluntly.

"Jack Howarth. He kidnapped them. I was the delivery man, a go between, but I thought they were going for adoption," Alfie sounded lame.

"Adoption?" Wilson gasped. He spat the word out.

"Yes, it sounds silly now I think of it, bloody stupid, but I believed him," Alfie put his head in his hands.

"For the tape please, Alfie. You were told that the twins were going to be adopted?" Crab was astounded.

"Yes, honestly."

"By who?" Wilson asked sarcastically.

"I don't know, rich Moroccan families that couldn't have children of their own," Alfie answered quietly.

The detectives exchanged glances and pressed on with the questioning. They weren't sure whether Alfie was genuinely duped by Jack Howarth, or a totally complicit player in the crime.

"Where are they now?"

"I don't know for certain," Alfie looked from one detective to the other, and he could see anger in their eyes. "The last time I saw them they were being put into a horsebox."

"A horsebox?"

"Yes, a big navy blue, wooden horsebox," Alfie expanded.

"What was the registration?"

"I don't know?"

"Who was driving it?"

"A Moroccan, I don't know his name," Alfie tried his best to answer, but he couldn't help sounding vague.

"Was the number plate British, or Moroccan?"

"British, I think."

"You think?"

"It was British, I'm sure. I think I would have noticed if it was foreign."

"How many wheels did this horsebox have?"

"What?"

"Was it a double wheelbase at the rear?"

"Yes, I think so."

"Was it being towed?"

"No, it was the type with a driver's cab, like a converted truck."

"What make?"

"I'm not sure, but the cab looked like the front end of a DAF truck."

"Were there horses in it?"

"Yes, they loaded the kids and then put a couple of horses into the back."

Crab turned to his colleague and nodded his head toward the door. His partner understood that he was to put out an immediate all ports bulletin to every police force in the country to look for a large blue horsebox. He stood up and left the room. It wouldn't be the first time livestock had been used to hide drugs or humans from border guards and customs officers.

"Detective Wilson has left the interview for a moment," Crab said for the sake of the tape.

"Were the twins alive and well?"

"Yes, they were sleeping."

"Were they sleeping, or drugged?"

"I'm not sure, they could have been drugged I suppose," Alfie didn't know because at the time he didn't care. He hadn't looked at the children that he'd transported as if they were somebody's sons or daughters. Not the way he did with his beloved nephews and nieces. Somehow, Alfie had been able to differentiate between the two, business, and family. Maybe it was akin to what the Nazis had done to the Jews, blanked all recognition of them as fellow humans, so that they could be complicit in their extermination without feeling any guilt. Now in the cold light of day it felt completely different. He felt very guilty indeed.

"How did you transport them to this, Hajj character?"

Alfie swallowed hard before he answered. He realised how it would sound. 'What on earth would his family think of him if this came out in court? ' 'Uncle Alfie the Child Taker'.

"In the boot of my car," Alfie said ashamed.

"You put five year old children into the boot of your car?" the detective repeated for effect.

"Yes."

"Could you answer a little louder for the tape please," Crab wanted this recorded with complete clarity.

"Yes, I put them in the boot of my car," Alfie felt sick.

"Where did you take them to?"

Alfie realised that he was digging a big hole for himself. The more he said the worse things sounded. He leaned over to Alan Williams and whispered to his brief. The brief took a deep breath and then spoke next.

"My client has been very helpful so far, Detective Crab, and now we'd like to know what's on the table if he helps you further?"

"Are you kidding me?"

"No, Detective, he's got some valuable information that he'd like to exchange for some leniency," the solicitor cleared his throat. He was uncomfortable with the situation, to say the least.

Crab sat back in his chair and linked his hands behind his considerably sized head. It looked almost too big for his body and was made to look larger by thick greying hair cut into a flat top.

"Your client, admits assault, carrying a firearm, and kidnap. He carried five year old children in the boot of his car, and sold them to a Moroccan paedophile ring, and you'd like us to consider making a deal?"

"Yes," Alan Williams undid the top button of his shirt and loosened his tie. He suddenly felt like he was choking.

"How does life without parole sound?"

"Obviously that's not for you to decide, Detective, but we'd appreciate your report being favourable to my client."

Alfie whispered again. The colour drained out of his solicitor's face as he spoke to him.

"I believe that my client can shed some light on a recent murder."

"How recent?"

"I believe it was today."

Crab stood up and removed the dogtooth sports coat. He undid the buttons on his shirts sleeves and rolled them up while he contemplated the issue. There were large sweat patches spreading beneath his arms.

"Let's just say that I believe a single word that your scumbag client has said, and I don't by the way. Why would we consider any deals?"

Alfie whispered to his brief again. The brief shook his head and was obviously disagreeing with his client.

"If you recover the twins alive, and my client divulges as much information as he possesses about the incident, will you recommend leniency?"

"I'll mention that he cooperated fully with the investigation, and that's as far as I'm going," Crab sat down and looked hard at Alfie Lesner. "Where did you take the twins, in the boot of your car?"

Alfie looked to his brief for guidance, and then paused before speaking. He was thinking of how to explain everything without digging himself any deeper. It was already obvious that his liberty would be taken from him, it was just a matter of how long now.

"The farm is called, Rookery Farm, it's near Delamere Forest."

"What Road is it on?"

"It's just off the A forty nine, in the forest," Alfie explained.

"How many men were there?"

"Half a dozen or so, maybe more, but he has hundreds of men working for him, all over the country, they're a nasty bunch."

"Nasty? Similar to people that transport five year old children in the boot of their car?" Detective Crab snarled sarcastically.

Alfie sat back in his chair and sighed. The situation was dire, and the more information he gave, the worse he sounded.

"Weapons?" the Detective carried on building a picture of the criminals that he'd be dealing with.

"Yes, he has everything from mortars to machineguns. Hajj deals them," Alfie shrugged.

"Deals weapons?"

"Yes, his men sell to most of the drug gangs in the city," Alfie explained.

"This gets better and better," Crab scribbled the details down as Alfie spoke.

"Is it his farm?"

"No, he rents a stable yard there for his racehorses."

"I wonder how many racehorses a five year old could buy me in today's climate eh?" Crab commented sourly.

"There is no need to be obtuse, Detective Crab. My client is trying to answer your questions honestly," Alan Williams interrupted. He tried to look sternly at the aging detective, but it barely registered.

Detective Crab thought for a second, and decided that if Alfie was on the level about the location of the farm that he'd taken the children to, then that's where they needed to start their search. He walked to the door and called to a uniformed police officer. He handed him a piece of paper with the address of the farm written on it.

"Get this to Detective Wilson immediately," he ordered.

"Yes, Sir."

"Tell him to organise a helicopter and an armed response unit there pronto." He closed the door and sat back down at the table. Detective Crab seemed edgy now, as he had enough information to be going on with, and he'd rather be out looking for the bad guys than sat sweating in this tiny interview room. "What else can you tell me?"

"Jack Howarth was paid to supply the Moroccans with

children to order," Alfie wanted the real kidnapper identified before the spotlight fell on him. "Myself and an associate, Brian Croft, were the intermediaries. We picked up the twins and took them to Hajj at the stables. Last night Hajj shot Brian with a Mach 10 machine pistol."

"You witnessed that?"

"Yes."

"How many times have you done this?"

"Done what?"

"How many times have you transported children to the stables?"

"I've just told you that Hajj shot Brian with a Mach 10," it was Alfie's turn to be annoyed. He thought that the revelation would have more of an impact than it had, but Crab was more interested in building a case against him.

"We'll look into it when we get to the farm, Alfie, if you play with fire then you expect to be burnt. How many times have you acted as intermediaries?"

Alfie's brief nudged him before he could answer. It had become obvious that the detective was trying to stitch Alfie up tighter than a drum.

"My client is here to answer questions about the events for which he has been cautioned, nothing else," the solicitor interrupted.

"Okay, I've got enough for now," Crab eyed Alfie suspiciously. "Tell me, why did you assault Jack Howarth?"

Alfie's solicitor shook his head again.

"No comment," Alfie replied.

Detective Crab stood and picked up his jacket. He opened the door and called a uniformed officer into the room.

"Put this scumbag back into his cell," he ordered as he disappeared down the corridor. The police officer motioned for Alfie to stand which he did without protest.

"I will not be requiring your services again," Alfie said

without looking at the duty solicitor.

"Thank god for that," Alan Williams muttered.

Alfie smirked as he walked down the corridor to the detention area. He didn't know why he found the solicitor's comment funny, but he did. The smell of stale urine grew stronger as he neared his cell. A hard shove in the back launched him forward through the doorway and he landed painfully on his knees. The police officer that had pushed him sneered as he slammed the thick iron door closed, and the sound echoed through the cellblock. Alfie grimaced as a tear ran from the corner of his eye. It would be a sound that he'd have to get used to for the foreseeable future.

21

TANK

John Tankersley waited outside Warrington General Hospital
for a taskforce vehicle to pick him up. The chopper that he'd
arrived in had been dispatched to pick up a unit who would
be on standby until they were required. The night had turned
cold and a drizzle began to fall steadily. Puddles of water
began to form, reflecting the yellow streetlights. The car parks
were empty bar a few isolated vehicles here and there. Tank
thought about the way things had progressed as he watched a
couple of drunks swinging punches at each other outside the
casualty department. The two men staggered back and forth
like human windmills in slow motion. The automatic doors
opened and two women staggered out of casualty to join
in the fray, and the action intensified. The drunken quartet
wobbled around hurling punches and abuse until two huge
black security guards managed to separate them.

A black Mitsibushi Shogun turned off the main road and
headed toward the foyer area. Tank recognised Grace as the
driver. She pulled the vehicle to a halt, much to the annoyance
of an ambulance driver who was in the vehicle behind her. He
honked the horn and gesticulated wildly to the double yellow
lines, which indicated that she should not have parked there.
Tank waved at him in apology and opened the passenger door,

climbing in as quickly as he could.

"Road hog," he joked.

"Do you think he's annoyed?" Grace added. She signalled and pulled the Shogun away from the curb, freeing up the lane again. The ambulance driver honked again, and this time Tank gave him the finger. The paramedic thought better of returning the gesture and steered his ambulance around the warring couples to the casualty department.

"What do we know?" Tank asked as he clicked the seatbelt into its socket.

"Well, the good news is we have a file as long as your arm on our friend, Hajj Achmed," Grace began.

"Why am I not surprised?"

"Is it because of your deep mistrust in human nature?"

"Probably," he grunted. Tank had a bizarre respect for the people that he usually hunted. Terrorists had a cause to fight for, a reason to cause others harm, in their own mind anyway. An organised business that dealt with paedophiles all over the globe was just plain evil in his mind. "Tell me about Achmed."

"He has been investigated for extortion, counterfeiting, arson, people trafficking, prostitution and, wait for it, arms running."

"What type of weapons?"

"Everything, he's in charge of British operations for a huge crime family based in Marrakesh. They have supplied several militias with weapons, ammunition, explosives, and according to the Americans, they sent a shipment of Stinger missiles to the Taliban. We have loose ties to extremist groups in Somalia, Afghanistan, Pakistan and The Yemen."

"Do we have enough evidence to justify stepping into the investigation?"

"No, and I think we're too late anyway," she slowed the vehicle before pulling out onto Lovely Lane. It was a ten-minute drive to the main police station in the town centre, where Alfie Lesner had just finished his amazing confession. She had a feeling that's where he'd want to go.

"Why do you think that we're too late?"

"Alfie Lesner has just spilled his guts to the Serious Crime Squad detectives," Grace brought up a liquid crystal display, which was built into the centre console and a series of communiqués from the Cheshire police began to scroll down. "He's admitted being an intermediary between Jack Howarth and a Moroccan Mafia family headed by Hajj Achmed."

"Where did he take the twins?"

"The uniformed division has despatched a chopper and three armed response teams to a farm near Delamere Forest. Lesner claims that the twins were taken away in a horsebox, they've issued an 'All Ports Bulletin' to find it. Every uniformed officer in the country will be looking for it."

"It should just be a matter of time before they find them then," Tank said.

"It might be time for us to step back and leave the police to their investigation," Grace glanced sideways to catch his reaction.

"Does the Major know?" Tank asked, ignoring her last remark.

"Yes, he's patched into everything."

"How are Karl and Hayley holding up?"

"Not good, she's thrown him out."

"Oops, not good, and not completely unexpected," Tank looked out of the window as they drove over the main West Coast railway line, a soap factory towered above the tracks. It looked like a metropolis illuminated in the darkness.

"What's next then?"

"I want to talk to Alfie Lesner myself," Tank was adamant that he wasn't going to walk away from the investigation yet. "He's just small potatoes in this, but he can tell me where Hajj Achmed is. Achmed and his employers are responsible for this,

I'm going to make sure that they don't do it again."

"The police will be all over them by now," Grace said.

"I don't think a man like Achmed will be that easy to find, especially if he knows that the police are on to him."

"If he's dealing arms to gangs in the city then the chances are that he has informers in the force," Grace carried on the thread.

"Exactly, in which case he'll be on the run already, but Lesner will know how he travels in and out of the country."

The Shogun turned a left hand, ninety-degree bend in the road. Bank Quay railway station was on the right, and the aging police station was on the left. It was a three storey redbrick building with a turret built on every corner of the roof. The station was built to act as a fortress in the event of civil unrest, and the turrets were in effect, gun towers. The rear of the building was surrounded by a high brick wall, which was topped with razor wire. There was not a single police car in the pound at the rear. It was obvious that the bulk of the force had been deployed to secure the stable block at Delamere Forest.

"It looks like no one's home," Grace commented as she pulled the Shogun around the front of the building. There were parking bays marked out along the front, and all the way around the right hand side of the police station. Private vehicles that belonged to on duty officers filled every parking bay. A public car park across the road was empty and Grace headed into it.

"They're on a wild goose chase in Delamere Forest," Tank laughed as he spoke.

"You think Achmed will be long gone by now?"

"Don't you?"

Grace was about to answer him when two cars, which were parked in front of the police station exploded.

22
WOOLTON VILLAGE

Patrick Lesner woke up with a start. It was pitch dark, which told him that it was the middle of the night. He rarely awoke before dawn, even though he was getting old. His prostate cancer was under control now, and he didn't need to pee every half an hour. The doctor had diagnosed him eighteen months earlier, and he and his wife, Margaret, had decided not to tell their children about his illness, to save them from the worry. Something had dragged him from his sleep but he couldn't work out what it was. He decided to get up and check that the house was secure, just for his piece of mind.

Patrick and Margaret lived in a gardener's lodge at the entrance to Reynold's Park, in Woolton Village. The park had once been part of a large estate owned by a rich merchant's family, but was now part of the city's portfolio of public parks. The park was twenty acres of sloping grassed areas, and plush gardens surrounded by a high sandstone wall, and the gardener's lodges guarded the entrances to the park. Patrick loved the park, and the village that it was situated in, and when the park's buildings came up for private ownership, they'd used their savings to buy the lodge. It was a dream home for them, and their grown up children visited them frequently. Christmas was a special time for them and they had to add chairs to the family table every year to accommodate their growing number of grandchildren. All of their children had kids now, all of them except Alfie. Alfie was always too busy 'chasing tail', as he so eloquently put it, to settle down with one woman. 'I'm still playing the field, dad,' he used to say whenever he was goaded about his philandering ways. Alfie was very different from the rest of his children, but Patrick loved him all the same. He worried sometimes, about where his money came from, but he'd decided a long time ago that it was better not to know.

Patrick swung his creaking legs out of bed and he wriggled his feet into a pair of red slippers. Although he had thin, blue, cotton pyjamas on there was a chill in the air. He could hear rain pattering on the roof too, which made him feel colder still. Patrick reached for a thick woollen cardigan that was on a wicker armchair next to the bed, and he pulled it on. He yawned as he headed for the bedroom door, trying not to wake his elderly wife.

"What are you doing?" she muttered as he opened the door.

"I'm sorry to wake you darling, something disturbed me, so I'm going to get a quick drink," Patrick lied.

"You're going to check the locks more like," Margaret chuckled. She always teased him about his obsession with security. He was continually checking that the windows and doors were locked tight. The problem was that age was dulling his mind and he couldn't remember if he had locked the doors or not, and so he'd have to check them all again.

"Better safe than sorry, you go back to sleep," he said as he walked out of the bedroom.

"Silly old fool," she called after him. She loved him dearly, but she could see his faculties fading fast. Arthritis was rotting his joints, and he couldn't walk far without a stick. The cancer treatment that he'd endured had stripped the muscle mass from his frame, leaving him frail. They had been together since school and it broke her heart to see the love of her life wasting away before her eyes.

Patrick was glad the lodge was all on one level, stairs would be a trauma for him to navigate nowadays. His walking stick was leaning against an ornate telephone table in the hallway, and he decided to use it while he did the rounds of locks and latches. He wasn't absolutely sure, but he thought that he'd felt a breeze on his face as he walked down the hallway. A creaking sound in the kitchen stopped him in his tracks. The lodge was hundreds of years old and creaking noises were not uncommon, as the ancient timbers expanded and contracted. The chances of there being an intruder in his home were slim, but he had to check. Many years ago he would have taken his chances with any would be burglars that invaded his home, and threatened the safety of his wife and children. Now though he was not as confident, age and illness had taken their toll on his body. He listened intently for any sound, but everything was still. Patrick gripped the walking stick like a bat and walked toward the kitchen door. It was closed too. He placed his ear flat against the cold wood and listened for any intruders. There was nothing but silence.

"Maybe I am a silly old fool," he whispered under his breath, but it didn't stop a chill running through him. Did he feel a draft on his skin again, or was it all in his imagination? He turned the handle and twisted it slowly. The hinges creaked as the door opened an inch at a time. Patrick peered into the darkness and gripped his cane tightly with his left hand. His right hand fumbled along the wall for the light switch. A blast of cold night air hit him, and he could hear the rain as if it were around him. The hairs on the back of his neck tingled as he realised there must be a door or a window open somewhere. He scrambled for the light in a panic and found purchase at last. The bulb flickered and then illuminated the kitchen.

Directly in front of him was the backdoor, and it was open wide to the elements. Rain blew into the kitchen at an angle and a puddle was growing across the red tiled floor. There was a wood burning stove in a stone fireplace to the left. The mantelpiece was shoulder high to a man of average height. There were deep recesses behind the stove, where a man could hide. He looked into them, but they were empty. On the right was a long pine table surrounded by eight chairs, and next to it were the sink and a wet area for a washing machine and a dishwasher. He couldn't see a burglar, or a bogeyman anywhere. All he could see was the backdoor flapping in the wind and the rain pouring in because a silly old man forgot to lock it. Patrick stepped into the kitchen to close the door. If he was honest he couldn't remember for sure if he'd locked it or not. Patrick lowered his walking stick and shook his head. He scolded himself for growing old and senile. He was a few steps in when he realised that he hadn't checked behind the door, in case someone was hiding there. Patrick had realised too late.

23
THE HOSPITAL

Constable Davis was gutted. He'd been a member of the armed response unit for nearly two years and he lived for the adrenalin rush that he got from combat situations. Three armed units had been despatched to a farm in Delamere Forest, tasked with rounding up a dangerous Moroccan Mafioso, and he'd been left at the hospital to babysit a scumbag paedophile. Davis had pleaded with his senior officer to be included in the operation, but he had denied his request. They had never seen eye to eye, and the constable felt that he'd been discriminated against on numerous occasions. He could find no reason for it, except that he was overweight. His senior officer had gone so far as to actually call him fat on his last performance review, and listed significant weight loss as his number one goal if he wanted to keep his place in the armed unit. Davis couldn't believe the effrontery of the man. Prior to his annual review, he was convinced that he was in line for promotion, and yet his superior was telling him that he was too fat to remain in the unit. Tonight was the biggest operation to be launched for years and he was sitting outside an operating theatre while a pervert had his testicles re-stitched. There didn't seem to be any justice.

His thoughts were disturbed as the theatre door opened

and Jack Howarth was wheeled out. An orderly pushed the bed toward the room that he'd been in previously.

"You still here, Constable," Jack asked sarcastically. His stitches had been replaced under a local anaesthetic, and although it had numbed the pain in his nether regions, it had done nothing to dull his whit.

"Don't push your luck, Howarth, I'm not in the mood for your nonsense," the constable said grumpily. He checked that Jack's handcuffs were secure as the gurney was pushed past him.

"Have you arrested Alfie Lesner yet?" Jack chuckled as he was wheeled into his anti-ward.

"Shut up Howarth," Davis said wearily. His heart was not in the task that faced him, not one bit. His colleagues had been buzzing with excitement and nervous anticipation, summoned to join the response teams. There was talk of heavily armed opposition, allegedly responsible for the kidnap of the Kelly twins, drug running and international arms deals. In comparison, he had to cope with the cutting jibes of an aging nonce. Initially there had been two rookie constables guarding Howarth until it became clear that he was somehow involved in the kidnapping, and then it was decided that he needed an armed officer, just in case. Rumours of Jack Howarth's previous record were being passed around the nursing staff like Chinese Whispers, and random employees were walking up and down the corridor trying to get a peek at the 'Child Taker' through his window. He had turned into the hospital freak show.

Constable Davis was parched and he wanted a drink. His colleagues hadn't even left him with a flask of weak tea to get him through his shift, as all thoughts had been of the imminent operation. He eyed a dark haired nurse that was doing her rounds further down the corridor, and so he decided to kill two birds with one stone, as it were. Number one he could try to coax a much needed cup of coffee out of her, and number two he could try to alleviate the excruciating boredom by chatting up a sexy young nurse. It seemed like a good plan. He closed the door to Jack's room and checked the corridor for strangers, a couple of orderlies dressed in mint green uniforms peered through the round viewing window in the door.

"He looks like a paedophile," one of the men commented to the other. They laughed as they carried on about their business.

The constable waited outside the room that the brunette nurse had entered. He checked his reflection in the glass, and sucked in his belly. It didn't make a great deal of difference; he still looked like a beer drinker squashed into a bulletproof riot vest. Perhaps his superior officer was right, and he should lose some weight. The door opened and the nurse walked out briskly. She was nearly past him before he'd composed himself enough to speak to her.

"Hi there," he said. "I hope you don't mind me asking you, but I've been placed on personal protection duties alone. There's not many of us qualified to work alone, you see, but I'm parched."

"Oh dear," She turned her head briefly as she walked. "I think you're getting me confused with the vending machine on the first floor."

"I didn't mean any offense, it's just that I can't leave my post you see, I'm gasping," he joked, but she was entering the next room before he'd finished speaking.

"Sorry, too busy," she called as she closed the door behind her.

"Just my luck," he muttered. He felt inside his combat pants for loose change, and he counted the grand total of forty-seven pence. A quick rummage through his other pockets netted him another two pence. He walked back to Jack's room and checked him through the window. Jack appeared to be sleeping, eyes closed and his chest was rising and falling rhythmically.

Constable Davis headed for the elevator and the smell of disinfectant intensified his thirst. He pressed the call button and jiggled the coins in his hand as he waited for the lift to arrive. The voices of two nurses passing the other end of the landing drew his attention, and he watched them walking toward the stairs, their starched uniforms clinging to all the right places. They were obviously taking the stairs because it would burn calories, and keep their figures trim. The sound of their footsteps echoed up the stairwell as they descended. He thought about following their example, but the lift beeped and the doors opened, and another opportunity to burn excess fat was missed. Two dark skinned ambulance men exited the car, leaving it empty, and Constable Davis stepped into it and pressed the button for the first floor. The ambulance men turned right as they exited and headed toward the stairwell. The doors closed and he felt the motors whirring into life, lowering him toward refreshment. The lift approached the second floor and slowed before stopping completely. Constable Davis straightened up and breathed in again as the doors opened, in anticipation of a gaggle of firm young nurses rushing through the doors. His imaginary scenario was shattered when a plump Asian doctor stepped into the lift. There was stethoscope hung around his neck and a collection of ballpoint pens in his top pocket. He brought the smell of coriander and spices with him; they lingered on him from his meal break. Constable Davis breathed out and returned his body to its natural slouch position.

The doors opened at the first floor and the fat police officer found himself confronted by a bank of six vending machines. There were two Cola machines, one containing chocolate, crisps and biscuits, and even a fruit vending machine. The constable made a mental note to avoid the fruit. There were half a dozen battered metal chairs with ripped seatbacks next to them, which, acted as a chill-out area for worried friends and relatives. The hot drinks machine was on the far left and a young couple dressed in hooded tracksuits were banging the coin slot and cursing at it.

"Hey, pack that in," Davis shouted to them as he approached. The young man turned aggressively, was about to unleash a torrent of abuse when he realised that the police officer was twice his size, and armed.

"The machine's swallowed my fucking money," the man said in his defence. Constable Davis could see from the size of his pupils that he was wired on some kind of narcotic, possibly ecstasy but probably heroin.

"Smacking it will not fix the problem, mate, so leave it alone."

"Yes, well we're going outside for a fag anyway," the female hoody sneered. They both giggled, but their demeanour was malevolent. Constable Davis had seen enough smack heads in his time to know that they were unpredictable and often violent if they were provoked. It didn't matter that one of them was female, because they could be just as violent when they were under the influence of drugs. The duo seemed to be waiting for a reason to attack, or retreat. The heroin was slowing their natural reactions, fight or flight. The male laughed and kicked the vending machine hard, before running off down the corridor, and his girlfriend tipped over a chair before following in his tracks.

"Who ate all the pies? Who ate all the pies? You fat bastard, you fat bastard, you ate all the pies," the duo sang in unison as they ran away.

"Everyone's a comedian today," Davis muttered. He ran his fingers over the selection buttons, until he found, white tea with sugar. The price required was sixty pence, eleven pence more than he was'd been carrying in his sticky palm.

"Shit. I do not believe this is happening to me today," he kicked the vending machine in frustration and a handful of coins clattered into the reject slot. The police officer looked up and down the corridor before retrieving the rejected monies from the machine. He chuckled to himself as he counted his winnings. There was enough for tea and crisps, and a chocolate bar too, happy days.

Constable Davis munched on salt and vinegar crisps and bit the first two inches from a Yorkie bar as the lift carried him back to the fourth floor. He slurped some of the hot liquid that was masquerading as white tea with sugar, and although it tasted like it was dishwater, it was welcome. When he arrived, the corridor was empty, and the prospect of spending the next few hours reading the newspaper and munching on confectionary did not seem too bad anymore. Things were looking much brighter, until he opened the door to Jack's room.

"Oh, my god," he spat a mouthful of potato snacks and tea across the room. The bed was empty and there was blood spatter on the floor. It made a narrow fan pattern up the wall and across the ceiling. A pair of shiny handcuffs was dangling from the bed frame, which he couldn't understand as the bracelets were still closed at either end. He put the tea down on the floor and scanned the room for clues. There was precious little to see with naked eye, forensic tests would obviously tell a more detailed story. He followed the blood spatter from the ceiling down to the skirting boards. Then he noticed a bloody lump of flesh on the floor, beneath the bed. Closer inspection revealed it was a human thumb, and it answered the question of how did Jack Howarth, the 'Child Taker' escape the handcuffs without opening them. Easily, either he, or someone else sliced of his thumb at the root, allowing the bracelet to slip over the hand unhampered. Constable Davis pulled the Glock fourteen from his holster and followed droplets of blood down the corridor.

24

TANK

Tank felt the vibration from the second explosion, and he instinctively sank lower in his seat. The ground floor windows at the front of the old police station were blown in, and flames from the exploded vehicles were flicking at the ceilings and walls inside. Thick black smoke was flooding through the shattered windows, filling the building with choking toxic fumes. A furtive figure ran across the car park to their left hand side, and darted down an alleyway. Tank couldn't make out whether they were male or female, white or black, because it was too dark and they were hooded.

"What do you think?" Grace said watching the police station intensely.

"I think that someone is using diversionary tactics, do you?" Tank replied.

"That's what I'm thinking, too much of a coincidence to be anything else," Grace took a small set of night sights from the glove box and scanned the area.

"You keep your eyes open here, I'm going to see why our friend is running away down that alleyway," Tank opened the door and sprinted down the road which ran parallel to the dark passageway. The road was well lit, and on the left set back was an arts centre, with a high glass foyer. A number of people had come outside to see what was happening at the police station. To his right was a row of terraced houses, and Tank figured that the alleyway ran behind them towards the town centre. He kept his weapon holstered as he ran between the houses and a never-ending line of parked cars. The sound of sirens wailing drifted on the night air. The fire brigade were obviously en route. Fifty yards further on there was a gap between the terraces, and Tank stepped into the darkness and listened. He could hear heavy footsteps echoing from the alleyway, and the sound of laboured breathing, but the runner was ahead of him further down the alleyway. Tank pushed his body away from the wall and sprinted along the pavement, nearly flattening a courting couple as he dashed past them.

"Hey, watch it!" the man shouted after him.

Tank ignored the warning and carried on toward the next break in the houses. A hundred yards on, he was panting for breath when he turned into the alleyway. He thought that he'd missed his target, maybe he'd been quicker, or maybe there had been another access road for the runner to escape down, but then he heard footsteps approaching. The runner was walking now, either too tired to keep running or thinking that they'd put enough distance between themselves and the police station. Tank walked quietly to the back entry, and waited in the darkness for the fugitive to appear.

"Why were you running away?" Tank stepped out of the shadows and blocked his path.

"What?" the runner was a young white man, maybe late teens or early twenties. He had a hooded sports top on, black tracksuit pants and dirty white trainers. Tank saw that his eyes were glazed and slow to react. "I'm not running away from anything, man."

"Take the hood off and show me some identification," Tank flashed his ID card and stepped closer to the youngster.

"Fuck you, man," the runner tried to step past Tank but a huge strong arm slammed into his chest, stunning him. Tank pushed the hood off the man's head and grabbed his face in his hand. There were spots and scabs around his mouth and his teeth were blackened and broken.

"Are you using crystal meth?" Tank pushed him against the wall.

"No way, man," he tried to look offended, but his eyes had a mind of their own.

"If I arrest you now, it will be twenty four hours at least before you're processed. Do you think that you can stay clean that long without really hurting?" Tank searched his pockets as he spoke.

"I didn't do anything," he whined. Tank pulled a Zippo lighter from one of his pockets, and five crisp twenty-pound notes from the other.

"You've got one chance to tell me who gave you this money, and this lighter," Tank waved them in his face.

"They're mine, give them back," he grabbed at them weakly.

"If they were yours, then you'd have already smoked this money, and swapped the lighter for more drugs, one last time, who gave you the money?"

"Fuck you!"

Tank brought his right hand up sharply and hit him across the face with the back of his hand. The runner's legs buckled at the knees. Tank grabbed him by the back of the neck, and he twisted the hood around his fist, before lifting the youth from the floor completely. He dangled in mid air and his legs kicked uselessly. His face turned purple and his eyes began to bulge from his head as he choked. Tank brought him level with his own face.

"Do you want to tell me where you got the money from?"

The youth couldn't speak but he nodded desperately. Tank lowered him to the floor, but maintained the grip on his clothes.

"A guy on a motorbike gave me the money, and the lighter, and a couple of rags," he rubbed his throat and gasped for air.

"Carry on," Tank lifted him an inch.

"Okay, okay. He gave me a ton to torch a couple of cars outside the station, man."

"What did he look like?"

"What?"

"What did he look like, black, white, old, young?"

"Black, well foreign anyway, youngish."

"What type of motorbike?"

"It was a beauty, man, a Fire Blade, red and white faring."

"When was this?"

"Five minutes ago, at the station," the youngster was beginning to get angst. His skin had become pallid and covered in a film of perspiration.

"At the police station?"

"No, man, at the railway station."

Tank had heard enough for now, and he pulled the young arsonist back onto the main road. He took two plasticuffs from his belt and held them in his left hand as they approached a concrete lamppost.

"Put your hands out behind your back," Tank grabbed his sleeve.

"What are you doing?" the junkie looked desperate. "I've told you what happened."

"You've just set fire to a police station my stoned friend, and you're looking at a long stretch in jail," Tank fastened his hands behind his back and then strapped him to the lamppost. "I'll tell the police where you are when I get back to the station."

"What about my money, you bastard?" the youth called after him.

Tank ran back to the police station and had to push his way through a small crowd of onlookers who had left some of the late night drinking clubs in the town. Fire engines were arriving en mass and the fire chiefs were directing the tenders to the front and back of the building. Grace had moved her vehicle to the main road, so that she could see both sides of the police station, and she was scanning the area through night vision glasses to see if she could spot anyone acting suspiciously, or paying too much attention to the goings on. He spotted a junior officer holding the crowd back, and directing traffic.

"There's a youth handcuffed to a lamppost a few hundred yards down the street," Tank said as he approached him. The officer looked confused even when Tank had shown him his Counter Terrorist ID. "He had this money on him and this lighter, and he started the fire by stuffing rags into the petrol caps, and then lighting them."

"Have you arrested him?" the officer asked.

"You can do that, Constable," Tank smiled. "It'll be a great collar for you, might even get you a sergeant's job."

The policeman smiled and nodded. He pocketed the evidence and headed through the onlookers to apprehend the arsonist, visions of a commendation in mind. Tank walked the short distance to the main road and approached Grace's vehicle.

"You seen anything?" he asked as he climbed in.

"Nothing of any note," she replied. "Did you catch him?"

"Yes, he lit the fires," Tank snapped the seatbelt into its anchor. "He said that a foreign looking man on a Honda Fire Blade paid him to torch the police station."

"I haven't seen any motorbikes," she said.

"Look over there," Tank pointed toward the railway station, which was only three hundred yards away, on the other side of the road. The station was situated on a sharp bend, the rails and platform thirty foot above the road, accessed by stairs and lifts. A line of white hackney cabs were standing on a rank to the left of the station approach, and to the left there were a few vehicles parked there by rail passengers. There had been some reconstruction work being carried out, and at the back of the car park there were two metal shipping containers, which were being used to store equipment and plant. Grace scanned the front of the station.

"Bingo," Grace said.

"What have you got?"

"Motorcycle, red and white faring, parked next to those shipping containers," Grace handed him the night sights. Tank looked through them and sure enough the motorcyclist was watching the rear of the police station intently.

"I've got him," Tank said.

"What do you think?"

"He's waiting to see what happens," Tank replied.

"How do you want to play this?"

"We'll wait and see what happens, but I think they're trying to get Alfie Lesner out of that police station," Tank settled down and waited. Whatever they were planning, they were about to show their hand.

25
THE TWINS

Sarah awoke from a dream-filled sleep when she heard a horse neighing. She opened her eyes and she was frightened by the darkness. Zak was next to her and she snuggled into him, trying to gain comfort from something that was familiar to her. She had a headache and a sore throat, and the feeling of motion was making her feel sick. The horse neighed again, and she knew that it was close by, but she couldn't see it in the darkness. She could smell the horses. Her mother had taken her riding as soon as she was old enough to walk and she loved every minute of it. The sounds and smells of the animals and stables were somehow comforting in this strange world that she had found herself in. She thought about her favourite pony, Misty, a grey with a pleasant temperament. Sarah took carrots to the stables every time she rode him, and she loved the sound of Misty crunching carrots, and the way his lips quivered as he munched them.

"Mummy," she whispered as loudly as she dared, scared that she might alert any monsters that were lurking out of sight in the darkness. Her foot was sticking out of the blanket, which covered them, and she pulled it back into the bed, out of reach of the snapping teeth of the ghosties and ghoulies that may live under there.

"Daddy," she whispered a little more urgently. The only sound was the horses, and the hum of a diesel engine. Sarah wanted to go back to sleep where she was safe, and she closed her eyes and waited for it to take her. Her brother stirred and moved closer still, oblivious to the darkness that surrounded him, and Sarah held him tightly as she drifted back to sleep.

26
THE HOSPITAL

Constable Davis reached for his radio as he followed the blood trail down the corridor. He needed backup to track down Jack Howarth. His superior officer would be over the moon that he'd let him escape. The constable knew that his boss wanted him out of the Armed Response Unit, and he would use this gaff to further discipline him for his poor performance. He would also crucify him for leaving his charge unguarded while he bought crisps and tea from a vending machine. There was no reason that he could think of to justify leaving Howarth alone.

"Constable two, two, three, five, to base. I require immediate backup at Warrington General, a suspect has absconded, I repeat, a suspect has absconded." The radio crackled in response, but there was no reply. Davis stared at the radio confused. The modern radio communicators that the police used were virtually fail safe, and they never went down. Nor were there many black spots where a signal could not be received. If there was no reply to a call, then there was no one in the police station, and that was impossible. The constable tried the call again, but there was no reply.

"How can there be nobody in the radio room?" he asked himself.

He hooked the radio back onto his utility belt and followed the trail. The blood had fallen in blobs at random. There didn't appear to be any pattern to it, which indicated that the wound had been wrapped to stem the blood flow, and that the blood was dripping from the sodden cloth. He stayed close to the walls as he tracked down the ward. A door opened to the right, which startled him. He pointed the Glock fourteen at the doorway and frightened the life out of the nurse that was stepping out. She screamed and slammed the door closed again.

"Stupid bitch, I nearly wet myself then," Constable Davis muttered under his breath. He reached the stairwell at the end of the corridor and pointed the gun into the landing area while he checked that it was clear. Globules of blood had dropped onto the beige floor tiles and there were smears on the stairs where someone had stood in them. From the smears, he gauged that there were at least two people, and probably three moving together down the stairwell, which meant that Jack Howarth had help. Davis approached a metal banister rail, which had been painted with pastel pink gloss, and he leaned over it to see who was on the stairwell. The floors above were empty. He looked down, two floors below he could see two men wearing green trousers, and a third was barefooted, wearing a dressing gown. Constable Davis figured that the green trousers belonged to ambulance men, and the dressing gown was obviously a patient. There was nothing unusual about seeing two ambulance men helping a patient down the stairs, but he remembered entering the lift earlier, and two paramedics had stepped out as he'd stepped in. Was it a coincidence or were they looking for Jack Howarth? He'd made enough of a cock-up of his posting today without adding wrongful arrest to the list. They were a long way down the stairs, and he could only see their bodies from the knees down. He decided to take a punt.

"Jack Howarth," he bellowed at the top of his voice. The men in the green trousers stopped walking, which was to be expected considering, but when they bolted he knew that they had Jack.

"Armed police, stop where you are," he shouted. The three men took absolutely no notice and kept running down the stairs, jumping them three at a time. Constable Davis launched himself down the first flight of stairs, like an Olympic sprinter out of the blocks; his considerable weight carried him down at breakneck speed. By the time he'd turned on the second landing he was puffing like an old steam engine, and he leaned over the banister to see how far ahead of him they were. One of the paramedics was looking up the stairwell directly at him, and he was pointing an Uzi nine millimetre machine pistol up at him. The Israeli built weapon is capable of firing nine hundred bullets a minute and Constable Davis threw himself onto the floor as it kicked into life. Bullets smashed into the stairwell all around him and ceramic floor tiles exploded into thousands of tiny shards as the volley of nine millimetres ricocheted off the concrete walls. The police officer waited until the deafening noise had subsided, sucked in a deep breath and took off down the next flight of stairs. He paused briefly before taking the next flight two steps at a time, as he reached the first floor landing he used the wall to slow himself down, and he had to swerve violently around a wheelchair bound woman who had been abandoned on the stairs by a frightened porter when the machinegun was fired. She seemed senile and completely oblivious to the fat police officer as he lumbered past her at full tilt.

He heard a clattering noise echoing up the stairwell and he risked another quick look over the banister. A nurse wearing a dark blue matron's uniform, with a stiff white headpiece was sprawled on the floor. She was surrounded by dozens of dark brown tablet bottles and sterilised dressing packs. To the right of her was the trolley that she had been pushing before she'd collided with Jack Howarth and his associates. It had been upturned and its contents were strewn across the corridor. Constable Davis had a clear view of one of the paramedics, as he'd fallen just a few feet away from the matron. He was lying on his back winded by the collision with the medicine trolley.

"Armed police! Stop or I'll shoot," he bellowed the warning which is required by police procedure. The dark skinned man looked straight into his eyes, but there was no fear in them, only contempt. He moved so that he was sitting up, resting on his hands with his legs out in front of him on the floor. He couldn't spring up to his feet from that position quickly, and Constable Davis had him cold in the sights of his Glock. His superior might think that he was overweight but no one could criticise his aim. He'd won the unit sharpshooter shield two years running for his skill with a pistol, but his boss said that all around fitness and stamina was more important to the unit. Davis wondered if he'd be saying the same thing now, faced with a foe armed with automatic weapons. Would it be more important to run a mile in under six minutes, or would being confident that he could hit his enemy square in the chest be more useful in this situation.

"Don't move a muscle," Davis trained his weapon on the Moroccan as he walked slowly down the last flight of stairs. Jack Howarth and the other man were making a break for it down the main corridor toward the casualty department. The matron scrabbled around dazed and tried to stand up; she was between the police officer and his prey.

"Stay down!" Davis called to her but she was panicked and concussed. She rose briefly, and then stumbled backward and landed firmly on her backside, looking shocked and slightly embarrassed. The Moroccan used the distraction to bolt in the opposite direction to his affiliates. He was up and running before the armed officer could get a shot off safely. There were too many nurses and patients milling around, watching the action as it unfolded.

The constable had to decide which of the fugitives were the more important to chase and he turned and sprinted after Jack Howarth. The corridor was wide and painted white, and the floor was red highly polished vinyl, buffed to a sheen everyday by an army of janitors. To the left it forked to accident and emergency, and to the right it opened out into a semicircle of shops and cafes, before leading out into the car parks via two revolving doors. He saw Jack Howarth fleeing through one of them as he reached the foyer. There was no way to get a shot off. His lungs were screaming at him for air and there was sweat pouring down his face. He wanted to stop and give up the chase, but the thought of his superior officer taking his weapon from him and sending him out on traffic duty permanently spurred him on. He took off as fast as he could and tried to close the gap between him and his quarry.

Jack Howarth and his associate were fifty yards across the car park as he reached the revolving doors, and they were heading toward the ambulance bays. The constable entered the doors and was about to exit the other side when the doors jammed suddenly. He slammed into the glass at speed, flattening his nose and splitting his lip. The armed officer was stunned for a moment, and he couldn't understand why the doors had stopped revolving, until he saw the two hoodies that he'd encountered earlier at the vending machines. The male hoody had rammed a waiting room chair into the doors, and he stood protected by the thick glass, puffing his cheeks out and mimicking the fat police officer. They ran back into the hospital laughing hysterically at him. The doors were jammed solid and he couldn't move them, no matter how hard he pushed them. He turned around and tried to push them in the opposite direction, to see if he could dislodge the chair, but they wouldn't budge. There were bystanders everywhere but people were too traumatised by the gunfire to come to his assistance. He banged on the glass to gain one man's attention, and pointed to the metal chair. The man thought about it for a second, and then rushed off in the other direction.

"Come back and move the fucking chair!" Constable Davis yelled. The man broke into a jog, desperate not to be dragged into a life-threatening situation. Police officer or not, there were guns involved and he didn't want anything to do with it.

Headlights lit up the foyer as they approached, and Davis looked to see where they were coming from. He thought that it could be an ambulance crew, in which case they would stop and help him. It was indeed an ambulance however, when he saw the Uzi being pointed out of the passenger window his heart sank. He saw the muzzle flash as the first nine-millimetre slug blasted out of the barrel, followed by twenty-two of the same, all of which were headed toward the front of the hospital. The muzzle flash meant that the bullet was already about to hit the target, and he dropped to the floor and curled up into a foetal position a split second before the plate glass windows disintegrated. Glass shards sprayed the foyer, slicing, cutting and stabbing anyone that was unlucky enough to be in their path. The bullets miraculously missed the fat police officer and the remaining onlookers, and they ripped through plate glass panes, aluminium window frames and plasterboard walls, before embedding themselves in the bricks that formed the exterior walls.

Constable Davis looked up and watched the hi-jacked ambulance speeding away. He stood up gingerly and wiped shattered glass from his hands and face; dozens of tiny cuts began to bleed as the glass shards were wiped away. Gripping the Glock tightly he closed one eye and aimed at the vehicle. He breathed in and steadied his aim by gripping his wrist with his free hand. The weapon kicked in his hand as he aimed three shots at the rear wheels. The first shot sparked off the sub-frame and then punctured a rear tyre. The rubber split, exploded and became nothing but ragged strips as the vehicle careered onward. The second bullet missed, but the third shredded the second tyre. The vehicle lurched to the right and bounced up the kerb, buckling the front wheel and ripping the front bumper from the chassis. Sparks flew skyward in all directions and tyre remnants were cast askew. The ambulance mounted a grass kerb and then smashed into a low brick wall in a shower of smoke and steam. The vehicle tilted violently before rolling completely onto its side, leaving a wake of sparking metal behind it in the darkness. When it finally crashed to a halt, there was nothing but silence all around it.

Constable Davis climbed through the ruined revolving doors and crunched across a thick carpet of shattered plate glass to reach the pavement outside of the main entrance. Ambulance crews from the hospital ran toward the crash site.

"Armed police!" The constable shouted. "Get back away from the vehicle." Some of the crewmen looked uncomfortable with the order, as it was their natural reaction to help, especially when it could be their own comrades that were injured.

"They're ambulance crew," one of the men shouted. The constable ignored him and approached the upturned vehicle with his gun raised.

"Stay back! They are armed fugitives," he shouted without taking his eyes from the vehicle.

"That's my ambulance," another voice shouted up from the back of the approaching ambulance men. "They must have stolen it."

Realising that the police officer was correct, they started to back away from the crash scene.

"Anything we can do to help?" one of the paramedics asked from a safe distance.

"Telephone the emergency services and hospital security, and tell them that I need help," he replied. The sound of broken glass shifting drew his attention back to the ambulance. "Move away, now!"

The armed officer jogged to the side of the ambulance and then approached the open rear doors cautiously. He peered quickly inside and a volley of bullets told him that the occupants were still functional and armed.

"Throw your weapons out, and step out of the vehicle, do it now!"

There was no reply from the fugitives. Davis tiptoed around the ambulance until he was level with the driver's cab. The windscreen was destroyed and he could hear the occupants scrabbling around inside. He took a deep breath and jumped into the field of vision. One of the Moroccans was waiting for him, and he blasted a volley of bullets at the armed officer. Constable Davis fired two well-aimed shots at the assailant; one smashed his sternum into pieces before ripping a lethal rent in the heart muscle. The second tore his lower jaw from his face, exposing his upper teeth and gums in a macabre grimace. Four bullets from the Moroccan's Uzi slammed into the policeman; two shattered his hip and pelvis before ripping a large piece of muscle from his buttocks. The other two were embedded in his stab vest, unable to penetrate his body, but the velocity of the impacts had caused dreadful internal injuries.

Constable Davis lay on the car park bleeding profusely. The Moroccan was dead but he could only watch helplessly as Jack Howarth picked his way out of the wreckage. He took the Moroccan's shoes and picked up the Uzi, before walking over to the dying policeman. His hand was strapped heavily with hospital gauze dressing. Blood was soaking through the bandages and dripping onto the tarmac.

"I have to go, Constable," Jack said as he stood over him. "I want you to know that I'm going to visit your children, just as a thank you for your kindness." He grinned an evil smile.

"You don't know where my kids live, you fucking pervert," the constable was fading fast, but he still had a little bit of fight left in him.

"Your right, Constable, I don't, but you're dying and I'm going to follow them home from your funeral," he smiled and ran off into the darkness. Constable Davis began to shake, maybe because of the blood loss and his body going into shock, but more likely because he believed that the Child Taker would make good on his threat. Darkness descended on him, and he worried no more.

27

ALFIE LESNER

Alfie was sat on a stinking rubberised mattress contemplating his impending incarceration when the first explosion rocked the ancient building. Showers of dust and plaster dropped from high above his head through cracks in the ceiling. At first, he thought it may have been a car crash or perhaps a gas explosion in a nearby house, but moments later the second explosion confirmed that it was something more sinister. The explosions were followed by a deafening silence, and then pandemonium broke out. He could hear several voices shouting, one of them in particular sounded as if he was in charge of the situation, barking orders and shouting for situation reports. Those of the prisoners that were in his neighbouring cells soon joined the raised voices of the police officers on duty, and the shouting became a cacophony of panicked voices. He leaned against the cold metal of the cell door and tried to make sense of what was going on. He heard someone shouting about a fire, and respirators, and he was almost certain that he heard the word evacuate several times. There was a distinctive odour of gasoline in the air and it was becoming more pungent as the minutes ticked by. Alfie was calm at first, but when the first tendrils of acrid smoke began to creep under the door then he too began to bang on the door and shout for his life. He could heard the viewing hatches in the cell doors being opened and closed further down the cell block, and he continued banging on his own door until his hatch was opened. As the metal hatch clanged open a police officer wearing a respirator appeared in his line of vision, and he was speaking to each inmate in turn. The vaulted ceiling in the cellblock corridor was thick with black smoke, and minute by minute, the smoke was becoming thicker.

"Take off your shirt and put it down the toilet, flush the chain to soak it, and then place it across the bottom of the door to stop the smoke coming in." The hatch slammed closed with a clunking sound.

"Are you fucking kidding me!" Alfie screamed. "Let me out of here you bastard!"

Alfie turned from the thick metal door and began to remove his jacket. Smoke was pouring under the door, and drifting up to the ceiling, where it was beginning to form a toxic cloud. He ripped the buttons from his shirt and wrestled it off, before holding it in the stainless steel toilet bowl. The thought of shoving his two hundred pound Armani shirt into that stinking orifice sickened him, despite the fact that it may prolong his life. He pressed the flush and held the garment there until it was saturated. The smoke was thicker still as he laid his shirt across the opening at the bottom of the heavy cell door. The advancing pungent smoke was abated momentarily, but it soon found its way through the smallest niches between the shirt and the floor. Stopping it completely was impossible. Seconds felt like minutes, and minutes felt like hours as Alfie tried desperately to stop the lethal fumes from filling his cell. He sat on the cold stone floor and pushed his back against the metal door. The turmoil beyond his cell was audible, and he could hear cell doors being opened and slammed closed, voices approached the cellblock. Suddenly the cell door was unlocked. Alfie had to stand up for it to be opened and a uniformed officer entered wearing a respirator appeared in the doorway.

"Hands out, Lesner," the officer showed him a pair of handcuffs.

"Are you serious?"

"If you want to get out of here, then you put these on, it's your choice," the officer coughed. The smoke outside of the cells was thick and black, and far worse than it had been inside. Alfie allowed himself to be handcuffed, and then the officer guided him through the blinding smoke.

"Keep your eyes closed and your head down," the officer's instructions were muffled through the respirator, but Alfie's eyes were already streaming. The fumes stung his eyeballs and tears blurred his vision as he stumbled through the custody suite.

"Where are we going?" Alfie tried to communicate, which was a huge mistake. He swallowed a lungful of acrid burning smoke and a coughing fit made him collapse to his knees in agony.

"Keep moving," another voice shouted from close by. A second pair of hands grabbed Alfie under the arms and he felt himself being lifted to his feet. He was carried forward through the choking fumes, and his feet were hardly touching the ground. His lungs were full of burning smoke and he thought he was going to suffocate, as he breathed out and sucked in another lung full of poisonous gases.

All of a sudden fresh air hit his face and he breathed in as hard as he could. His oxygen-starved brain registered that he was outside of the main building. Alfie blinked his eyes and tried to clear his vision, but they were stinging badly and he had to close them again. He could hear men coughing and spluttering all around, and one man was vomiting repeatedly. The police officers were barking orders to each other as the burning police station was evacuated. One voice close by seemed to be more prominent than any other was.

"Get them into the bus, come on move them!" the voice ordered. The order heralded a flurry of activity around him. He could hear men walking past him, and he could hear prisoners swearing and cursing. There seemed to be people everywhere that he couldn't see. He tried to clear his vision once more and this time he could keep his eyes open. His surroundings were bleary but he could make out shapes and shadows. There appeared to be uniformed officers guiding people toward a white prison van, which they affectionately called a bus. Strong hands grabbed his arms and pulled him up to his feet.

"Move it, Lesner," an officer shouted through his respirator. Alfie could hear the wail of approaching fire tenders approaching. He stood on his feet and immediately collapsed again. Chest wrenching coughs rattled his body, and although he tried to respond, he could not. Alfie knew that more people died in fires from smoke inhalation than burns, but he didn't really understand how disabling acrid fumes were until now. He could barely move.

"I said move it, Lesner!" the muffled voice ordered him again. This time there were two sets of hands lifting him up to his feet. He could feel tarmac beneath his feet, and realised that his shoes had come off when he'd been dragged out of the building. It confused him at first, but he realised that it was because they'd taken his laces from him when he'd been processed. The shoes had cost him four hundred pounds from a Versace boutique in Manchester, and losing them irked him. He scrapped his shins painfully on the steps at the rear of the prison bus, and his feet peddled in thin air trying to gain a footing. There was a narrow passage through the centre of the bus, with tiny cells fitted on either side. The cells were only big enough for a man to sit on a seat just three inches wide. They were encased in thick clear Perspex that was perforated with air holes at head height so that the prisoners could breathe. Alfie was still struggling to gain his breath, and being pushed into the claustrophobic cell was a torment that he couldn't bear, however he didn't have the strength to fight. The door was slammed closed and within fifteen minutes, the bus contained every prisoner that had been in the custody unit. Alfie slowly regained his composure and slowed his breathing down as the rear doors were closed and the diesel engine started. He felt the bus moving forward across the compound. There was a tiny window level with his eyes, which was supposed to alleviate the feeling of claustrophobia, and he could see the compound gates being unlocked to allow the prison bus out, and to give the fire engines access to the rear of the burning police station. A firefighter was directing the prison bus toward the gates while a second was waving the tenders toward the burning building.

It hadn't been a good night on reflection. Alfie leaned his head against the Perspex and tried to draw in as much cold fresh air as he could through the holes. It was like being inside a giant pet carrier. He looked around the bus and soaked up the scene. There were sixteen men in total, all shapes and sizes, and a mixture of ages and ethnic origins. The one thing that they all had in common was a look of complete exhaustion on their blackened faces. Most of them were gazing into the night, and the others were snoozing. Alfie looked out of the window and saw that they were heading out of Warrington town centre and from the direction that they were taking it seemed that they were taking the expressway toward Risley.

"Hey, mate," a gruff voice called him from across the aisle. Alfie looked toward the man and vaguely recognised his face.

"Alright?" Alfie said. His throat was sore from coughing, and his voice sounded three octaves lower than it had before.

"What you in for?" the man asked. His accent told Alfie that he was from the city of Liverpool.

"Drugs, you?" Alfie lied.

"I thought I knew your face. You sell blow to the doormen at the State Ballroom, right?" the man laughed.

"I think you've got me mixed up with someone else," Alfie joked. "You never know who's listening, and the company in here isn't great is it?" He nodded to the other inmates.

"Yes, I know what you mean," He laughed. "What do you think happened back at the station?"

"Fuck knows, sounded like a bomb to me," Alfie guessed.

"I'm not sure, but I'd rather be having a kip in my cell than crammed into this box," the man shook his head.

"Can't say I miss my cell to be honest," Alfie sneered. His nostrils were full of fumes but he could still smell urine, it seemed to linger on him.

"Hey, did you hear about the nonce they brought in?" the man lowered his voice, so that the other prisoners couldn't hear what he was about to say. "One of the screws told me that the bloke that kidnapped the twins from the Lake District, you know the ones that have been all over the telly, well, he told me he was in the nick with us."

"Really?" Alfie tried to sound surprised. It was obvious that he was going to be tarred with the same brush as Jack Howarth. The cons and screws would think that he was a nonce, a pervert, a 'Child Taker'.

"Straight up, that's what he told me. I'd like five minutes alone with the bastard, wouldn't you?"

"Too right, I would," Alfie tried to sound convincing. He leaned back and closed his eyes. Images of being locked up in jail, surrounded by hundreds of convicts that wanted to kill him, and being protected by prison officers that wanted to kill him too floated past. There would be nowhere to hide once he reached prison.

The bus turned a corner and Alfie could see a cricket ground through the window. The road was unlit and lined with trees on both sides. He was familiar with the tree lined dual carriageway, as he'd driven along it many times before. It was the road to Risley, no doubt about it. There was a remand centre there, which would be ideally situated to accept a busload of refugee prisoners. The bus slowed as it approached a roundabout, and then the driver had to slam on the brakes as a small saloon car pulled out of the junction. The brakes squealed and bus fishtailed and threatened to turn over. Alfie was flung forward and cracked his head against the Perspex. There was a chorus of profanity hurled from the prisoners in their tiny cells as they were tossed about like ice cubes in a cocktail shaker. Alfie touched his face and felt a lump rising on his forehead immediately.

"For fuck's sake, can today get any worse!" he moaned as he glanced out of the window again. His mouth opened in shock as he saw a huge yellow JCB digger hurtling out of the trees. It was headed toward the stationary prison bus at full pelt. Alfie closed his eyes and waited for the impact.

28
MAJOR STANLEY TIMMS

The Major stood in the kitchen of his daughter's house. It was the only room where he felt that he could think about the situation clearly. The house seemed cavernous and empty without the twins in it; their two tiny forma had left a huge void behind them, that simply couldn't be filled. He could hear their laughter echoing around his mind, and everywhere he looked there was something which reminded him that his grandchildren were missing and in terrible danger. The bedrooms upstairs smelled of the twins, stuffed toys lurked in every corner, discarded dolls and cars acted as both memories and trip hazards. Hayley wouldn't allow anyone to pick them up, and she wanted everything left as it was the day they had left for the Lake District. The strain was taking its toll on her, and the pressure on the marriage had been too much for her to cope with. The front of the house was still besieged by paparazzi, and so the curtains were closed against the prying camera lenses. The kitchen was the only safe haven.

Hayley appeared in the doorway, and the Major could tell that his beautiful daughter, the apple of his eye, his sunshine and his rain, was deteriorating fast before his eyes. Once a keen hockey player and athlete with attractive muscular curves, she now looked more like an anorexic teenager. He'd managed to get her to eat some fruit and hot soup, but the trauma was sapping the life from her. Her face was gaunt, her cheeks were hollowed and dark circles were entrenched beneath her eyes. Prior to the abduction, Hayley was always smiling but now the corners of her mouth seemed to be pointing down permanently. She was carrying a bundle of dirty laundry, and she tried to smile as she entered the kitchen, but she couldn't hide the pain that was in her eyes.

"Why don't you have a rest, Hayley? You look exhausted," the Major stepped forward and took the washing from her.

"I'm fine, Dad, please don't fuss," Hayley frowned and opened the washing machine door. There was a load already in, which was ready to be dried and she began pulling at it frantically. "I'm better off if I keep myself busy."

"Have you heard from Karl?" the Major made a clumsy attempt at changing the subject.

"Yes, he called this morning," she stuffed the clean load of washing into the tumble drier as she spoke.

"Where is he staying?"

"At his brother's house in Chester," she slammed the drier door closed with much more force than was required.

"What, with that woman, isn't that a little bizarre, bearing in mind the reason why you told him to leave?"

"What, more bizarre than screwing your brother's wife you mean?" she slammed the detergent drawer closed angrily.

"You know what I mean, Hayley," the Major was embarrassed by his daughter's turn of phrase, but he couldn't really blame her for being angry. Her children had been kidnapped by a prolific paedophile, and her husband had left the family home and moved in with the woman he was accused of having an affair with. "What on earth is going through the man's mind?"

"You tell me."

"What has Steve had to say about it?"

"His brother thinks that the whole thing is a figment of my imagination, and that I'm cracking up," she laughed bitterly.

"Is there a chance that you're mistaken?" the Major asked calmly.

"Not you as well, the bastard is fucking his brother's wife!" Hayley shouted.

"I believe you, but I don't need to hear that language from my daughter," he scolded her gently.

"I'm sorry, Dad, but I'm finding it hard to cope," she stopped and tears flooded down her cheeks. The Major put the washing onto the kitchen top and held her tightly. "I want my babies back, Dad."

"The police know where they are now, it's only a matter of time until they find the vehicle that they're in," he spoke softly in her ear as he rocked her gently. His cell phone buzzed in his pocket, and Hayley wiped her eyes and stood back from him.

"Answer it, Dad, it could be news," she sniffled.

"Major Timms," he answered the call. The number on the screen was withheld, which meant that it could be any of his team, or someone using the taskforce network.

"Can you talk?"

"Yes," the Major recognised the brash tone as the Minister of Defence. He was the only member of the cabinet that knew roughly what the taskforce was doing at any particular point in time, and then he was only told the bare minimum. As long as the objectives were achieved, and enemies of the state were neutralised, then the politicians wanted to be spared the details. He shook his head at Hayley to let her know that the call wasn't related to any progress in the investigation.

"One of your operatives is ruffling feathers, Major," the Minister said abruptly.

"I see, can you be a little more precise?"

"The Chief   Constable of Cheshire police is raising merry hell that one of our counter terrorist personnel is interfering in his investigation into the kidnapping of the Kelly twins."

"Ah, I see, Minister."

"Why would one of your agents be interested in that case, Major?"

"It would appear that the people responsible for the kidnap are also involved in the movement of sophisticated weaponry and munitions to some of our more extremist friends," the Major twisted the truth slightly.

"Really?"

"Yes, Minister, a Moroccan outfit working out of Marrakesh."

"What are you planning to do?"

"We don't want to interfere with the safe return of the children, Minister, but we want to follow up on the Moroccans' business interests, and stop them operating within our shores."

"Good show, Major, carry on," the Minister ended the call as abruptly as he'd begun. The kitchen was long and fitted with upper and lower dark oak units. He walked to the coffee cupboard and opened the door, switching on the kettle with his spare hand.

"What was that about?" Hayley asked.

"John is making waves and irritating people," the Major smiled as he removed a jar of Nescafe.

"I bet that they don't complain to his face, do they?" she tried a smile again.

"Not very often," the Major smiled too. He grabbed two cups and held them up. "You want one?"

"Does he know where the twins are?" she folded her arms across her chest, holding herself for reassurance. She looked like she had as a young girl when her tortoise had died. The Major had told her that it had gone back to the jungle to visit its family, but she'd seen through the lie. Naturally, the Major wanted to protect his daughter from the pain, as any father would.

"No, Hayley, but I think that we can be assured that he's

trying his hardest to find out," he looked at his cell phone again thoughtfully. He opened the back door and stepped out into the night. "I'm going to call him, I'll be two minutes." The Major stabbed the speed dial number that would link him to John Tankersley, but the line was completely dead.

29
THE PRISON BUS

Grace indicated and then turned at the traffic lights, keeping a safe distance behind the Honda Blackbird that they'd been following from the railway station. They'd waited patiently as the fire engines arrived and began to spray thousands of gallons of water into the burning building, creating towers of boiling steam which spiralled upward into the night sky. Eventually a white prison bus was allowed to leave the police compound, and the suspect motorcyclist had followed its progress.

The red, amber and green of the traffic lights were reflected in the rainwater that was pooling on the roads. The motorcycle was still tailing the white prison van which was loaded with the prisoners from the police station cells, and rainwater sprayed from the bike's fat back tyre as it accelerated away. Tank pointed to a brown signpost that was fixed below the main road signs.

"The signpost said that Risley Remand Centre is four miles away, they must be taking the prisoners from the cells there," Tank said.

"That would make sense," Grace nodded.

"If they're going to try to spring Alfie Lesner, then they need to do it soon," Tank commented.

The prison bus had turned down a tree-lined expressway, and it was approaching a small roundabout. The stretch of road was wide, but unlit, and the trees offered a myriad of hiding places for a potential hi-jack. Suddenly the motorcyclist dropped the bike down a gear and twisted open the throttle, accelerating the machine at incredible speed, and overtaking the white bus. He guided the two-wheeled machine around the island and took off at speed down the right hand exit.

"The tail has disappeared," Grace said.

"It could be show time," Tank commented as he watched the motorbike roar off into the distance.

"This is the perfect place for an ambush," Grace nodded and she slowed down and pulled the vehicle into the verge. They were five hundred yards behind the prison van as it reached the traffic island.

A set of headlights appeared from the first junction, and a small salon car pulled out into the road directly in front of the van, blocking the exits. The brake lights illuminated as the prison bus slammed on the anchors, trying desperately not to plough into the vehicle on the roundabout. Grace switched the lights off and brought the Shogun to a standstill. Tank scanned the area with night sights, trying to second guess what was going to happen next.

"There's movement in the trees to the left," he said, passing the sights to Grace.

"It's a digger, and it's headed straight for the prison van," she pulled her Glock nine millimetre from its holster, and readied the vehicle for action.

"Wait a minute Grace," Tank put his hand on her arm and squeezed it gently. She looked surprised, as it was not like Tank to miss the opportunity for a fight.

"Someone has gone to an awful lot of trouble to spring Alfie Lesner, I vote we wait and see who it is, and where they're going to take him. They could lead us straight to the twins."

Grace was uneasy with allowing the situation to progress unchecked, but she could see the sense in what he was saying. The twins were the priority, and so she unwillingly slid the pistol back into its holster and watched events unfold. A huge yellow JCB trundled out of the tree line onto the road and its giant back wheels spun in the mud as it dropped onto the tarmac. The gigantic metal bucket, which was attached to the front of the digging machine, began to rise as it neared the side of the prison van, and it smashed into the passenger side in an earth-shattering broadside. The metal teeth that lined the edge of the bucket sliced through the driver's cab, and the rear container simultaneously, and the force of the impact rocked the prison bus onto two wheels. It shook violently and almost tipped over completely. There was a second or two of silence before the digger reversed slightly, readying itself to ram the prison van a second time. The sound of men screaming drifted to them on the night air, as the prisoners inside the bus began to panic. They were pinned inside their Perspex prisons, with nowhere to run.

"Are we just going sit and watch this?" Grace asked. She was itching to stop the attack.

"We need to follow Alfie Lesner to the Moroccans, as long as no one gets hurt, then we shouldn't get involved," Tank said.

"What about the prisoners in that bus?"

"They're not our priority, Grace, what's the matter with you?"

He didn't look at her as he spoke, and he carried on watching through the night sights. Two men were getting out of the saloon car that they had used as a roadblock, and they started running to the back of the prison van. A huge gaping rent appeared in the side of the prison container as the JCB struck again, and the vehicle tilted dangerously, threatening to tip over. The driver of the prison bus opened the door and jumped out of the stricken vehicle, trying to avoid the deadly metal teeth that were piercing the cab. His face was bloodied, cut by shards of flying glass. He was not a real police officer. He was a community police volunteer, employed by the police department to drive vehicles to and from mechanical services, and body repair shops. With most of the force deployed to Delamere Forest in search of the twins, he'd offered to drive the prison bus to the nearby remand centre. He staggered as he ran away from the scene as fast as his legs would carry him, but he couldn't out run a bullet. A volley of automatic gunfire rang out and the part time police officer dropped onto the road mortally wounded. Two fat nine-millimetre slugs had punctured his back, splintering his ribs and ripping lung tissue to shreds. He managed to get up onto all fours, crawl a short distance, desperate to escape with his life, but a second volley stopped him in his tracks, and his body collapsed twitching in the gutter. Blood pooled around him and began to wash away with the rainwater down a storm drain.

"Now we have to get involved," Tank shook his head at the cruel shooting. The part time police officer was unarmed and running away from the scene. He was no threat to the hijackers, and his death was unnecessary. Tank felt a tinge of guilt for reacting too late, and he could tell from the look in Grace's eyes that she thought so too.

Grace flicked on the lights and gunned the engine, and the vehicle lurched forward. Tank lowered the window and leaned out, aiming his nine millimetre as they hurtled toward the stricken van. Raindrops crashed into his face, feeling more like small pebbles than water droplets because of the speed. The men from the saloon were firing their weapons at the rear door lock, and jagged holes appeared in the white metal as the bullets ripped through the prison bus. It appeared to Grace that they were not too concerned who was on the other side of the metal as the bullets drilled through it. They were so taken with their own task that they didn't see the taskforce vehicle approaching until it was too late. One of the men grabbed at the rear door and he wrenched it open, while the second man tried to scramble inside. Tank closed one eye and lined up the sights. He squeezed the trigger twice and the Glock kicked in his hand. The first bullet ricocheted off the prison bus, and sparks flew through the air. The shot alerted the two bandits to the presence of the speeding vehicle, and they turned toward it a split second too late. Tank's second shot smashed into the chest of one man, lifting him from his feet and slamming him into the prison bus. He slid down as his legs buckled, leaving a red smear on the white metal. His colleague aimed his nine-millimetre Uzi sub machinegun at the Mitsibushi. It was the weapon that had been used to slay the volunteer police officer. Tank squeezed the trigger again and the bullet smashed into the bandit's right eye. The back of his head exploded like a ripe melon, spraying the bus with grey matter, and bloody mucus.

"The prisoners are escaping," Grace shouted as she approached the traffic island. They could see arms and legs clawing at the jagged split in the bus, ripping the hole wider and wider, so that they could scramble out of it.

"Get me around the other side of the van," Tank shouted back to her. The heavens opened and rain hammered down against the windscreen. The road was wet and sheen in the headlights as they speeded past the prison van. Grace had to swerve violently to avoid the saloon car which was still blocking the road. A prisoner dropped from the shattered bus onto the road, directly in front of the speeding Mitsibushi. Grace stamped on the brake. The tyres squealed and the rear end slid across the wet road as the black Shogun went into a spin. Grace twisted the steering wheel full lock to try to stop the skid, but the momentum was too great. The Mitsibushi slammed into the kerbstone with a sickening bump, and Tank was thrown against dashboard. His head cracked off the plastic and his Glock was thrown into the foot well.

"Are you okay?" Grace glanced at him. There was a deafening roar and she twisted around to see where it was coming from. The huge yellow JCB had disengaged from the attack on the prison van, and it was reversing across the traffic island at speed.

"Move it!" Tank shouted as he realised what the JCB driver had in mind. The yellow digger stopped and there was an audible crunch as the driver selected the forward gear. "Now, Grace."

The Shogun juddered as Grace's foot slipped off the clutch and the vehicle stalled. The JCB lurched forward and began to gain speed as it hurtled toward them.

"Get out!" Grace shouted. She realised that there wasn't time enough to start the vehicle. The JCB driver lowered the jagged bucket so that it was level with Grace's window, and the huge machine accelerated toward her.

Tank opened the passenger door and rolled out onto the grass verge. He stopped for a fraction of a second to recover the Glock, but he couldn't grasp it in time. Grace swung her feet out of the Shogun, and she dived to the back of the vehicle. The digger crashed into the Mitsubishi and almost removed the roof with the force of the impact. The teeth sheared through the door pillars and the windscreen as if they were made from rice paper, and Grace was showered with shattered glass. She placed her hands over her eyes to protect them as the digger engine screamed above her. The machine shuddered as the driver slammed the JCB into reverse, and a second wave of twisted metal and splintered glass shards fell onto her.

"Give me your hand!" Tank screamed over the deafening noise of the JCB. The yellow machine backed off twenty yards to ready for a second charge. Grace looked up and reached out a bloodied hand. The digger's engine roared again and with a grinding of gears, the JCB thundered toward them a third time. Tank grabbed her by the wrist and pulled her to her feet.

"Run for the trees," he shouted over the engine noise as they cleared the rear of the Shogun. Tank dived headlong into the trees, carrying Grace with him, seconds before the digger smashed through the wrecked Mitsibushi and bashed it over onto its roof. The vehicle flipped as if it was a toy and it crashed against a sapling, snapping it before it finally came to a standstill.

"Give me your weapon," Tank dragged Grace further into the trees as the JCB reversed clear of the shattered Mitsibushi. He reached under her jacket and removed the Glock from her holster. The yellow digger roared again as the driver tried to pinpoint them in the tree line, but he couldn't locate them, and so he switched on the machine's headlights. The lights were dazzling and Tank was left exposed as the shadows disappeared.

"Move Grace!" Tank hissed as the huge machine began to pick up speed as it careered toward them. There were fine rivulets of blood running down her face, mixing with the rainwater that soaked them.

"Split up," Grace shouted. She turned and ran to the left, while Tank ran to the right, weaving through the branches as fast as his legs would carry him. The tactic confused the JCB driver enough to give them a few valuable seconds, and he swerved the machine to the right picking Tank as his target. Tank stopped behind a large tree trunk, raised the Glock and fired three times. The bullets pinged off the huge metal bucket without leaving as much as a dent in the thick steel. The driver raised the bucket higher still, narrowing the angle of the shot, and protecting him from the nine millimetre bullets. Tank darted to the right again, tying to make himself a moving target, but the JCB was closing the gap between them quickly. It bounced in the air as it hit the kerbstones and mounted the verge, and the bucket felled half a dozen trees without losing any momentum. Tank ran deeper into the trees, illuminated by the JCB's headlights. Tree branches scratched his hands and face, and a small gash opened over his left eye. Blood trickled down his face and into his eye, carried by the rain, blurring his vision and impairing his aim. He could hear trees groaning and cracking as the huge machine pursued him relentlessly, and from the increasing noise of the diesel engine, Tank could tell that he was losing the race.

A gunshot rang out and suddenly there was only half as much light as there was before. Tank side stepped a sycamore tree and bolted in the opposite direction to which he'd been running. He risked a glance over his shoulder, costing him vital seconds. One of the headlights had been shot out, and Tank figured that Grace had recovered his weapon from the Shogun, and had stalked the vehicle from the shadows. The change of direction slowed the digger's progress and Tank gained a few precious seconds to aid his escape from the massive machine.

He turned and raised the nine-millimetre, closing one eye and steadying his hand, he squeezed the trigger twice. The first bullet disappeared into the darkness but the second one found its target, and the remaining headlight was blasted to smithereens. He ran toward the roundabout, away from the sound of the roaring diesel engine, but the gargantuan digger kept on coming. The tree line was thinning out as he ran at full pelt, and he was almost clear of the bruising tree limbs and branches, when he caught his right foot beneath an exposed tree root. His own momentum flung him headlong, and his head struck the base of a chestnut tree, stunning him and sending bolts of white light through his brain.

The JCB thundered through the tree line, and the noise of the huge engine and the splintering wood was deafening. The driver was steering the machine blindly, following a course that would bring him back onto the road. The volume increased tenfold as the machine neared him, and Tank tried to find his feet but concussion had dulled his reactions. His head span, and he felt dizzy. A wave of nausea swept through him, as the digger threatened to overwhelm his position, and crush him to a pulp. He closed his eyes and waited for the inevitable.

Two gunshots rang out from the melee, barely audible over the noise of the approaching digger. Tank opened his eyes and through the darkness, he could see a huge shadow looming, parting trees with ease, and crushing everything in its path. It was yards away when it swerved to the left and the brakes let out a high-pitched squeal that hurt his ears. The digger ground to a halt noisily five yards to his right, and the engine spluttered as it was turned off. The driver was sat slouched at the controls and as the cab door opened, his body tumbled out. It bounced off the huge rear wheels before crashing into the undergrowth next to Tank. The dead man stared sightlessly at him, and blood ran from his nostrils.

"Are you okay?" Grace asked as she stepped off the rear of the digger. She had waited until the machine paused to change direction, and then climbed up onto the rear arm of the machine. Two well aimed bullets had shattered the driver's spinal column and sprayed his brain stem all over the cab windows.

"Fine, I was waiting for you," Tank moaned, trying to make light of his near demise.

"Ah yes, the old decoy trick was it?" she smiled as she climbed down.

"That's the one, you remember it from training right?"

"Of course, split up, make several targets instead of one, and then decoy and destroy."

"Correct, I was the decoy."

"Okay, so where does bashing your head on a tree trunk come into it?"

"I was improvising."

"You've got a bump on your head, but it doesn't look too bad," Grace ran a thumb over the swelling, and Tank winced at the pain.

"I think we're going to need a new truck," Tank pulled himself up, and dusted his clothes down. They were soaked, cut, battered and bruised.

The sound of a well-tuned Honda engine caught their attention. Through the trees, they could see the headlight of a motorbike, and they watched as someone exchanged a few brief words with the driver, before climbing onto the back of it. The engine purred and the motorcyclist weaved through the debris on the road before speeding his pillion away. They limped out of the trees and walked cautiously toward the shattered prison bus. Their Shogun was upside down on the verge to the left, and the small saloon car, which had blocked the road, was gone.

"They must have left the keys in the ignition," Grace said. She realised that the prisoners from the crippled bus had probably used it to escape.

"Careless, to say the least," Tank commented. "No prizes for guessing who the bike rider came back for."

They stepped around the body of the police volunteer, and approached the prison bus. The vehicle creaked and groaned as the rain hammered down onto its shattered carcass. They peered into the wreckage, but there was nothing to see but twisted steel and shattered Perspex.

30
DELAMERE FOREST

Peter Knowles had been the head of Cheshire's Armed Response Unit for nearly eighteen months now, and things weren't going too well. He had climbed through the ranks quickly, joining as a university graduate on a fast track programme. The programmes were designed to attract the brightest students into the police force by offering them accelerated promotion prospects, but the candidates were also targets for resentment and criticism from officers that had followed the traditional career paths. Knowles was confident and assertive, which was translated by his critics as arrogance. He had his own ideas on how to run the elite firearms unit, and his own ideas on who should be selected to serve in it. When he'd taken over, the unit was full of long serving officers who had been selected for the unit as a reward for their loyalty to the force, and not because they were the best candidates for the job. Knowles had a very different view of how the selection process should work. He was of the opinion that his team should the sharpest, fittest, and brightest officers in the force, and he had made enemies of both junior and senior officers as he rang the changes through the unit.

Now he was leading one of the biggest operations in the Armed Response Unit's history. Four fully armed teams, plus hundreds of uniformed officers in support, would be operating under the watchful eye of the Divisional Commanders and the county's helicopters. The night had begun on a high when his unit had successfully captured the two men thought to be responsible for the kidnap of the Kelly twins. Unfortunately he had purposely left one of his unit at the hospital to guard the paedophile, Jack Howarth, and that decision had come back to bite him on the ass. He had never rated Constable Davis, and his poor opinion of him had affected his better judgement, and now his superior officer was breathing down his neck.

"Why was Constable Davis left at the hospital to guard Jack Howarth?" the Divisional Commander asked in a crisp no nonsense tone. He had a twitch that made his eyes blink rapidly when he was annoyed, and they were twitching ten to the dozen.

"I've questioned his suitability for the firearms unit, Sir, and so I thought that he would be best used at the hospital," Knowles answered. His men were in position around the forest, and he was ready to move. He really didn't need an inquest into what had happened at the hospital right now.

"So you have had issues with his performance?"

"Yes, Sir."

"Then why did you leave an incompetent officer in charge of the most wanted man in the country?"

"With respect, I would hardly call Howarth the most wanted man in the country, Sir."

"Oh really, perhaps you could give me the benefit of your wisdom then, Knowles, what would you call him then?"

Knowles struggled to answer his superior, and his face flushed red with embarrassment. He remained silent, rather than let the issue deteriorate into a slanging match. The commander wasn't going to let him off the hook though.

"He's obviously a high profile prisoner, Sir," was the best answer he could muster, without causing his boss offence.

"High profile?"

"Yes, Sir."

"The abduction of the Kelly twins has caused a national outcry from the public that is completely unprecedented," the commander was so annoyed spittle was flying as he spoke. There were junior officers around in earshot, and rumours of trouble between the top brass were spreading like wild fire through the unit.

"I'm aware of the news furore that the case has created, Sir, however with respect I do not make my decisions on the back of what the newspapers will think, Sir."

"Really and how do you make your decisions, Knowles?"

"I'm not sure now is the time for a debate, Sir."

"You left an incompetent officer in charge of a high profile criminal, resulting in the death of that officer, thousands of pounds worth of damage, and the subsequent escape of that criminal. I will take charge of this operation with immediate effect, and you will follow my orders to the letter, Knowles, do you understand?" his rant ended with a flurry of eyelid activity.

"Yes, Sir," Knowles flushed purple with anger, but there was little point in arguing the point now. His decision to leave Davis alone was flawed, and the blame for the deaths and the resulting collateral damage would land squarely on his doorstep. He would deal with it when the job in hand was completed.

"Then get your men into position, and let's get this farm cleared as quickly as possible," the commander removed his flat peaked hat, and replaced it with a combat helmet. Then he took a bulletproof vest from the equipment rack and struggled into it. "Get me the helicopter on the radio."

"It isn't in the area yet, Sir," Knowles replied curtly.

"What, why on earth not?" the commander whined.

"We wanted to take the farm by surprise, Sir," Knowles was concerned about the engine noise alerting any remaining gangsters.

The farm was situated in ten acres of valley clearing, surrounded by dense pine forest. The police had set up an operations centre in a mobile trailer, which was used to control operations for major incidents. Across the road was a stagnant lake that was surrounded by rotting trunks of trees that had been killed by the acidity of the water. The stable block was in clear view from their vantage point.

"You can't allow your men to walk into that area without any aerial reconnaissance," the Commander said.

"I have spotters on each side of the stable quadrant, Sir, and we have scanned the buildings thoroughly," Knowles stood his ground.

"What have they found?"

"The stable block is built in a wide U-shape, with an access track from the main road here," Knowles pointed to an ordinance survey map as he spoke to his furious superior officer. "Our heat sensors are picking up four horses in this block here, a fire, which seems to be contained in an oil drum here, and two humans in this stable here."

"Could it be the twins?" the Commander asked excitedly.

"No, Sir, they're adults," Knowles spoiled his fun.

"Have your men secure the area, and we'll move in and neutralise those targets," the Commander ordered, and his eyelids fluttered rapidly. The two senior officers stepped out of the incident room, and they barked orders as they moved toward the farm to lead the unit into action.

Ten minutes later the officers were lying face down in the grass, approaching the stable block from the north. The oil drum fire was still burning fiercely, and from the smell, the police officers feared the worst.

"What do you think?" the Commander asked nervously. He had seen service with the Royal Navy in the Falklands conflict, where British ships were constantly the target of Argentine missile attacks. The unmistakable smell of burning human flesh would stay with him forever.

"I'm not sure what to think, Sir," Knowles didn't want to admit that he thought the twins were probably dead already, and that the evidence of their demise was being torched in the oil drum inferno.

"Have our heat sensors picked up any movement from that stable?" the Commander asked, referring to the two humans that had shown up on the scanners.

"No, Sir, they seem to be stationary, probably asleep."

"Okay, let's stop messing around. Send your men in," the Commander stood up and began to walk toward the stables. Crawling on his elbows through wet grass was losing its appeal, and the driving rain had dampened his enthusiasm to return to the helm of the operation.

"With respect, Sir, we don't know who is in that stable, or what they're armed with," Knowles tried to restrain his superior. "A forced entry and frontal assault would be rash, Sir, to say the least."

"Nonsense!" the commander said. "Is the stable door bolted from the outside?"

The radio crackled as the spotters were asked for their opinion.

"No, Sir, the door isn't locked," Knowles replied uncertainly.

"Exactly, so whoever is in there is not a prisoner, and we must assume that they're our targets. Send a unit in immediately," the Commander nodded his head to reinforce his orders.

"Sir, I think we should air on the side of caution," Knowles stuttered. He wasn't sure why he was wary, but he had a bad feeling about the situation, a policeman's hunch.

"Move in," the Commander brushed past him as if he wasn't there.

A unit swept through the stable block in a silent formation, and another surrounded the area, blocking any escape attempts and acting as cover for their exposed colleagues. The first team reached the stable door without incident, and they positioned themselves to open the door and swarm the occupants inside. The commanding officers moved to the corner of the stable block, yards away from the stable door as the unit moved in. The lead man opened the door and covered the immediate space inside with his weapon as his colleagues swept through the door in deadly unison.

"Armed police! Drop your weapons!" the response team members cried in unison as they barged into the stable. The combination of shock and awe threw suspects into a state of confusion. Two things became obvious as the armed unit assessed the situation inside the stable. One was that the two people inside were no threat to them, and number two was that they had seconds to live.

There were two camp beds several yards away from each other, and tied to them with several rolls of gaffer tape were Patrick, and Margaret Lesner. Hajj had taken them from their home as insurance against Alfie Lesner talking to the police. If he kept quiet, then no one would know about the farm. If he talked then he would lead the police straight to the farm, and his parents. Patrick and Margaret were surrounded by fifty kilos of fertilizer and hydrogen peroxide, which is a very unstable mixture. When the stable door was opened, the pin was pulled from a phosphor grenade, and when that ignited, it acted as the detonator of a massive fertiliser bomb. Patrick, Margaret, Peter Knowles, the Divisional Commander and two units of the Armed Response team were blown to pieces. Human remains were still being dredged from the acidic lake a fortnight later.

31

THE HORSE BOX

Geraint Jones was driving home from a long shift in the customs sheds. He had worked for the port authority as a customs officer at Heysham ferry terminal for over ten years. Heysham was situated on the North West coast of England, and was a key container port connecting Ireland to Europe. The port had always been busy, and trying to stop weapons and hard drugs crossing the Irish Sea was a twenty four hour, three hundred and sixty five days a year operation. Tensions at the port had been heightened by the all ports bulletin being issued, in response to the kidnap of the Kelly twins from a tent in the Lake District. No one thought that they would be brought back to the north, and the ports on the south coast were favourites to find the suspect horsebox.

Geraint lived in a rural area, inland from the port, and his journey home took him over a single-track bridge, which crossed the River Lune. The water was high at this time of year, flooded further by the heavy rainfall that had been falling for days now. The road wound through miles of green open farmland separated by dry stonewalls, and hilly wooded areas, which couldn't be farmed. Agriculture was the biggest industry in the area, outside of the port. He was listening to the news on the radio and looking forward to getting home, and opening a bottle of Merlot, when he past an abandoned derelict petrol station, one of many which were dotted all over the English countryside. The rise of petrol monopolies, and supermarket domination had scuppered thousands of small garage businesses across the country, and rural farming areas were the worst hit. Geraint glanced at the rusty pumps and the shattered signage, which swung gently in the wind. He had taken his first car there once for a head gasket change, an old Mini Cooper that he thrashed around the country lanes until it fell to bits. The garage had been a big part of the community back then, but now it was a dangerous eyesore. The metal grids, which covered the underground tanks, had long since been stolen and sold for scrap, leaving treacherous deep holes in the ground. Behind the single storey frontage was an old workshop, one used to house a servicing and minor repair business, and Geraint was certain that he'd seen a large blue vehicle parked in it as he glanced sideways. He slammed on the brakes and brought his Ford to a stop. His watch said it was five o'clock in the morning and horizon to the east was starting to brighten as the sun began to rise.

Geraint reached for his hands free kit. The icon on the screen told him that he had no signal, normal service for that part of the world. The network was patchy at best in rural England. He made a decision and slipped the gearstick into reverse, slowly rolling the car backward to the garage forecourt entrance. He looked over the building; it was filthy and the paint was blistered and peeling. He swung the vehicle onto the forecourt and his headlights illuminated the petrol station and the workshop beyond it. There was no mistake. He had seen a blue truck parked inside the old workshop.

Geraint edged his car forward at a crawl toward the rear of the building, and as he rounded the corner, the dark vehicle came into full view. It was a navy blue horsebox, which was the vehicle that they had been alerted to be on the lookout for. He was looking directly into the deserted driver's cab. The hair on the back of his neck stood on end as he weighed up his options.

Geraint was no coward, but he was no hero either. He had a wife and three children at home, and they were his number one priority in life. The faces of his three daughters flitted through his mind, and anger began to build up inside him. The thought of a paedophile ring stealing his precious daughters and subjecting them to unthinkable things made him feel nauseous, and he knew that he had to act. He opened the door and went around to the back of his car. He popped the boot and reached inside to remove a torch, and a tyre iron. The iron felt cold and strangely comforting in his hand, and he flicked on the beam and walked toward the horsebox. The ground beneath his feet was blackened with engine oil, and air was heavy with its smell. Geraint froze as a loud creak reached his ears, but when he turned, it was just the old signage caught by the breeze. His heart was pounding ten to the dozen as he neared the workshop. He played the torchlight all over the vehicle, checking beneath it and illuminating the furthest corners of the building. Nothing moved, but he was sure he could hear the sound of laboured breathing coming from inside the horsebox. The conundrum that he faced now was a difficult one. He could hear life in the vehicle, but dare he enter the building, risking his own life to see, or did he leave now and drive somewhere that he could get a signal and alert the authorities. If he did that whoever was inside the horsebox could die, and he was not sure if he could live with that. If it was his own daughters in that vehicle, and a passerby left them to die because he didn't have the courage to help them, would he be able to forgive them because they were scared for themselves?

The answer was simple and he began to tiptoe around the horsebox. He reached the back of the vehicle, and he could see that the ramp was lowered. As he shone the torch beam over the wooden ramp, he could see that it was coated in thick sticky liquid. Geraint bent closer to it and he could smell the thick coppery odour of blood. There were gallons of it dripping from the vehicle through the sides of the horsebox, onto the oil stained concrete. He felt very scared as he stepped gingerly onto the ramp. The breathing sound stopped suddenly and the silence deafened him. He shone the torch inside, frightened by what he would find, and the scene which met him was worse than anything that he could have imagined.

The carcasses of four large horses lay butchered on the floor of the horsebox. Their underbellies had been slit from the breastbone to the groin, and their innards had been pulled from their bodies and dumped on the straw next to them. The intestines had been ripped apart as if someone were trying to find something. Geraint had seen similar scenes in photographs during his training. They were used to demonstrate the lengths drug smugglers would go to, in order to recover their contraband if something went wrong with their operation. The stench of offal and excrement cloyed at his nostrils and he had to grab at the handrail to stop himself from being sick. There was no sound at all except the driving rain outside.

32

ALFIE LESNER

Alfie sipped a cup of boiling coffee and pressed a tea towel filled with ice to a large bump on his forehead. He was shaking like a leaf and his nerves were shot. The trauma of being inside the prison bus when the sides were ripped open had been matched in ferocity by the motorcycle ride away from the scene. He had closed his eyes and clung on for dear life as he watched the speedometer climbing over one hundred miles an hour. He was over the moon to be free initially, but now reality was hitting home and he had to ask why anyone would go to such lengths to free him. The coffee burnt his lips and he spat it back into the cup. He looked to his rescuer, but there was little information to be gained from him. He had barely said three words to him since they arrived. They were in a detached factory unit somewhere north of Crewe, about forty miles south of the Delamere farm. It was set in similar countryside, isolated yet conveniently situated close to the major motorway networks.

"How long do we have to stay in this dump?" Alfie tried to make conversation. The Moroccan shrugged and sipped his tea.

"Hajj will have an escape plan right, to get me out of the country for a while?"

The Moroccan shrugged again, and this time he smiled as he drank. The sound of a vehicle approaching diverted their attention.

"Thank god for that, I don't think I can stand anymore of your riveting conversation," Alfie frowned as he placed the ice pack back onto his bruised head. He heard footsteps approaching the unit, and then a door opening echoed through the building. Hajj appeared in the doorway of the room that he was in, and Alfie could tell from his expression that he wasn't happy at all.

"Hajj, thanks for getting me out of there," Alfie stepped forward and offered his hand toward the Moroccan mafia boss. Hajj ignored the offer and punched Alfie in the teeth. The blow rocked Alfie backward. Hajj grabbed the iced towel and wrapped it around his knuckles, before punching Alfie a second time.

"Hajj!" Alfie shouted as he spat a tooth covered in blood and saliva onto the floor.

"What did you tell the police, Alfie?"

"Nothing, honest," Alfie spat blood again. He hesitated before continuing, which was his undoing. "I wouldn't tell them anything, Hajj, I've got too much to lose."

"Did they question you?"

"Yes, of course they did, but I didn't tell them anything, honestly," Alfie stressed the last word. He knew that it would only be a matter of time before Hajj found out the truth. The police would be swarming all over Delamere Forest by now.

"Did they ask you about the children?"

"Yes."

"What did you tell them?"

"Nothing, that bastard Howarth had told them that I kidnapped the twins," Alfie played for time.

"How do you know that he told them that?"

"They were waiting for me at his caravan."

"Where was he?"

"They had already taken him away. I walked right into a trap, and that fucking pervert is to blame," Alfie pretended to be annoyed, but his fear was tangible.

"You think that Jack telephoned the police?"

"Yes, he did, and he tried to set me up for the kidnap."

Hajj laughed and paced up and down for a moment. He was mulling over the situation, as he understood it.

"Good old Jack! He's not stupid is he?" Hajj laughed again, but there was little genuine mirth in it. "What did you tell them about the twins?"

"I told them that I didn't know anything about them."

"And you think that they believed you?" Hajj's eyes darkened as if he was trying to see the truth inside his head.

"I think so," Alfie felt beads of sweat running from his temples, and his lip was swelling painfully.

"Did they get your car, Alfie," Hajj spoke quietly.

"Yes."

"You put the twins into your trunk."

Alfie could see where the conversation was going. Hajj didn't believe that he hadn't said anything and he was fishing for clues in his story.

"They were wrapped in the sleeping bag, Hajj. There isn't any evidence of them being in the car," Alfie flapped.

"There will be skin, and hair. It will not take them long to prove that you transported the twins, and then you'll be looking at a long stretch in jail. Then it would be in your own interest to tell them everything that you know," Hajj shrugged as he spelled things out the way that he saw it.

"You could get me out of the country, Hajj, then they'd never catch me."

"Every policeman in Europe will be looking for you and Jack Howarth, you're far too much of a liability I'm afraid."

"What do you mean Jack Howarth?"

"He's on the run somewhere, but I'm not worried about him."

"How did he escape?" Alfie was shocked by the news, with Jack Howarth in the wind all the fingers of blame would be pointing at him.

"That's of no consequence now, I've taken a small insurance policy out, Alfie, just to make sure you haven't said anything."

"What are you talking about?" Alfie looked worried and confused.

"You parents are at the stables, Alfie, surrounded by enough explosive to send them to kingdom come and back," Hajj dropped a Polaroid that had been taken earlier. It showed the terrified elderly couple strapped to a set of camp beds. Alfie sat down and put his head in his hands, his own pain forgotten for the moment. "You're quiet, Alfie, what's the problem?"

Alfie started to cry like a baby, his hands shook and tears streamed down his face. Hajj didn't need to hear any more, it had become obvious that Alfie had given away the location of the stables, which he'd anticipated anyway. He pulled a shiny Bulldog revolver and pointed the huge gun at Alfie's head. Alfie closed his eyes tightly as a forty-four calibre bullet smashed into his brains.

33
THE HORSEBOX

Detective Crab drove over a narrow grey stone bridge, which crossed the River Lune. The drive north had taken him nearly two hours, and his head was still thick with a hangover from the whisky that he'd drunk the previous night. Leading the investigation into the abduction of the Kelly twins had given him sleepless nights, and whisky numbed his senses and gifted him a few hours of fitful slumber. The investigation itself had spiralled out of control over the last few days, as their two main suspects had been sprung from custody, resulting in the deaths of one armed officer and one special volunteer constable. The police station had been torched, which caused the destruction of their main investigation room, and hundreds of witness statements connected to the case had been lost in the blaze. Last but not least, two senior officers, the head of the armed unit and the Divisional Commander, had been killed in an explosion along with ten firearms specialists. The loss of so many of his colleagues had devastated the morale of the division, and set the investigation back in the process. The major incident team were trying to set up a new operations centre at a neighbouring police station, but it was going to take time to be organised, and many of the witness statements that had been lost could never be replaced. The discovery of the blue horsebox was a major breakthrough, and he had to go to the scene himself to see what evidence could be recovered.

It was close to midday and the sun was getting hot, as he navigated a tight bend in the road and almost drove past the entrance to the derelict petrol station where the horsebox had been found. Yellow crime scene tape flapped in the wind and a uniformed officer was keeping a gaggle of photographers away from the overgrown forecourt. Crab indicated that he wanted to drive onto the weed strewn garage, and he honked his horn to get the policeman's attention. The constable waved to him and walked over to the car, bending to the window as he lowered it.

"I'm Detective Crab, Cheshire Division, I'm here to meet your forensic team," Crab could smell whisky on his own breath, and from the look on the young constable's face, so could he. The uniformed officer frowned and lifted the yellow tape.

"They're round the back of the building, Sir, and I'd get some mints if I was you, Sir," the officer said as he passed by.

"Smart arse," Crab muttered as he pulled the vehicle on to the tarmac. He closed the window and reached over to his left. There was half a packet of extra strong mints in the deepest darkest reaches of the glove box, and after a few dredges he felt them in his grasp. The wrapper was tattered and torn, and the top mint was dirty so he tossed it into the back seat, and then crammed the next two from the pack into his mouth. Crab checked himself in the rear view mirror before opening the door and climbing out of the vehicle. His eyes were not as red as they had been earlier, so at least his liver and kidneys were getting to work on the alcohol that was coursing through his bloodstream. The sunshine was warming, and he had to squint against the glare. He breathed in deeply, and the country air lightened his mood considerably. The rainfall from the previous night was evaporating quickly, making the atmosphere moist, and fresh.

"Detective Crab?" a female voice disturbed his thoughts.

"Yes, and you are?" Crab was taken aback by her appearance.

"Doctor Peters, crime lab, come this way please," she almost purred when she spoke, a gentle Southern Irish lilt to her voice added to her attractive demeanour. Doctor Peters was a stunning brunette, and despite the fact that she was wearing a blue paper jump suit, Crab could tell that she had the body of a glamour model. "If you could put this on I'd appreciate it."

Crab stopped at a second line of tape, where he was handed a similar paper garment to put on. He ripped open the packet and struggled into it clumsily. The doctor took the empty packaging from him and smiled as he pushed his legs into the jumpsuit.

"Whoever invents one of these things that is easy to get on will make a fortune," the pretty doctor joked.

"I'm with you there, Doctor," the detective replied. He closed the zip up to his neck, and then smoothed the paper suit down with his hands. "Ready when you are."

"We've found something interesting, my colleagues are about to open it now," the doctor sounded excited as she worked toward the derelict garage. "Have you been brought up to speed with what we have found so far?"

"Not really, my information was sketchy to be honest. That's why we requested a visit to the scene," Crab was staring at the doctor's rounded behind as he walked.

"Watch that manhole," she pointed to one of the open tanks, which stopped him from disappearing into the earth.

Detective Crab blushed and sidestepped the hazard. They rounded the corner of the petrol station, and the old workshop came into view. A navy blue horsebox was parked inside, barely visible from the road. Lying on the tarmac were the carcasses of four horses. They had been placed onto plastic sheets, and a forensic officer was probing a slimy pile of intestines with gloved hands. It looked like they had been disembowelled.

"What happened to them?" Crab grimaced as the thick stench of offal and excrement drifted across to him.

"They were obviously being used as mules, if you'll pardon the pun," the doctor explained.

"I don't follow."

"They were force fed condoms full of crystal meth. It would appear that the smugglers changed their plans and had to recover their drugs from the horses' intestines before nature could take its own course. They must have been in a hurry," she pointed to the piles of intestines, and a swarm of flies took off as they neared them.

"Jesus," the detective muttered.

"It's common practice nowadays detective, especially now sniffer dogs are so prevalent. The dealers have developed new ways to trick the dogs, horses are often used."

"Why here though, how was the vehicle found?"

"According to our uniformed officers a local man, who knows the area like the back of his hand, was passing on his way home from a shift on the docks at Heysham. He's a customs officer and they had been alerted to keep an eye out for the vehicle earlier in the week. He saw it parked here, thought it was unusual and called us."

"Do you think that the port was their destination?"

"Without a doubt, thoroughbred horses are shipped over to Ireland everyday of the week to be used for breeding racehorses," the doctor stepped into the workshop away from the smell of the rotting horses. "This vehicle and those horses would have sailed across the Irish Sea without a hitch if there hadn't been an alert put out."

The detective nodded, and processed the information that he'd been given. Their investigation had been focused on the ports to the south, assuming that the twins were destined for the continent. He followed the doctor around to the back of the horsebox. The walls of the building were made from corrugated iron, and it was covered in rust and a thick curtain of cobwebs. The smell of congealing blood filled the air, and he longed to be back in the sunshine away from the stomach-churning stench. The ramp of the vehicle was sticky, and he could feel blood squelching beneath his shoes.

"We think there is a hidden compartment behind that wall," the doctor pointed toward the bulkhead of the stable box. "There seems to be about eight feet of space missing from the inside of the vehicle when it's compared to the exterior dimensions," the doctor smiled at her colleagues who were clearing bridles and saddles from the tack wall. They walked past the detective and nodded silent hellos, and the bridles clinked as they placed them into neat piles on the workshop floor.

"It would be the ideal place to smuggle two small children," Crab said excitedly.

"We didn't notice it at first, but don't get your hopes up we haven't heard any signs of life in there I'm afraid."

"We're ready to pull the wall down, Doctor," one of the scientists said, as he stomped back up the ramp. He was a portly grey-haired chap, and his paper suit was stretched to its outer limits.

"Okay, if we're all ready then let's see what's behind there," the doctor sighed. She turned to the detective and rolled her eyes. "I'm not looking forward to this," she said.

"How long would the twins have been in the horsebox, assuming that they are actually in there?" the detective asked. Two forensic officers set to work with electric screwdrivers, and the high-pitched whining noise that they made reminded him of a dentist drill. He pressed his teeth together at the thought.

"Who knows?" she shook her head without committing herself to a speculative guess.

The panel came away easily once the screws, which held

it in place, were removed, and the secret compartment was revealed.

"Dear god," the pretty doctor said under her breath. She put her hands over her nose and pressed her fingers into the corner of her eyes, trying to stem the tears that were forming there. One of the forensics began to click photographs of the terrible scene before them, and it was all detective Crab could do to stop himself from vomiting.

"That's identical to the sleeping bag that the twins were taken in," the detective said to himself referring to a blood soaked quilt.

"How could anyone do that to another human being?" the doctor shook her head.

"I guess she was a mule too," the detective sucked air between his teeth as he looked at the carnage. Ramah had been a sexy young woman when she entered the horsebox with the twins. Her role was to nurse them on the ferry journey across the Irish Sea. She was also made to swallow fifteen condoms full of cocaine. It would appear that she had suffered the same grizzly end as the horses had when the deal went sour and the voyage had to be cancelled. She was lay spread eagle on a cot bed, her chest had been ripped open from her neck to her groin, and her intestines had been sliced open and strewn across the floor. The compartment was small and compact, and apart from Ramah's savaged corpse, it was completely empty. The twins were gone.

34

TWO DAYS LATER/SYLVIA LEES

Sylvia Lees crushed out a cigarette in the overflowing ashtray of her car as she tried to gather her thoughts. The nicotine hit had only succeeded in making her feel lightheaded, and hadn't calmed her nerves one bit. She reached for her packet of Benson and Hedges Gold, and swore when she realised that it was empty. That meant that she had smoked twenty cigarettes since teatime yesterday, considering that she was trying to give up, it wasn't good.

She had parked a few hundred yards down the road from the Kelly residence, in order to avoid the crowd of paparazzi that were still encamped outside, waiting for a shot of a devastated mother to plaster on their front pages, or a snippet of information about the case. The disappearance of the twins was news enough to cause a media storm, but the torrent of violence and intrigue which had dogged the investigation over the last week was unrivalled by anything that had happened before. The fact that Karl Kelly hadn't been seen at the house for a few days had not gone unnoticed, and it had fuelled speculation of a marital split, and that wasn't helping to quieten the furore either. The police were not coming out well in the newspapers, as the broadsheet editors dissected one blunder after another.

Sylvia had been briefed in a very long meeting by her superiors about the findings at both Delamere, and Heysham, and now she had to relay the bad news to an emotionally broken mother, who was grieving for her children and for the breakdown of her marriage simultaneously. This had been a particularly difficult assignment for Sylvia, complicated by betrayal within the marriage and the arrival of Major Stanley Timms and his affiliates, and she was not looking forward to being the bearer of such bad tidings.

She opened the car door, took a deep breath and prepared herself to run the gauntlet of the press. Sylvia was less than fifty yards away from the house when the first reporter spotted her approach. He broke away from the pack and ran toward her, camera clicking and voice recorder thrust in her face. It was seconds before the others joined him in the scrum.

"Is there any news on the children's whereabouts?"

"No comment."

"Can you confirm or deny if the explosion in Delamere Forest is connected to the investigation?"

"No comment."

"Are the incidents at Warrington police station and Warrington General Hospital connected?"

"No comment."

"How many police officers lost their lives in the forest?"

"No comment."

"Can you confirm whether the main suspects in the kidnapping have escaped from custody?"

"No comment." Sylvia had finally reached the garden gate and a burly uniformed officer opened it for her and let her through.

"Stand back and let the lady through please," the officer shouted. The reporters continued to fire questions at the back of her head, despite her obvious insistence on remaining silent.

"Has Karl Kelly left his wife?" The last question was the most cutting, and she treated it with the same silent contempt as she had with the others. She reached the door and rang the bell. The curtains in the front window twitched as Hayley looked out to see who her visitor was. Sylvia waved her hand and offered an empty smile, but Hayley didn't return the gesture. This was going to be a difficult encounter, especially if Hayley's father was around. Sylvia needed to speak with him urgently, but she didn't know how to go about it, without compromising herself and the investigation. The fact that the investigation was in such turmoil had forced her hand, and after a sleepless night tossing the options around in her head, she had finally made her decision. It would be very difficult to broach, but she had to try. The handle twisted and the Major opened the door.

"Good evening, Officer Lees," he said curtly as he stepped back to let her in.

"Good evening, Major," she replied. Sylvia wiped her feet and waited to be asked for her coat, but the Major didn't offer to take it. She took it off anyway, and hung it up. "I need to update Hayley on the investigation."

"Rather you than me from what I've heard," the Major frowned. He nodded his head toward the hallway, and walked into the living room, and Sylvia followed him nervously at a distance. Hayley sat on a brown leather corner unit, which matched the colour of the wooden laminate floor. A white woollen rug covered half of the room, and Sylvia reckoned that it would need vacuuming everyday at least if Hayley wanted it to remain that colour, especially if the twins were recovered. A large plasma television was fixed to the wall opposite, and Sky news was replaying a roll of the latest pictures which suggested there was a link between the previous week's events and the abduction of the Kelly twins. Hayley held the remote, and she lowered the volume as Sylvia walked into the room.

"How are you holding up?" Sylvia asked sympathetically.

Hayley picked up a cushion and hugged it, but she did not reply. She was shattered, and emotionally devoid, being polite was not on her list of priorities right now. The Major seemed to be just as on edge as his daughter was, but at least there was no sign of his huge colleague, despite being built like a Greek god there was something about him that Sylvia found intimidating.

"Do you have anything new for us, Officer Lees?" the Major broke the ice.

"How much do you already know, Major?" Sylvia fronted him. She didn't like the fact that he always seemed to be one step ahead of the police, and the death of her colleagues had frayed her patience to zero. She wasn't in the right frame of mind to play mental chess with the Major.

"We know what we have seen on the news, pretty much the same as yourself really," Hayley said sarcastically.

"Okay then I'll tell you what I've been told, ask me whatever you like, and I'll answer you honestly," Sylvia sat back and tried to build some kind of trust in them. There was an awkward silence for a few moments.

Hayley looked at her father and held out her hand. The Major took her hand and sat down beside her. Hayley tried a half smile, but her lips were quivering as she spoke.

"I'm sorry Sylvia, but I'm at my wit's end," Hayley apologised for her hostility.

"I'm not surprised, Hayley," Sylvia replied. "I don't know how you're holding yourself together."

"I'm not sure that I am to be honest," tears filled her eyes. "I believe that they found the horsebox, didn't they?"

"Yes they did, not far from the ferry port at Heysham," Sylvia replied. Only the Major could have known that it was the vehicle that they were looking for. The press had been told that it was similar, but they couldn't confirm that it was the actual vehicle at this stage.

"Do they know if my babies were in it?"

"They found a sleeping bag which matched the description of the one that you said had been taken with them." Sylvia watched the Major's reaction, and she was certain that he didn't know about the sleeping bag. Hayley glanced sideways at her father, questioning him silently, and that confirmed it to Sylvia that he didn't know the details from the scene yet. "The twins had been moved somewhere, but there was no sign that they had been hurt in any way."

"So the vehicle was empty?" the Major asked.

"No, Major it wasn't empty," Sylvia would have to pick her words very carefully. "We found evidence that the horsebox was being be used as the carrier for a large drug consignment destined for Northern Ireland, but the perpetrators aborted the journey before they reached the port."

"What kind of evidence, you said you would tell me what you know, Sylvia?" Hayley squeezed the cushion again. Her cheeks were hollowed and her eyes were bloodshot from crying.

"I'm sorry, Hayley, we found four dead horses, and the body of a Moroccan woman that we can't identify."

"Oh God," Hayley said. "Sarah loved horses, I mean she loves horses. Why would they kill them?"

"The drugs were placed into condoms and the force fed into the horses' stomachs. The idea was to pass them off as breeding stock, and to take them to Ireland in the horsebox, and then sell the drugs over there."

"So what happened," Hayley asked naively. The Major shifted uncomfortably on the seat, as he had an idea what was coming.

"We think that the smugglers aborted the run when the news broke about the horsebox, and they killed the horses to recover their drugs," Sylvia was as honest as she could be, leaving out the gory details.

"What about the woman?" Hayley was open mouthed as the images went through her mind, and it became obvious how the smugglers would have recovered their drugs.

"The same thing happened to her," Sylvia replied to the question that she was hoping Hayley wouldn't ask.

"What if they did the same to my babies," Hayley's face greyed, and she stared at her father for reassurance.

"We think that the twins had already been moved before the horses were killed, Hayley," Sylvia jumped in and rescued the Major from an awkward question. "The woman was found in a secret compartment that had been screwed back into place by the smugglers. We don't think that they ever planned to take the twins to Ireland."

"You're saying that they're still in this country, aren't you?" Hayley whispered. A spark of hope glinted in her eyes and she squeezed her father's hand tightly.

"We have no reason to believe that they're not at this stage," Sylvia replied and tried a smile. Hayley broke down into tears and buried her head into the cushion that she held.

"How did Jack Howarth escape?" the Major held his daughter and stroked her hair. "Did he have help?"

"The Moroccans cut his thumb off to slip him from the handcuffs, and they helped him out of the hospital dressed as paramedics. We lost the officer that tried to stop them, I'm afraid he was shot during the escape," Sylvia replied.

"I'm sorry about that."

"It's a pity that your colleagues weren't around to help out, Major."

"Why do you say that?"

"One of our uniformed officers has reported a large built man, with a shaven head, who apparently apprehended the arsonist that petrol bombed the police station, and left him handcuffed to a lamppost, sounds like your colleague, John Tankersley to me," Sylvia raised her eyebrows questioningly.

The Major shook his head, and remained silent. He was mulling over the information that Sylvia had parted with. The fact the twins may still be in the country reassured him somewhat that they could find them.

"I'm assuming that it was your people that intervened with the hijack on a police prison bus near Risley, which was transporting Alfie Lesner," she pressed.

"I doubt that my people had anything to do with it, Officer Lees," the Major batted the question away. There would be no comebacks, because there were no witnesses.

"Really, this Mitsibushi was found at the scene," Sylvia took a Polaroid from her pocket, and passed it to the Major. The picture showed the wreckage of a black Mitsibushi Shogun being craned onto a low-loader. "We ran the usual checks on this vehicle, and guess what, we hit a dead end. It's registered to the Ministry of Defence, full stop, we can't access any further details."

"There are limits to everyone's access levels, Officer," the Major replied abruptly. He wasn't sure where Sylvia was headed with this conversation. Hayley had stopped sobbing and she was listening intently to the conversation.

"I've been trying to do some research into your unit, Major, but I can't find anything to suggest that one exists," Sylvia sat forward. Hayley wiped her eyes and stood up, she'd heard enough.

"If John Tankersley is out there looking for my children then I for one don't care what he does," Hayley walked out of the room sobbing like a baby.

"I can't find any information on you or your team, Major," she grinned nervously. The Major remained silent.

"If your people are as good as I think they are, tell them to follow this," Sylvia handed him a folded piece of paper. "Our computer geeks were working on this, before the station burned down that is. I'll go and make us all a drink."

The Major watched Sylvia Lees walk out of the living room, and he could hear her voice in the kitchen, soothing Hayley and offering words of encouragement. She meant well that was for sure, and she obviously had empathy for his daughter's plight. He ran his fingers over the fold in the paper and then opened it up. There were several web site addresses written on it, but they all had the same keywords in them, forbiddenfruitcompany.com. He took out his cell phone and called Tank.

35

24 HOURS LATER/TANK

Tank walked out of the elevator, into the government bunker where they were based. The bunker had been carved from the red sandstone bedrock, which was deep below the city of Liverpool. The bunker was home to several hi-Tech listening posts that were tasked with monitoring communications between suspect terrorist cells, the world over. It also housed the taskforce trace laboratory, where computer searches and e-mail monitoring was carried out. Today the team was working on something completely different. He waved a brief hello, and headed to a bank of screens, which were being monitored by Tara and one of their boffins. Searching the net for ghost sites is a thankless task and they had been at it all night. Tara looked tired, but her face lit up when she saw him coming.

"Have you found anything?" Tank smiled back at her.

"We're making progress. We have eliminated thousands of sites which have been confusing our search, and we've narrowed it right down," she replied.

"How can you tell which ones could be of interest?" Tank asked. There were nine screens processing information and he couldn't make head or tail of any of it.

"Okay, let's pretend that you're someone who has a porn

site or you're a webcam studio owner, and you want to make your films or pictures available for anyone to view, but you don't want to charge any money, then we can filter them out immediately," Tara explained.

"How many sites come up when you enter that domain name?" Tank asked.

"It would appear that forbidden fruit is a keyword linked to over three million sites," she frowned.

"Yes, but how many of them are child porn sites?"

"That's the problem, Tank, we can't tell because they ghost the pay per view sites, and it would appear that not all their broadcasts are child pornography," she pointed to the screens as if it would all be made clear if he looked at them. He looked and it was as clear as mud. "They broadcast everything from hard core porn to live snuff videos."

"You mean they are killing people in these broadcasts?" Tank shook his head in disbelief.

"It appears that all their broadcasts appeal to the most violent end of the sexual spectrum, and the snuff broadcasts that we have found look very convincing. I'm convinced they're not actors," Tara sounded tired. "They're making millions out of these sites, and their customers are paying hundreds of Euros each to watch the real hard stuff, and even more if they want to join in," she explained.

"Join in?"

"Yes, the sites are totally interactive, and the action is guided by a majority voting system, and the longer they watch the more they pay."

"You wouldn't believe there were that many sick bastards out there would you?" Tank was sounding worried now. "How do these things work?"

"There is software available now which can allow anyone from a private person who wants to show his own video stream with a web cam, to a full blown agent or a webmaster.

They can stream their images from multiple cameras and collect payments from all over the globe. They show the images, and then they shut it, take the money and then close the whole show down and disappear.

"Can you trace them or not?" Tank wasn't the most patient person in the world.

"I'll cut a long story short," Tara smiled again and tossed her blond hair.

"We're looking for sites that have more than just standard interactive features, and if we can identify them then it will narrow down the search. A site like theirs needs webcam chat software that has lots of special functions like: special show facility that allows them to have many cameras in one room, hot-or-not photo and video on demand matched with an auto-translator that changes messages to and from ten different languages."

"How many people watch these things?" Tank was amazed and sickened at the same time.

"Tens of thousands, world-wide," Tara replied sadly.

"Once they take the site off line then you can't trace it, right?"

"Right, they set up simulated streams, which are bounced off several stream servers at once, and they attach the streams to fake servers, it's impossible once they stop broadcasting," Tara finished explaining as best as she could.

"There's no hope then?" Tank leaned on the desk, and Tara couldn't help but look at his bulging triceps.

"Oh, I didn't say that," she teased.

"Tara, what have you got?"

"Look here, this site went live yesterday, it has all the features that we would expect on that type of broadcast, and it has been set up to be a pay per minute channel,"

"What's the significance of that?"

"A Pay per minute site fitted with an interactive facility is used predominantly for live streaming, so that the action can be guided by the viewers' wishes, or votes, and if they want to carry on watching then the price goes up and up as the action accelerates," she stared at the screen.

"You mean as the level of violence accelerates?"

"Yes."

"I've got something here," the boffin spoke for the first time. He was sat in front of a tray of chocolate sprinkled donuts, which were half eaten, and he tucked into another one as he printed off some information.

"Please tell me it's an address," Tank said.

"Well I have good news and bad news," the Tech guy said.

"What's the good news," Tank asked.

"I have a GPS position for four different servers in this country, but only one of the servers has been used for every broadcast," he said. Tank took a print out from him and nearly walked away, before he'd finished speaking. "The bad news is that they have started broadcasting a live feed."

Tank stopped in his tracks and turned around. One of the screens showed a young girl, thirteen or so, Tank guessed. She was blindfolded and handcuffed by one hand to a metal link that was set into the wall behind her. The thin mattress that she was lying on was heavily stained, and by the coppery colour of the stains Tank guessed that forensics would identify it as blood from several different secretors. Two hooded men appeared, one either side of the mattress. They were naked and aroused as they looked at the camera and then suddenly the screen changed completely. 'Pay now to view the action live' began flickering across the screen, along with the instructions on how to make a payment. For an extra fifty Euros the viewer could become a voting customer, which would give the power to influence what horrors would be inflicted upon the young victim. Tank looked at the server address again and left the bunker without saying a word.

36
THE TWINS

Sarah had been awake for hours now and the effects of the drugs were wearing off. She reached for a plastic beaker, which was full of milk, and she drank it greedily, leaving a white tidemark on her top lip. Zak giggled at her and clumsily wiped the milk from her mouth. She passed the beaker to him and he took his turn to drink from it. It was uncanny how the twins shared their food and drinks, preferring to use one cup and one plate between them rather than one each. Most twins have an emotional bond, and Sarah and Zak were no different. They'd taken great comfort from each other during their strange journey, sleeping close to each other and seeing their identical sibling there next to them when they awoke had reassured them. Sarah missed her mother terribly and she was teary and scared. Zak sensed her fear and he held her and tried to keep her occupied. He smiled at her despite feeling a terrible unease himself. They were five years old, but they knew that something was very wrong.

Their surroundings had changed dramatically. Sarah remembered the smells and sounds of horses, but the memories seemed dream-like and unclear. Now they were bathed and they had been fed well, spaghetti hoops on toast, and milk to drink. A DVD player played a myriad of their favourite programmes and there was an enviable toy collection. Although it hadn't been used much, neither of them felt much like playing with toys yet.

The door opened and the twins fell silent for a moment. They looked longingly toward the door, desperate for their mother to walk through it and to take them home. It wasn't their mother, and Sarah began to cry again. Zak looked at his sister crying, and he patted her chubby leg to soothe her but it didn't work. The DVD player was turned off and Zak started to cry too.

37

TARBOCK GREEN/PRICE'S PIG FARM

John Tankersley left the bunker in his own vehicle, a dark metallic pickup truck, and he headed out of Liverpool on the main arterial route, the M62. The address that he'd been given by the Tech team was a postcode which related to a group of buildings in a leafy greenbelt area of the county called, Tarbock Green, and it was only twelve miles out of the city. He pulled up Satellite pictures of the village that showed a small group of industrial units, two petrol stations, a pub, three big residential houses, and a large pig farm surrounded by a heavily wooded area. Tank had no idea which one of the structures could be housing the server, or if the film studio was actually situated there, but he had to investigate it as there was no time to lose. He had the image of the frightened young girl handcuffed to the wall in his mind, and the banner headline on the payment page had a digital timer counting down from sixty minutes. That meant he had one hour to stop anything happening to the girl. He could only assume that the twins would be used as the main event.

Tank was going to the village alone. Tara and the trace team were searching for any other possible server addresses, and Grace was charged with selecting and moving in on any other potential targets that appeared. They had decided to leave the

Major out of the loop for now, as pressure from Westminster was mounting, especially since the taskforce vehicle had been found at the scene of the prison bus hijack. So far, the police had blown their cover every time they had moved in on the paedophile ring, and the Moroccans had proved to be slippery customers with access to inside information from informers within the police force. There wasn't enough time to risk letting them know that they had found the main server, if they did the Moroccans would be in the wind again, and they would never find the twins.

Tank pulled off the motorway and within minutes, he was driving down country lanes, which weaved, between acres and acres of bright yellow rapeseed crops. There was a sharp bend in the road and Tank saw a brass post box fixed to the wall of a thatched cottage, which was the post office for the surrounding area. Entering Tarbock Green was like stepping through a time warp. It was a rural oasis inhabited by a farming community unchanged by modern society for decades. The road straightened and to his right was a white bricked pub called the, Brick Wall Inn, opposite was one of the petrol stations that he'd seen on the map, and directly across the road was the entrance to the woods. Tank pulled onto the pub as it had a large car park and seemed to be the centre of the village. He pulled up the aerial pictures of the area, and he looked around to get his bearings. The industrial units were hidden from view behind the petrol station, and while they could easily be used as the site for the illicit studio, his attention was drawn to the pig farm. It was situated through the woods to his left, and was hidden from the road by residential properties. Tank could see the top of a large metal silo, which looked like it was part of the pig farm. The trees concealed the other buildings. Tara said that during their search they had seen evidence of snuff films being broadcasted from the server. If they were being made here then the film makers would have the problem of disposing of their victim's bodies. Pigs would eat anything that was put in front of them, and it was that fact which made the pig farm favourite in Tank's mind. He decided to investigate the farm first.

Tank opened a lockbox that was situated between the front seats of his pickup, and he took out his spare Glock seventeen, slipping it into his waistband next to his standard issue weapon. It was rare that he'd ever needed two handguns, but losing his Glock during the hijack had left him feeling uneasy about carrying one weapon, especially as he was going in alone. He removed four full clips of nine-millimetre ammunition and slipped them into his pocket, before strapping a Smith and Wesson boot knife to his ankle. Tara and the team knew roughly, where he was, but there were at least a dozen buildings, which came under the same postcode, and so Tank activated a GPS tracker, which was built into his spare Glock. The taskforce would already be aware that the weapon had been removed from its safety box, and now they would know if it was discharged and how many times it was fired. 'Better safe than sorry,' he thought. If the twins were in the pig farm then there was only one way that he was going to get them out, and he didn't believe that he'd be arresting anybody in the process. He was used to being judge, jury and executioner, but this time it was personal.

The pickup beeped and the indicator lights flashed as he walked away from the vehicle. He checked the road was clear and apart from the sound of music, which was drifting from the jukebox in the pub, everything was quiet. Suddenly there was a loud concussion noise, which came from the direction of the pig farm, and it was followed quickly by the sound of a second blast. Tank thought that a twelve-gauge shotgun had been discharged, and huge flock of starlings took to the air from the woods. They formed a huge black cloud, ducking and darting across the sky in a panic.

"Bird scaring machine," a voice said behind him.

"I beg your pardon?" Tank turned around surprised. The noise of a shotgun had startled him, and he was ready to draw his weapon in response. He eyed the man that had spoken, and relaxed.

"That noise, it's a bird scaring machine. I could see you were confused, most visitors are," the old man said drawing deeply on his hand rolled cigarette. He had obviously stepped out of the pub to have a smoke.

"I see," Tank said. "Are you local then?"

"Lived here all my life, Sir," the old man replied. "They have to keep the starlings away from the pigs' food because they carry disease you see."

"Who owns the pig farm?"

"It used to be the Price brothers, until swine foot and mouth wiped out all the animals about five years ago, everyone still calls it Price's farm though," the old man explained.

"Who owns it now?"

"Foreign company owns it now, brought their own herdsman too, and fired all the locals."

"Do they keep any horses?"

"They do, couple a sheep in the back fields too, you should never keep horses and sheep together with pigs," the old man began to explain, but his voice trailed off when the big man turned and walked into the woods. "Charming I'm sure."

Tank was fifty yards into the woods when he came to a fork in the path, and there was a sign was nailed to a tree that declared the land to the right as private property. He ignored the warning and ducked off the access road into the trees, heading toward the outer perimeter of the pig farm. He pulled out his cell phone and texted Grace, telling her to run a check with the land registry department, to find out who owned the pig farm, and more to the point where they were from. The results wouldn't stop him from searching it himself but it may speed things up for the traditional law enforcement agencies, especially if there was a Moroccan connection. He pressed send and then moved on through the woods.

To his left was a thicket of hedge, and it had grown unchecked to at least head height. Through it he could see manicured lawns and the rear gardens of the houses that he'd seen earlier on the road. To his right the trees thickened, but he could see the shapes of farm buildings through them. He picked his way toward them following narrow paths that had been flattened by woodland animals and the poachers that stalked them. The sun light was filtered through the tree canopy into bright shafts of light, and squadrons of midges and gnats seemed to hang in the air enjoying the warmth of the sun. Five hundred yards further on he came to a small pond, and he kneeled down in the long grass to look at it. It was silted up, and polluted with pig excrement and green slime. It blocked his path and he looked for a way around it. As he progressed the bird scaring machine retorted again, it had been fired every ten minutes or so, and although Tank knew what it was, it still made his nerves stand on end when the blank shotgun cartridges were discharged.

He circumnavigated the pond and the thick brambles that grew on its banks, and at the other side, he reached the out buildings that were on the periphery of the pig farm. Two rolls of razor wire spiralled their way as far as he could see in either direction, forming a barrier between him and the farm. Tank searched the immediate area and found a thick rotting tree trunk beneath the dark green foliage of a rhododendron bush. He slid his fingers underneath it and lifted the heavy log with ease. An army of wood louse and black beetles scurried for cover as their microscopic universe was exposed to the daylight. Tank shifted the tree trunk onto his shoulder, waiting for the bird-scaring machine to roar again, and then with a huge shrug he tossed it across the razor wire. The wire was flattened and it rattled and vibrated beneath the crushing weight of the trunk, but the bird-scaring machine smothered the noise. Tank stepped along the rotten tree, crossing the wire and breaching their defences.

The outbuildings were nothing more than wooden storage sheds, which harped back to another era of farming. Hand held sickles and scythes hung from rusted brackets on the walls, and huge swathes of spider silk hung from the ceilings. There were dust-covered workbenches laden with wooden planes, and metal vices, handsaws and chisels that looked like they had laid there untouched for decades. Tank moved quietly across the dusty floor and reached the doorway of the first building. He looked out across the main farmyard. To his right was a deep cesspit about one hundred yards wide, filled to the brim with pig sewage. The smell of excrement filled Tank's nostrils and the strength of the ammonia in the urine made his eyes water. A load gurgling sound turned his attention to a tall metal silo on his left. It was the one that he had seen from the road earlier. Beneath the silo a bulldozer was busy pushing tons of rotting vegetables and supermarket food waste into an enormous metal vat, were it was boiled into tons of liquid pigswill, before being piped into the silo. Tank knew that the two businesses could fit hand in glove. A human body could be dumped into the vat, and it would disappear in the boiling process in minutes. The gurgling sound became louder as thousands of gallons of pigswill poured through a network of pipes, finally being sloshed into over three hundred pig troughs across the farm. The pigs could smell the swill boiling and they anticipated their food being delivered. The hungry animals were becoming excited and the noise of the pigs squealing became a deafening cacophony of grunting sounds.

Tank stayed hidden behind the out buildings and looked to the left. There was a central building made up of animal pens, stables and storage lofts, and behind that was a newer, modern brick built block. Tank was about to double back and make his way to the new building by skirting behind the animal sheds, when a different type of scream rang out across the farm. Tank knew that it was human, probably female although it could have been a child. He looked at his wristwatch, and guessed that the internet show was about to begin. He drew his Glock and bolted straight across the farmyard. There was no time left for stealth.

Tank was fifty yards across the yard when the bulldozer driver spotted him. He began shouting in a foreign language that Tank couldn't decipher, and as he ran, from the corner of his eye Tank saw the vehicle change direction. He turned toward the advancing machine, dropping to one knee. He had no wish to repeat the episode with the JCB digger, and he wanted to make his first shot count. He closed one eye as he aimed, squeezed the trigger twice, and the Glock kicked in his hand. The retort was barely audible over the sound of the screaming pigs, and the bird-scaring machine fired again, adding to the racket. The bulldozer veered wildly to the right and it trundled across the yard toward the cesspit. The driver was slouched over the steering wheel, mortally wounded, but not quite dead. Bubbles of blood and phlegm seeped from a deep hole in his throat, and he tried in vain to steer the bulldozer onto a different course, but it smashed through a low breezeblock wall before dropping over the edge and plummeting nose first into a million gallons of pig excrement. The heavy machine disappeared in a matter of seconds, swallowed up by the septic sludge.

Tank bent low and ran toward the new building. He was out in the open, and as such, he was a sitting duck for an accomplished sniper. He tensed his body as he ran, and visually scanned the area around him, looking for the most likely position for a shot to come from, but none came. Tank reached the corner of the new building, and another scream rang out. This time there was no doubt that it had come from inside the newer block, and despite the deafening noise of the pigs, he knew that it was a young girl that had screamed.

The building was two storeys high, square, and had a flat roof. It was built from grey, prefabricated concrete slabs, and although there were several windows, they had all been blanked out from the inside. Tank let his breathing calm down and he wiped perspiration from his brow with his sleeve. His heart was racing and he knew that he had to rescue the young girl from her torture, but he couldn't throw caution to the wind or he would wind up dead, and so would she. He checked the surrounding area, and it was clear. Tank bolted for the door with his weapon pointed skyward, at the ready. He reached for the handle and twisted it, but it wouldn't budge, it was locked from the inside. Another scream from inside rocked him, and he ran to a ground floor window to his left. There was a large rusty oil drum beneath the windowsill, and he rocked it to test if it was full or not. The oil drum was about a quarter full of diesel engine oil. Tank holstered his Glock, tipped the oil drum, and slipped his fingers beneath it. He breathed deeply as a weight lifter would in the Olympics, and then he heaved the metal barrel up above his head, pausing for only a second before he launched it at the glass. The window imploded completely, shattered glass was catapulted into the air, and the wooden panel that had blanked out the window splintered into pieces with a load crack.

Tank ran and used both hands to vault the window ledge, and he cleared a narrow table before landing on a hard bare concrete floor. The brick walls were painted white, and were completely bare. Three long laboratory workbenches, cluttered with chemistry equipment, separated the room. There was a sudden movement to his left and Tank pulled out the Glock from its holster, and spun around to face it. A man dressed in a white laboratory technician's coat, wearing a protective face mask stood frozen to the spot. He instinctively raised his hands above his head as Tank levelled the weapon at him. The crashing sound of braking glass had alerted everyone in the building, and raised voices were coming from the first floor. Tank waved the Glock at the technician and he moved to the left away from the door. A quick look around told him that he had smashed his way into a crystal meth lab, and he realised that a stray bullet in this room could cause an explosion big enough to blow the roof off the building.

Suddenly the lab door opened and a small dark skinned man ran into the lab. He waved a Mach 10 machine pistol in front of him. It was obvious from the expression on his face that he was not expecting to see Tank in the room. He had run downstairs expecting to find that there had been an explosion in the meth lab. Accidents were common during the manufacture of crystal methamphetamine. Tank used the element of surprise and before the man had realised his mistake a nine-millimetre bullet blew the back of his head off. The technician reached under his bench and pulled out a twelve-gauge Mossberg pump action shotgun, but before he had chambered a cartridge and lifted it clear, Tank fired two shots from his Glock. The nine millimetre bullets slammed into the man's chest, and the impact knocked him off his feet, dark red patches began to bloom across his lab coat as he landed on the cold concrete.

The lab became silent, but Tank heard multiple sets of footsteps stomping down the stairs from the first floor, and he jumped over the workbench and snatched the shotgun off the floor. He aimed the Mossberg at the doorway and waited. Two men charged into the lab and they walked into a deadly spray of twelve-gauge buckshot. One of the men collapsed in a heap instantly but the second man was blasted backwards into the hallway. Tank chambered a second cartridge and he pulled the weapon tight into his shoulder before he fired the shotgun again. The lead shot hit the man square in the face, ripping his lower jaw from his head, and severing the jugular vein in his neck. Arterial spray splattered the walls as a crimson plume jetted from the ragged wound.

The hallway was silent as Tank crossed the lab and stepped over the dead bodies. He peered around the doorframe and looked up the stairs, and the young girl screamed again but this time it was a blood-curdling wail. Tank rushed through the door toward the stairs when a strong hand grabbed at his ankle. He tripped and fell heavily on his elbow, and the shotgun clattered down the hallway out of his reach. The man that had grabbed him was bleeding from his nose and mouth, and there was blood pooling beneath him from a wound in his chest, but he was still alive and dangerous. Tank couldn't reach his holstered weapon, and so he grabbed the second Glock from his waistband. The man's eyes widened in shock as Tank fired one well aimed shot, which hit him in the centre of the forehead, leaving a jagged hole the size of a walnut. His grip was released instantaneously, and Tank scrambled up to his feet. He grabbed the shotgun and checked that it had ammunition left in it. There were two cartridges remaining. Slipping the Glock back into his belt, he began to climb the staircase as quickly as he dared. The building was bare concrete, and the walls and floors had been left uncovered. The light was provided by rows of strip-lights. When he reached the top of the stairs, he checked that the room nearest to him was clear, another scream gave away the location of the studio. Tank couldn't understand why the filming was still going on, hadn't they heard the shotgun being fired? The bird-scaring machine retorted again and it became clear that the men involved in the filming hadn't distinguished the gunshots as anything to worry about.

Tank moved down the empty corridor to the studio, took

a breath and opened the door. The scene that confronted him was like the vision from a nightmare. One man was raping the young girl, while the other cut her skin with a hunting knife. She was bleeding from several wounds already. They had removed the blindfold so that the victim could see what was going to happen to her, and who was doing it. Her eyes were like those of a wild animal, trapped by a predator, and going through its death throes. There were four cameras, one in each corner of the room, and two more on tripods either side of the filthy bloodstained mattress. The man with the knife had been smiling when Tank walked into the room, but his smile disappeared when Tank levelled the shotgun at him and pulled the trigger. He was standing over the girl, and the buckshot hit him square in the stomach. The force of the impact lifted him backwards and he fell doubled up onto the floor, clutching at a wide rent in his torso. The second man pulled out of the girl and turned to face the intruder. He was a muscular build, and under normal circumstances, he fancied his chances against any man, but the sight of Tank carrying a Mossberg cooled his ardour. The young girl scurried into a foetal position against the wall, and Tank could see blood running down her thighs. He looked into her eyes, and he see the desperate pleading in them, 'for God's sake, please help me'.

"Don't shoot," the rapist held his hands up in surrender, but he glanced at his colleagues discarded hunting knife, which was on the floor nearby. "I can explain everything."

Tank chambered the last shell into the breach and squeezed the trigger. The lead shot hit the man low in the abdomen, ripping the top of his dangling penis off, and shredding his right upper thigh. He dropped like a stone and screamed like a banshee, clutching at his ruined genitals. Tank tossed the shotgun to the side and stepped over the writhing man. The young girl backed away from him as he approached her. Tank realised that she was terrified, traumatised by her experiences, and he backed away from her. He reached down to the screaming man and grabbed him by the left foot.

"Where are the keys for the handcuffs?" Tank growled. He grabbed a large bloodstained towel from a wooden chair close by and tossed it to the girl. The chair had handcuffs attached to it too, and was obviously used as another part of the film set to restrain which ever poor soul that was the star of the show. Tank repeated the question but the man didn't answer so Tank twisted his little toe three hundred and sixty degrees, dislocating the small bones and snapping the tendons and ligaments in one movement.

The man howled and pointed a bloody hand toward a pile of clothes that were piled in the corner of the room. Tank tossed him to the side, and recovered the silver key from a pair of Wrangler jeans. The girl had pulled the towel around her tightly, and she tucked her hands under her chin, leaving nothing of her body exposed, expect her face.

"What's your name?" Tank asked as gently as he could. He leaned over her and inserted the key into the handcuffs. The girl didn't answer the question, she just began crying. "It's okay now, no one will hurt you while I'm here, do you understand me?"

The girl nodded, but Tank couldn't be sure that she spoke English. There were deep grazes were the metal bracelet had cut her as she struggled, and she rubbed at her bloody wrist as the handcuffs came free. The cuts on her body were shallow, made to cause pain rather than to kill her.

"What is your name?" he asked again, reaching down and lifting her gently by the arm. "Are you okay to walk?"

Tank kept an eye on the door, he figured that the cameras were still running, and therefore the Moroccans would be aware that their broadcast had been interrupted. If he had to carry the girl it would impede their escape, and he needed his hands free in case he encountered any resistance. He was desperate for the girl to talk, so that he could find out if there were any more children on the farm, especially if the twins were here.

"Were you kept on your own?" Tank asked her. She looked at him blankly. "I need to know if there were any other children with you."

The girl looked confused and then she opened her mouth and began to gabble incoherently. Tank wasn't sure what language it was but he figured she was probably Albanian, and that she wasn't going to be able to answer his questions. He reached back down to the wailing man. His cries had subsided a little, but the volume began to rise as Tank grabbed his injured foot. He twisted the big toe violently to the right, dislocating it at the first knuckle. The rapist howled in agony.

"Are there any more kids on this farm?" Tank asked, ripping the second toe from its socket. The man nodded his head rapidly, his eyes bulging as if they were about to explode. There was saliva drooling from the corner of his mouth, and tears streamed down his face.

"Where are they?" Tank twisted the third toe and it cracked as it popped out of place.

"Down the stairs in the cellar!" the man cried in a thick guttural accent. He may have been a Moroccan, but then again he may not have been, Tank couldn't tell and he didn't care. He pulled out the Glock and fired it twice into the man's face. His skull exploded into three big bloody lumps, and brain matter oozed across the concrete. The first man had stopped moaning minutes before, probably already dead, but Tank fired two nine millimetres into his back just to be sure. The young girl looked shocked as she watched the body twitch twice before becoming still for the final time, but she clung to his arm like a limpet as he led her from the studio into the corridor. He waited a second and the sound of his own breathing was all that he could hear. The building was still.

The bird-scarring machine retorted twice, making Tank jump a little, as they descended the stairs. The young girl covered her eyes as she stepped over the dead bodies that lay at the bottom of the staircase. The sightless eyes staring accusingly frightened her, and her grip on Tank's arm tightened. Tank looked around the hallway, trying to spot the entrance to the cellar, but he couldn't locate an obvious doorway. It crossed his mind that the rapist had lied to him about the children's whereabouts, but it was too late to worry about that for now. He edged backwards down the hallway, away from the crystal meth lab, and the front door. A corridor ran behind the staircase, and he followed it, guiding the frightened young girl as he went. The building looked grey and stark, almost unfinished, but considering what it was used for, decor and decoration were hardly a priority. He peered into a doorway on the left, covering the space inside with his weapon. Then he moved over to the right hand side, of the corridor and repeated the process, pressing the girl against the cold concrete walls as he progressed. Both rooms were completely empty, and looked as if they had never been used. Tank saw a metal door at the end of the corridor. It was a steel grey colour, and the young girl flinched as he approached it. She pulled at his arm as if to stop him going near to it, and she rambled urgently in an unrecognisable language. Tank placed his index finger onto his lips and shushed her. She understood and calmed down a little, but he had to peel her fingers from his arm before he could move any closer. The door had bolts fitted at the top and bottom of it, and Tank slid them out of their keeps. He pushed the door open and peered into a deep, dark, stone stairwell. There was a light switch fixed to the wall on the right and he flicked the light on illuminating a cellar area below. A shuffling noise came from somewhere, which was out of his sight.

"Hello," Tank called out.

The silence was deafening. From the top of the stairs, he could only see an area of concrete ten feet square, and he knew that he would have to descend into the cellar to see if the children were there. He checked that the young girl was ok, and he pointed to his watch and held up two fingers.

"I'll be two minutes, okay," he said hoping that she would understand, and he was relieved when she nodded as if she had. She slid down the wall and sat on her haunches, the towel pulled tightly around her. He moved quickly down the stairs, taking them two at a time, and when he reached the basement, he had to catch his breath as he looked to the far wall. There were four tear stained, dirty little faces staring at him from the corner of the room. His heart flipped as he realised that he had saved these poor urchins from at the hands of the monsters in the film studio. He approached them slowly, and held out his hands to reassure them.

"I'm not here to hurt you," he said, and his eyes filled with stinging tears as he looked at the fear in their eyes. He picked them up one at a time and stood them on their feet. "Come on we're going to take you home."

The kids shuffled across the cellar, frightened by this big man, but trusting him at the same time. As he reached the top of the stairs, the young girl came to them and helped him to take the little ones down the corridor. One of them, a little blond boy, began crying and she comforted him, her own fear and pain forgotten for the moment. Tank unlocked the front door and checked the farmyard outside, but it seemed that apart from the hungry pigs the place was deserted. He reached for his cell phone and dialled Grace.

"John," she answered urgently.

"Send in the cavalry," he replied stroking one of the little girl's blond hair with his big gnarled hand. "This is where they were broadcasting from."

"I know, the police are already on their way to you, the Tech guys saw you entering the studio on-line, and they figured that you might need some help. Is the girl okay?"

"She needs a hospital, she's bleeding and there are four toddlers here to that need to be checked over," he felt totally drained.

"The twins?" Grace was frightened to ask the question.

"They're not here, Grace," Tank sighed. He was about to speak again when the meth lab exploded and blew him off his feet.

38

SYLVIA LEES/TWO WEEKS LATER

Sylvia looked through her car window, and sucked deeply on her cigarette, savouring the soothing smoke as it filled her lungs. The rain was hammering down on the roof of her vehicle and it added to the feeling of melancholy that she had felt since this investigation had begun. She had joined the police force because she felt that she could make a difference, but this time around, she had felt totally useless. Despite the fact that she had given Major Timms and his team a lead on the paedophile website, it had not helped to recover the twins. Granted four children and a toddler had been saved from hideous abuse and death, but the twins had vanished into thin air. John Tankersley had tracked the paedophiles to their lair, and recued the children, but the building had been totally destroyed in the process, and any evidence that it contained had been lost beneath tons of concrete, and twisted steel reinforcement bars. Forensics teams were sifting through the debris piece by piece, but it would take months to recover anything useful. The Moroccans had shut down everything they owned in the United Kingdom and gone into hiding. There was simply nothing left to trace which could lead them to the twins. Sylvia doubted very much if they were still alive, although she never told Hayley that.

Through the torrential rain, she watched Steve Kelly

opening his front door, and then staggering down the steps of his townhouse onto the pavement. He looked like he hadn't washed or shaved for a week. Sylvia sucked on the cigarette, stubbed it out, and opened her car door.

"Steve," she shouted him as she slammed the car door.

"Leave me alone," Steve slurred. He stumbled and fell onto his knees. "Now look what you made me do," he mumbled as he tried to get up.

"I need to talk to Karl, Steve," Sylvia said. She grabbed his arm and pulled him up. "Is he in?"

"Get lost," Steve tried to push her off him but he only managed to knock himself backwards onto the soaking wet pavement, banging his rump hard as he fell.

"How much have you had to drink?" Sylvia grabbed his hand and pulled him up onto unsteady legs.

"Not enough thanks, now get lost," Steve wobbled, made an about turn, and then set off back toward his front door.

"Is Karl in?" Sylvia repeated.

"No, he's gone fishing in the Lake District," Steve sneered. Sylvia thought it strange that he would return to the Lakes when his kids were still missing. Steve slid his key into the lock on the fourth attempt, and he tumbled into his hallway as the door opened. Sylvia waited on the stone steps for a moment, rain pouring down her face and neck.

"When did he go to the Lakes?" Sylvia asked as she followed Steve into his mock brownstone terrace. Steve stumbled down the hallway and then crashed into a doorframe before entering his living room. It looked untidy to Sylvia, as half-empty take away cartons were strewn across the floor. The carpet hadn't been vacuumed for a week at least, and there was an ashtray that was overflowing onto an expensive glass coffee table in the centre of the room. There was no way a woman had been here for days.

"I can't remember," Steve mumbled. He collapsed onto a

black leather armchair

"Where's Louise?"

"Working away, she's on a course," Steve mumbled, but his face told another story.

"Where?"

"Where what?"

"Where is Louise working away?"

"What the fuck has it got to do with you?"

"I'm finding it odd that Karl has gone fishing when his kids are missing and your wife is working away at the same time, and looking at the state of you I think you find it odd too," Sylvia crossed her arms and glared at him.

"I guess you've been talking to Hayley, silly bitch, thinks Karl is screwing everything that walks," Steve protested.

"No, Hayley doesn't think that he sleeps with everything that walks, but she does think that he's screwing your wife, Steve," she went for the jugular.

"Well if it makes you feel any better, Detective, if I'm really honest with you then I think that he's screwing my wife too," he stuck out his tongue like a petulant child, but Sylvia could see the pain in his eyes.

"How long have you suspected this?" she asked softly.

"I don't know, I didn't believe it first, well you wouldn't would you?" He smiled a haunted smile. "I mean your own brother, would you believe it?"

"Stranger things happen, Steve," Sylvia replied.

"Not to me, not to good old boring sensible Steve," he lit a cigarette with a shaking hand, and breathed in deeply. "Maybe that's why she's looking elsewhere, because I'm boring?"

"Have you spoken to Louise about it?"

"Of course I have, do you think I'm stupid?" Steve was beginning to get annoyed.

"And what did she say about it?" Sylvia sat down opposite him.

"She said I'm being paranoid," Steve slouched in his chair and pulled on the cigarette again, ash tumbled down his shirt. "Karl says that I'm being paranoid, but then what else would they say?"

"Do you think you're being paranoid?"

"I think that you should fuck off and leave us alone, that's what I think."

"This is serious, Steve, where is she?"

"None of this would have happened if you lot hadn't come sniffing around, blaming Karl for taking his own children."

"You're hampering a police investigation, Steve," she persisted.

"Ooh, are you going to arrest me, Sherlock?" Steve muttered.

"I might do, Steve, where is she?"

"Dublin," Steve mumbled.

"Pardon?"

"She's working in Dublin, you know the capital of Ireland," Steve sneered sarcastically.

"Have you got her hotel details?"

"What is your problem?"

"I need to speak to her and Karl," Sylvia pushed the point. Steve stood up and staggered over to the telephone. He pressed redial on the handset and a ringing tone sounded.

"Here ask for Louise Kelly, room three, two, five," Steve said very slowly labouring the issue.

"Hello, Dublin Hilton, how can I help?" a woman with a Polish accent answered.

"Could you put me through to room three, two five," Sylvia asked. She picked up a dirty sock from the settee with the tips of her fingers, and twirled it in her free hand. Something wasn't right.

"Hello," a voice answered.

"Louise Kelly?"

"Yes speaking," Louise sounded surprised.

"Louise, it's Constable Sylvia Lees, here, I'm with your husband Steve, and I need to speak to Karl urgently," Sylvia went out on a limb trying to provoke a response.

"I suggest you call him on his mobile then, why are you calling me, have they found the twins?"

"No, they haven't, I'm sorry to bother you," Sylvia hung up and stared at the sock and the overflowing ashtray. She figured that Louise had been gone a while, and Steve was in some kind of denial. There was a picture of Louise and Steve in happier times on pine bookcase next to Sylvia's chair. Louise looked stunning, jet-black hair, deep brown eyes, and tanned skin. Her smile revealed perfect white teeth, which added to her model looks.

"She's a pretty woman, your wife," Sylvia commented. Steve shook his head and closed his eyes. Tears formed and he rubbed at them angrily. "Where was this photo taken?"

"At a restaurant in Chester," Steve sniffled.

"Oh, I thought it was abroad somewhere, as she looks really tanned," Sylvia said.

"She had just come back from a girlfriend's hen do in Tenerife," Steve answered, looking longingly at the picture of his beautiful wife. He stubbed his cigarette out and lit another one immediately. Sylvia noticed that his index finger was turning yellow, stained with nicotine, a sign that he was chain smoking.

"How did Louise get to Dublin?"

"Canoe," Steve sneered. He sniffled and then wiped his nose on his sleeve.

"Have you spoken to your brother since he left for his fishing trip?"

"Karl is in the Lakes, where cell phone signals are like gold dust. I told you that my wife is in Dublin, and you have phoned my wife to see if she is actually in Dublin, and guess what, she is indeed in Dublin, just like I told you, now what more do you want, Sherlock!" Steve shouted sarcastically

"I'd drink some coffee if I were you," Sylvia said as she left the room. She opened the front door and paused before stepping out into the pouring rain.

39

MAJOR STANLEY TIMMS

Major Timms sat in the rear passenger seat of a Nissan Navarra. The dark pickup truck was travelling south on the M6 motorway at ninety miles an hour. The evening sun was fading away, and a half moon was arcing across the sky.

"I don't understand where all this has come from," the Major said confused. He looked at the large satellite navigation screen that was built into the dashboard, and read that they were nearing Wolverhampton. They had rushed him into the vehicle promising to explain everything on the way. On the way to where, he didn't know.

"Sylvia Lees went to see Karl at his brother Steve's house on a routine visit, as part of her family liaison duties," Grace explained from the front passenger seat. She twisted her body on the grey leather seat, so that her shoulders were facing the Major. "When she got to his brother's house, he was drunk and obviously upset about something. Sylvia said that from the condition of the house it looked as if Steve had been on a bender for a week or more."

"Louise was in Dublin, working away, and coincidently Karl was allegedly fishing in the Lakes on his own," Tank indicated left and the Navarra moved over onto the slip road, which would take them off the motorway toward the city of Wolverhampton.

"Okay so she was suspicious that the affair is in fact a reality?" the Major asked.

"Right, but not only that, because she became even more convinced that Karl's behaviour has been unusual to say the least," Grace carried on. "So she went to see Hayley and got some details about Karl's work, and social life recently."

"Sylvia found out where Karl usually stays when he's fishing, and she checked all the hotels that he would normally use, and the campsites around them, and she came up with nothing," Tank said.

"So she thinks that he's in Dublin?" the Major asked, still confused.

"She did, but she couldn't get access to the airport and ferry manifests without a warrant, and so she contacted us, because she knows that we can," Grace added. "We ran all the checks and we're convinced that there has been no Karl Kelly travelling to Ireland in the past few weeks, but guess what?"

"Louise Kelly has been coming back into the country from Dublin?" the Major guessed.

"No, but Louise Scolari has flown budget airline from Dublin to Wolverhampton twice in the last week," Grace said.

"Scolari is her maiden name?" the Major asked.

"Correct," Tank added. The Nissan navigated a huge roundabout and then Tank followed a brown sign that took them onto a narrow minor road. The brown sign had the picture of a boat on it.

"With a name like Scolari, I'm guessing her parents were Italian?" the Major was racking his brains to understand where this was going.

"Her father was Italian, her mother was Moroccan," Tank filled in the details. "And she was born in Marrakesh."

"We know for an absolute fact that Jack Howarth, or Alfie Lesner took the twins, I just can't see anything past that," the Major argued. "Why are we going on a wild goose chase?"

Tank looked at Grace and smiled, shaking his head. The Major was a stalwart, a doubting Thomas, and he never believed anything until he could see it for himself.

"Sylvia saw a photograph of Louise and her husband, she was tanned and he wasn't. Steve said that she had been on a girlfriend's hen do in Tenerife, but when Sylvia checked up with the friend she told her that Louise hadn't gone on the trip. She had fallen out with Louise over the fact that she pulled out at the last minute. Louise told Steve that they had fallen out on the Tenerife trip because the bride to be was being a little too frivolous with other men. They didn't go to the wedding, and so there were no uncomfortable questions to answer about not going to Tenerife."

"What's the significance of that?" the Major asked.

"Louise Scolari bought a flight from Manchester airport to Marrakesh, and guess who else was on that flight?" Tank said. He caught the Major's eyes in the rear view mirror, and he could see him processing the information.

"Karl?"

"Correct," Grace said.

"What did he tell my daughter?"

"Golf trip to Marbella," Tank replied.

"I remember him going, and I remember him bringing presents back for Hayley and the twins," the Major spoke quietly.

"We think that they went to Marrakesh to arrange for the twins to be kidnapped, via relatives of Louise in Marrakesh," Grace said. "We think that Jack Howarth was employed by the Moroccans to capture the twins. Karl was planning to leave Hayley, and he was terrified that she wouldn't let him see the twins."

The Major nodded and turned to look out of the window. The industrial city of Wolverhampton was sprawled out behind them and the countryside was opening up in front of them.

"Why here, why in Wolverhampton?"

"The police found the body of Alfie Lesner at an industrial unit near Crewe, and it is situated on the Shropshire Union canal. We checked credit card transactions with all marinas in the area, and we found an eight berth narrow boat that has been paid for by......"

"Louise Scolari," the Major interrupted; his voice was acidic. Karl's bank transactions had all been checked thoroughly as a routine part of the investigation. It had to be Louise that had paid for it, and she had to have used her maiden name to avoid any obvious connections being made. "The canal network is the ideal place to keep the twins out of the public's gaze."

"It is, and all the hire boats are chipped for GPS tracking, to stop vessels being stolen. We know exactly where the boat is, fingers crossed that we're right, Major," Tank said.

They travelled in nervous silence for the next twenty minutes, and the road ran parallel to the canal. Brightly painted longboats were dotted along the banks, some covered and empty and others were lit up like Christmas, and had smoke coming from their chimneys.

"We're here," Tank pulled the Nissan into a gravel car park, and the white stones crunched beneath the wheels. The sun was nearly gone and electric lights, paraffin lamps and candles illuminated the occupied narrow boats in the marina. There was an array of different hues and colours coming from inside the vessels. They climbed out of the Navarra and Tank locked the pickup with his remote. A small curved footbridge took them over the canal to the opposite bank and they scanned the moored boats for the vessel that they were looking for.

"The Lady Ruth," Grace said pointing to a boat, which was moored about a hundred yards further up the canal. "Look."

A lamp attached to the bulkhead illuminated the front of the boat. A pair of glass-pained doors had been left open revealing a cosy living space within. The interior was lit by amber light and the occupants were seated around a small kitchenette table eating a meal. Sat on a padded bench next to each other giggling, were the twins. Karl and Louise sat opposite them, and they clinked long stemmed wine glasses and smiled lovingly at each other as they watched the twins eat.

"We'd better call the police," Grace said.

"I don't want the twins upset, by being taken into care while this mess is sorted out," the Major said. A tear ran from the corner of his eye and he wiped it with his sleeve. "We take the twins back to Hayley, Grace, and John can stay with them until the police get here."

"Fine by me," Tank agreed. "Take them to their mother, Major, where they belong."

"Don't shoot him, John," the Major patted him on the back as they walked up the towpath.

"I wouldn't dream of it, Major," Tank smiled.

40
THE CHILD TAKER

The hearse stopped at the gates of the church, and the crowd fell silent as the funeral directors removed the coffin. A reef of white roses, crafted into the word 'DAD' was taken from the hearse and placed on top of the walnut coffin. Eight police officers in full dress uniform moved to the coffin, four each side, and they lifted the casket onto their shoulders. The winding path to the church was lined with police officers, as is the tradition when they have to bury one of their own, and the cortege prepared to carry their fallen colleague into the red sandstone brick church.

Jack looked up at the steeple, and he couldn't help but be impressed by its scale. A series of wooden ladders were tied to the pointed spire, allowing a steeplejack access to maintain the weather vane and the lightning conductors. The throbbing in his hand was becoming a dull ache now. A doctor friend of his, that shared the same sexual interests as he did had stitched up his hand and given him antibiotics to ward off any infections. It had been incredibly painful when he left the hospital, and as the local anaesthetics from his operation had worn off, the pain in his groin had become intolerable. It had taken him two days to get help from his doctor friend, but the pain had been the price he had to pay for his liberty, and it was worth every second of agony that he had suffered.

The sad procession at the front of the church began to move and Jack smiled as the dead policeman's family filed behind his coffin. His widow was nearly as fat as he had been, and his son was a younger look-alike of him. The daughter however was a different matter. She was prepubescent, just the age that he liked them, and although she was plump, he would enjoy making her do the things that he liked. He had promised Constable Davis as he died that he would visit his children, and he intended to keep that promise. Jack knew that he would be taking children for profit soon enough, but this one would be purely for his own pleasure. There is a 'Child Taker' in every community, look after your little ones.

Author's Note

2007 a little girl was taken from her family, and the world held its breath as we waited for news. My wife, Ruth, and I were embarking on an extended tour of America, and we watched the news programmes hoping for good news from home, but none came. When I hear her name, or fresh cases of child abduction appear on television, my stomach tightens, and one can only imagine the pain a parent must feel in that terrible situation.

For, Ruth and Evy, my girls.